How to Climb
the Eiffel Tower

a novel

ELIZABETH HEIN

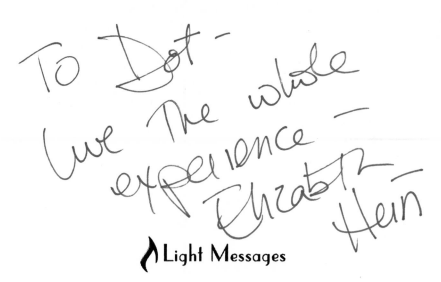

To Dot —
Live The whole
experience —
Elizabeth Hein

Light Messages

Published 2014, by Light Messages
www.lightmessages.com
Durham, NC 27713
Printed in the United States of America
Paperback ISBN: 978-1-61153-102-2
Ebook ISBN: 978-1-61153-103-9

To all the doctors and nurses who shepherd cancer patients through the Valley of Death and out the other side.

Acknowledgements

Moving a book from idea to printed page is a marathon and requires many team members along the way. I would like to acknowledge just a few of the people who helped me carry this book forward. First, and foremost, I would like to thank my darling husband, Ted, and daughters, Katherine and Emily, for being my biggest cheerleaders and listening to me talk about Lara as if she is another member of the family. I'd also like to thank my many critique group buddies who challenged me to keep moving forward by reading chapters and nudging me toward the right path—Rebecca White, Samantha Dunaway Bryant, Sarah Sugg, Elizabeth Carroll, Kimberley Workman, Amy Overley, Dawn Taylor, Robert Byrd, Noelle Granger, Becky Abbott, Grace Wetzel, Stepheny Houghtlin, Sarah Wilkins, and Jennifer Madriaga. And lastly, I'd like to thank Elizabeth Turnbull and all the people at Light Messages Publishing for getting this novel over the finish line.

Part One

1

The Colors of Cancer

Ellery Cancer Center protruded from the hospital's facade like a glass tumor. The night before, a Kafkaesque voicemail told me to report to the reception lobby by 7:00 for my 9:00 appointment. I left the house at 6:00 sharp even though the hospital was twenty minutes away. An appointment with some strange specialist wasn't going to make me deviate from my routine.

My footsteps echoing through the brightly tiled lobby accented the nervous murmuring of the people waiting in line as I strode past them to the reception desk. The receptionist didn't even look up when I said, "Blaine. Lara Blaine. I have a 9:00 with Dr. Lander." She robotically found my file in the tall stack to her left, handed me the itinerary clipped to the front, and moved my file to the short stack to her right. My itinerary said to report to the red waiting room by 8:00.

I stood to the side of the room and watched people until I

understood that the lines of multicolored tiles in the lobby's floor were not decorative. They were paths to the color-coded areas of the Cancer Center. I followed the line of red tiles from the reception desk to the red waiting room. A clot of people sat on crimson and burgundy couches clutching their itineraries. I sat just inside the doorway and watched as people disappeared one by one through the slick red doors at the far end of the room. No one came back. An hour later, it was my turn. On the other side of the red doors, an old man with hairy knuckles checked my name against his orders then jabbed a needle in my arm. We didn't say a word to each other. I liked that.

The next stop on my itinerary was the green waiting room. A line of green tiles in the floor led me back to the lobby and up two flights of stairs to another room with worry worn carpeting and faded couches sagging under the weight of their occupants' despair, but all in green. I'd roamed the Ellery Cancer Center for nearly an hour and had yet to speak to a soul. I slipped into the crowded room, commandeered the pea green love seat in the corner, and opened my dog-eared copy of *Great Expectations*. I held the tattered pages in front of my face, yet couldn't read. I watched the elderly couple across from me over the top of the book.

I don't belong here. I'm not like these people. I'm young. I crossed one leg over the other and clenched my thighs together. *There's nothing wrong with me. It's just a false positive. I'm fine.*

The elderly man's hand shook as he lifted a cup of tea to his wife's lips. The limp paper label dangling over the edge of the foam cup taunted me. I should have been researching the effect of the recent earthquake in Northern China on the green tea crop for my boss's presentation the following week, not sitting in that waiting room. *This is such a waste of time. So what if I have weird periods? Doesn't everyone?*

I turned away from the old people and focused on the normal looking woman in a black suit slowly making her way down the corridor. I assumed she was a doctor or pharmaceutical salesperson until she stopped in the doorway to hack into a tissue. She saw me looking at her and lurched over. "May I sit with you?" I expected the woman's voice to be as smooth as her grey silk blouse, but it sounded as scratchy as wool against bare skin. I moved my battered leather backpack to let her sit down.

"Jane Babcock-Roberts."

"Lara Blaine," I replied with a curt nod.

"I think you sprinted past me on the stairwell earlier," Jane sighed. "I used to be able to run up stairs like that."

"I'm good at stairs. I climb the Eiffel Tower every Tuesday."

Jane dabbed perspiration from her upper lip with a clean tissue and tucked it in her sleeve. "I climbed the Eiffel Tower once. What a view, huh?"

"I haven't actually been to Paris," I replied. "It's a setting on the stair stepper at my gym."

"That doesn't sound nearly as fun." Jane flipped her long silver-blonde hair over her shoulder. "And there wouldn't be any croissants when you finished."

A couple entered the room and perched on the edge of the moss colored couch next to us. The stench of fear wafted off them. The wife stared at a stain in the carpet while the husband repeatedly flipped through the pamphlets in his hand as if they would miraculously reveal some new information that wasn't there a moment before. Jane shifted her weight to turn away from the couple and face me. "How well do you know these doctors?" she whispered.

"I've never been here before. I'm just here to get some test results." I recrossed my legs and tapped the toe of my scuffed black flat against the side table. "I'm sure it's nothing though. The first doctor I saw is making me see this specialist just to cover her ass."

"I'm here for test results, too. Although, I'm pretty sure there's something wrong. Busy medical practices don't give you a next-day appointment when there's nothing wrong."

I bounced my novel on my knee. The first doctor had scheduled that day's appointment for three days after I saw her. I didn't think it meant anything; I thought they were efficient. "Maybe they had a cancellation."

"Maybe." Jane absently twisted a scratched men's watch around her thin wrist three times.

A brawny orderly appeared with a wheelchair to collect the elderly couple. Jane and I watched the old man carry his wife's pocketbook over his arm as he followed her through the sliding green doors. Jane cleared her throat. "What are you reading there?"

"*Great Expectations.*" I stopped bouncing and tapping. "I read a Dickens every summer. *Nicholas Nickleby* is my favorite. This one is good, but the girl really annoys me. I like Magwitch, but—" I was cut off when an aide called Jane's name. She smiled a quick goodbye as she got up then disappeared through the green doors.

Maybe I should just leave. Which color tiles leads the way out of here? If I walk out now, will they come looking for me? I turned toward the wall and reopened my book. My book friends would protect me from the room full of bewildered people clutching their itineraries like shields against bad news.

✷✷✷

Nearly an hour later, a nurse in tired pink scrubs called my name and ushered me into a small room for a health interrogation. The first six pages of questions about my sleeping and eating habits didn't faze me. When the nurse flipped to the seventh page and asked, "When were you first sexually active?" I panicked. *Shit, what did I tell that other nurse the other day? Certainly not the truth. I bet she's got my answers on that clipboard and is trying to catch me in a lie.*

"I was twenty-one, so eight years ago?" The nurse did not look up from her clipboard. *That must have been the right answer.*

"Number of sexual partners in the last five years?"

"Zero." *That one was easy.*

"And before that?"

My mouth went dry. My abdomen clenched as the old sense of terror slithered up my spine. *None of your God damn business!* I slid forward on the cold metal chair.

"Just two. And, we always used protection so I've never had any STD's." All lies. I leaned forward, ready to bolt if necessary. The nurse flipped the page and moved on to questions regarding drug use. I could relax. The metal chair felt cool against my sweaty back when I slid back again.

Once she was finished with me, the nurse shoved a paper gown in my hands, and demanded I strip from the waist down. I didn't want to, but it was easier to let them poke and prod my body than talk about my past. I quickly pulled off my chinos and folded my panties inside them. I didn't realize how much I was sweating until the cold air in the Pepto-Bismol pink room hit the backs of my bare legs.

A light knock on the door startled me. I swung around to face the door as an efficient blond strode in and thrust her hand toward me. "Lauren Blaine?"

I ignored the gesture. "It's Lara."

The doctor walked around me and dropped my file on the desk. "I'm Karen Lander." The nurse came in and closed the door. "This is Stephanie. I believe you were referred to us by Dr. Bonnerheim?" Dr. Lander meticulously washed her hands and pulled on a pair of blue latex gloves. She stepped around me again as if I was an ill placed piece of furniture. "I see you've had a number of abnormal Pap smears. And Bonnerheim did a colposcopy?"

"I don't mean to be any trouble." I held the thin paper gown together behind my back while Dr. Lander opened a drawer lined with glistening instruments. "Dr. Bonnerheim is just being overly cautious."

"That's a good thing." Dr. Lander said over her shoulder. "She caught it in the early stages."

"What?" The walls felt like they were caving in. "What do you mean, caught it?" I swallowed hard.

"The colposcopy found cancerous cells." The doctor pulled a gooseneck lamp to the foot of the examination table. "Didn't Bonnerheim tell you that she saw abnormal cells?"

I searched my memory. I remembered the gynecologist saying that I had failed a test and that I had to go see a specialist, but I didn't remember her actually saying the word cancer. I would have remembered the word cancer. Cancer had stolen my grandparents.

Dr. Lander pulled the stirrups out with enough force to move the examination table several inches. "Why don't we take a look?" I considered running, but the nurse was leaning on the door. I was naked. My clothes were out of reach. I was trapped. I had to submit.

I pulled myself up on the exam table and lay back. By the

time my head hit the surface, my mind had disengaged from my body. I didn't feel the thin paper gown slipping down my thighs or the nurse positioning my feet in the stirrups. I had escaped with my book friends. While Dr. Lander dictated copious notes into a handheld recorder, I wandered through Narnia eating Turkish delight with Edmund Pevensie and the White Witch.

✷✷✷

An astringent smell filled my nostrils as cool fingers grasped my shoulder. I blinked a few times. The nurse helped me to sit up. The light seemed harsher, the walls pinker. Dr. Lander sat at a small desk with her back to me. "We should schedule you for a LEEP procedure right away. My exam verifies Dr. Bonnerheim's diagnosis. It is cancer. We had hoped it was pre-cancerous, but I'm afraid not. I'll send off some tissue samples to pathology to tell us if the cancer has spread beyond the cervix itself, but…" I didn't hear anything beyond "cancer" and "cervix" before my mind shut down again.

By the time the nurse shook me out of my stupor again Dr. Lander was long gone. "Miss Blaine? I'm afraid we need to clear the room now."

"Okay, I'll go now." I massaged my aching jaw. I didn't remember clenching my teeth.

The nurse dropped a thick folder on the empty pink plastic chair. "Here is a hard copy of the information the doctor went over. You might want to read that at home." She placed an orange form beside my backpack. "Take this to the orange check-out desk on your way out. They'll give you a blue sheet with the appointment information for your procedure." *Information? Procedure? What the hell is she talking about?* The nurse glanced up at the wall clock. "Can I call someone for you? Your husband? A friend?"

"No. I'm better off alone."

Once the nurse was gone, I snatched a handful of tissues from the box on the desk and wiped the remaining lubricating jelly off my thighs. My skin still felt sticky. I ran the water in the tiny sink until it scalded my fingers, then scrubbed my body with a wad of brown paper towels.

Cervical cancer? But it was just a false positive.

A line of orange tiles led me out of the maze of examination rooms to an exit lobby. Gripping the instructions for my next appointment, I stumbled toward the banks of elevators, nearly walking into Jane. "Oh, wow... excuse me."

"That's okay. I'm okay," Jane replied. She brushed a long silver hair off her face with a trembling finger. "Where are you off to in such a rush?"

"Work. I left a note on my monitor saying I'd be in by noon."

Jane glanced down at her scratched watch. "It's half past one. It's already too late." Jane sniffled loudly and turned away. She wiped a tear away with a French manicured fingernail before she stabbed the elevator button. The doors slid open and, stunned, we both entered. "How was your appointment?"

"Awful. I have cancer."

"Me too," Jane snorted. "The nice young doctor actually apologized when he told me."

"My doctor's a spiky haired bitch." As we slowly descended, laughter rose in my chest like bubbles in a simmering pot. The heat inside me rose with every floor the elevator fell.

I have cancer.

By the time the doors opened on to the first floor, my tittering progressed into uncontrolled howls until my chest and belly burned. The doors began to close again, but I couldn't move. I just stood there in the elevator hugging my backpack to my chest. Jane clumsily shoved her shoulder against the door. "Are you all right? You're frightening me." She stepped back inside and lightly tugged on my shoulder. "I can't just leave you here in hysterics. Would you like to get a cup of coffee or something?"

"I need to get back to work." I tried to catch my breath.

"You can't go to the office looking like that. What would your colleagues think?"

"I can't?" I looked down at my rumpled white blouse and wrinkled chinos. I ran my fingers through my disheveled hair and twisted it behind my head. "I can't go back looking like this. They'll know."

"Come on. I'll buy you a coffee."

I stepped out of the elevator. "Okay, but not the cafeteria. I saw a Starbucks off of the lobby earlier."

"I'm surprised you can remember anything in your state," Jane said.

"I have exemplary retention skills," I muttered as I followed her across the crowded reception lobby.

In Starbucks, I ordered a sweet frozen concoction topped with whipped cream and chocolate syrup. Jane ordered a small black coffee. Jane handed the young man a ten-dollar bill and carelessly threw the change in the tip jar. We found a table near the window and passed several awkward moments silently sipping our drinks. Jane watched a woman step outside and stagger back from the wall of heat and humidity. "August in North Carolina. It'll get you every time," she said. Other than the gravel voice, Jane appeared fine. She looked like a successful businesswoman in her sixties at the top of her game. She didn't look like a person with cancer.

"What kind of cancer do you have?" I asked.

Jane dabbed her lips with a paper napkin. "Lung. You?"

"Cervical."

"Oh." Jane ran her finger around the rim of her cup. "I'm sorry, I don't know anything about that kind."

"Me either," I replied. A blast of frigid air blew up my pant leg as the air conditioning kicked on. "I guess I'll learn though. They gave me a packet to read."

"Me too," Jane sighed. She pulled a bulging folder from her bag and ran her long fingers over the large watercolor picture of a sun on the cover of the packet. "This thing looks like the prospectus for a preschool, not a 'so you have a potentially fatal disease' packet. I should really sit down and study this information. Probably won't. Anyway, I still need to have more tests before they can even come up with a plan."

"Me too." I moved to the chair further away from the air conditioning vent and closer to Jane.

Jane tapped two fingernails against her lips. "I want a cigarette so bad. I finally quit just last year and then, look what happened. I got cancer." Jane's breath hitched and she began to cough. Droplets of bloody sputum speckled the tissue she held in front of her mouth. "Oh my God, I have lung cancer! This cough is cancer! What am I going to tell my mother? You know she's going to say this is my fault."

Mama would certainly find a way to make this my fault, if she knew.

"She always said my smoking was a filthy habit. If she hadn't been such a shrew about it, I probably would have quit when I was teenager." Jane twisted her watch again. "I wish my dad were still alive."

We both turned to stare at the bright sunshine playing off the fountain in the courtyard. A little boy ran around trying to catch the rainbows formed by the mist. "I should call my son, Tom." Jane popped the top off her cup and drained it. "Or, maybe I should wait until after I get more specific results."

"That might be best. Don't tell anyone until you're sure."

We both stared out the window for a few more moments until Jane asked, "When?"

"What?"

"When are your tests?"

I checked the blue appointment sheet sticking out of my backpack. "Thursday."

"I'm Friday," Jane replied. "Too bad. It would have been nice to see a friendly face."

The cell phone on Jane's hip rang. "Jane Babcock-Roberts," she whispered into the mouthpiece. "No Candace, we will not pay that invoice until they deliver the product—all the product." She spoke with authority. "We sent a purchase order for six pallets of stone and only received four. When we receive the remaining two, then I will pay... make sure they come from the same lot of stone... No, I can't call them... Tell them I'm in a meeting. Off-site." Jane tucked her phone back in its holder. "I'm sorry. That was rude of me. How are you feeling now? Better?"

"Is it a problem for you to be away from the office?"

"Yes and no, I've lost some time on several projects but it'll be fine." Jane flipped the plastic coffee cup lid absently in her hand. "I'm more concerned about how today will affect the company long-term."

"What kind of company is it?"

"We build custom homes." Jane's hand went to her wrist again. "I took over after my father's death."

"At least you won't get fired. My boss will fire me if she

finds out I'm sick." I stirred my drink trying to come up with a good excuse for where I'd been all morning.

"It's not as easy as you might think to fire someone for something like this. There are employment regulations," Jane said. "What kind of cancer did you say you had again?"

"Cervical."

"Did you know something was wrong?"

"I collapsed at the gym one night, so they made me go to the hospital in an ambulance. The ER doctors wouldn't let me leave until I saw a gynecologist." I didn't tell Jane that the nurses kept asking me questions I didn't want to answer. "How 'bout you, did you know you were sick?"

"Oh yeah." Jane rolled the wrapper from my straw into a snail. "I've had this nasty cough for a while. I just kept putting off having it looked at. I thought I was prepared to hear bad news, but I guess you're never fully prepared for news like this." Jane dabbed at her lips again before smearing on a coat of merlot lipstick. "I'm sorry. I can't remember the last time I was so emotional. Probably when my son went off to school. Do you have kids?"

"No children. No husband; just me."

Jane pulled her bag onto her shoulder. "Do you have family in the area?"

"No. My mother lives up north. We're not close," I said.

"Believe me, I understand about difficult mothers." Jane made a show of looking at her cell phone and stood up. "Well, if you're feeling better, I really should be getting back. I need to salvage at least part of this day."

2
Cubicle Chaos

Hurricane Mavis saved that afternoon. I needed something exigent to drown out the sounds of Garlic Breath playing Spider Solitaire in the next cubicle and Dr. Lander's voice bouncing around inside my head. Five minutes into my drive to Bettel Occidental Commodities, NPR reported that Mavis was building strength to the east of the Dominican Republic. By the time I sat down at my desk, I was planning charts and graphs on the storm's impact on regional shipping routes. As a commodities analyst I needed to consider the effect of a direct hit to the southeast dependent on the tides, ports and evacuation routes. I was giddy with the possibilities.

My happy bubble of concentration popped when the elevator doors slid open and my boss, Letitia, clattered out. The entire eighth floor peeked out of their cubicles like doughboys watching for incoming grenades. Everyone looked to see what kind of cup Letitia held. We knew that fattening coffee drinks meant her presentation went well, where iced tea meant it was time to hide under your desk. She held a Venti iced tea against the hip of her sleek black dress. I was relieved to hear the sound of Letitia's stiletto heels tapping out someone else's fate on the other side of the eighth floor. Analysts had a short life span in Letitia's department. She had a way of sucking the life out of them and scattering their empty shells around the building. Earlier that week, I found a file box filled with picture frames and coffee mugs protruding from Bald Guy with Twin Girls' cubicle. He had put the decimal point in the wrong place on his monthly report. A fat woman with cropped grey hair had pinned pictures of kittens to the walls of Bald Guy's cube. I gave her six weeks.

Letitia's footsteps stopped on the other side of the room. "You call this a market analysis?" She paused to make sure we were all listening. "Where are the long-term trends? The seasonal overview? When did you send this to Blaine?"

"I ran out of time, so I added it to the end of Blaine's PowerPoint this morning," a woman's voice wailed. I recognized it as belonging to Short Red Hair who sat next to Pathetic Dog Owner. I made a mental note to password protect the presentations.

"Swenson asked me a question about the global impacts that I couldn't answer because you didn't include any background notes. You made me look like an idiot in front of the executive committee!" The entire room sucked in their breath as if watching a cheetah taking down an impala on the outer edge of the herd. "Why can't you be more like Blaine? They loved the bauxite presentation."

I smiled. I had done a particularly good job on that PowerPoint; the bullet points were animated, the graphs were detailed, and the data points overlaid my projections.

"Oh come on," Short Red Hair said. "That's not fair. That guy is a machine."

"Listen to that, Blaine," Garlic Breath clucked through the cubicle wall. "They think you're a dude."

"Blaine is a machine," Letitia replied with a flip of her sleek black ponytail. "She works harder and is smarter than all y'all combined." The recognition felt hollow when used against someone else. "You know, if you spent less time shopping for shoes—"

"What?"

"It's a corporate firewall, you idiot. IT tracks your browser history and alerts me to any irregularities. Unless you're preparing a report on leather futures, there is no reason to spend so much time on Zappos." The room exhaled in relief. If Letitia could make light of the situation, then she wasn't that angry. No one would be fired that day.

✳✳✳

As soon as Letitia was safely encased inside her glass fortress of an office, Pathetic Dog Owner lumbered into Garlic Breath's cubicle. "Did you hear that? Letitia called Blainiac over here a machine."

I stared at the hurricane rotating in the Atlantic, but I couldn't concentrate anymore. I wished Garlic Breath would choke on one of the pork rinds he was always munching.

"Do you think Letitia will give her another big bonus?" Pathetic Dog Owner grumbled.

"Keep your voice down," Garlic Breath hissed. "I told you that on the down low. No one's supposed to know that Letitia gives her a little extra here and there in exchange for compiling everyone's reports for her presentations. Letitia doesn't know I overheard Blaine whining about not getting credit for her work."

"Like that's ever going to happen," Pathetic Dog Owner said. "Letitia's no idiot. If it means throwing Blaine a bone every once in a while, she'll do it."

Little did Garlic Breath and Pathetic Dog Owner know, Letitia had thrown me far more than a bone. Every quarter our department successfully predicted market trends, Letitia received a bonus that more than doubled her salary. In exchange for me doing most of her job for her, she shared those bonuses with me.

"And, could you see Letitia ever letting that train wreck stand up in front of the steering committee?"

Why can't you just leave me alone and let me do my work? I looked up and saw Pathetic Dog Owner peeking over Garlic Breath's cubicle wall. I winked at him. His head popped back down behind the wall as the two of them guffawed like the football players who would make faces at me through the library stacks in high school. I put my headphones on and listened to the emergency weather messages about the hurricane to block them out.

✳✳✳

At 5:01, everyone else shut down their workstations and head for the exits as if the building was on fire. I waited for Garlic Breath to gather his lunch box and sundry electronics, then picked my way down the line of cubicles to Letitia's glass walled office. The late afternoon sunshine reflected off Letitia's diamond earrings, projecting rainbows across the slick glass and steel desk. I pushed open the frameless glass door. "Excuse me, Letitia?"

Letitia startled and automatically whipped her reading glasses off her nose. She spun around in her chair to block her screen. "Blaine! What's up?"

"I'm sorry I didn't make it back this morning but—"

"You weren't here?"

"I left a note. Didn't anyone—"

"You okay?"

"I'm fine." I checked that everyone had indeed left before I whispered, "Well, actually, I need to take Thursday off. I am having some 'woman troubles' and need to have a procedure. I can dial in from home and post my reports before the close of business."

Letitia crossed her spindly legs and rolled one slender ankle as she mused, "I had a cyst on my ovary a few years ago. It was nothing serious, but boy, was I crampy for a few days. If you want to just lie on the couch Friday, you can work from home."

"That won't be necessary. I'll be fine."

Letitia uncrossed and recrossed her legs. "Hey, good job on that bauxite report. They really liked it."

I rolled my eyes and turned to leave. *Of course they liked it. It was an awesome presentation.*

"So what're you working on now?"

"There's a hurricane coming. I'm analyzing the ramifications. That's what I do, the research and analysis that you present as your work."

"Come on Blaine, I know you're mad that I didn't have you present the bauxite research yourself but... well ... that's just not going to happen." Letitia shrugged and flipped her long ponytail over her shoulder and flashed me a brilliant, capped smile. "Frank Mariano did imply that there would be a bonus in the works for me. I'll share it with you."

I bit the inside of my cheek to keep from pointing out that the entire bonus should have been mine. I had done all the work while Letitia got all the glory. "I want my half in cash this time. I don't like having to go to the bank to deposit your checks."

✳✳✳

Even though my day had been disrupted, I left work as usual at 6:18 and drove to Silver Star Fitness for my daily workout. If I didn't get a full hour of aerobic exercise, the nightmares would get me. Tuesday was a stair stepper day. I changed into a pair of bike shorts and oversized T-shirt in the locker room and mounted my preferred machine, the one in the corner away from the television and nattering housewives that hogged the recumbent bikes. As I set the machine's program for the Eiffel Tower, I thought about Jane Babcock-Roberts.

I didn't know anyone actually climbed the Eiffel Tower anymore. View or no view, that can't be safe. You could get trapped way up there with an axe murderer. No way. I'll stick to my nice predictable, safe machines.

The next thing I knew, the machine beeped indicating that I had climbed to the top. My long hair was plastered to my head and my muscles ached, yet I didn't feel the sense of release I usually got from my workout. I moved to a treadmill to warm down by running a couple of miles.

I wonder how that Jane woman is now. Did she tell her son about the cancer?

I hoped not. The longer her son didn't know Cancer, the better. I knew Cancer. He stole my grandparents. He made my mother come back from wherever she'd been for the first seven years of my life and pack my little life into the trunk of her big yellow Plymouth. Cancer killed the only people that ever loved me. And now he'd come for me.

After my workout, I stepped into Lucky Lee's Chinese Restaurant, conveniently located two doors down from the gym. As soon as I opened the door, the tiny woman behind

18

the high counter put a hand on the red plastic bag in front of her. "Hold on just a sec, Miss Lara. I think Helen forgot your Pineapple Surprise. Can you wait a few minutes? Do you have time?"

I don't know. Do I?

"That's fine, Mrs. Lee. I can wait." I put my gym bag down and picked up the takeout menu. There was no real reason to read it. I ate the same thing every night - Moo Goo Gai Pan, white rice and Pineapple Surprise. Over the years, the Lees had learned to have it waiting for me. I appreciated their efficiency.

"Good workout tonight?"

"Some old lady set the treadmill to the slowest setting and I had to reprogram the whole thing. But, it was fine."

Susan Lee straightened the already straight stack of menus next to a waving cat statue. "It's supposed to rain tonight. My garden sure needs it."

"We are 3.6 inches below average right now but that is 30% better than—" The arrival of a ten-year-old girl in a bright yellow soccer uniform spared Susan Lee any further discussion of North Carolina's annual rain fall.

"Here you go, Miss Lara."

I smiled at Helen Lee. "Game today?"

"Just practice." Helen tightened the yellow bow around her long ponytail. "Hey, guess what? I got an A on that spelling test today. Thanks for helping me study."

"Thank you for sitting with her when you came in last night."

"It's okay." I tucked a strand of my dishwater blonde hair behind my ear. "I like helping Helen with her vocabulary. I was always wicked good at English." Little did the Lees know, drilling Helen on her spelling words had been the highlight of my week.

∗∗∗

Seven and a half minutes after leaving Lucky Lee's, my reinforced steel garage door squealed and thumped closed behind me and Ruby, my precious red VW Bug. I lingered in the garage to wipe some dirt off Ruby's hood. On this terrible day, I wished the little car could give me back some of the love I poured into her. Ruby's paint gleamed, her leather was supple and her engine well tuned. In her trunk, I kept a neatly packed bag with a change of clothes and photocopies of my important documents. It took me less than a minute to unlock the three deadbolts between the garage and my apartment, enter, and lock myself inside. I hung my keys and backpack on their respective hooks next to the door. Everything I needed was at hand in case my stepfather tracked me down and I needed to make a quick getaway.

I dropped the bags of food on top of the three moving boxes full of books I used as a makeshift coffee table. The food could wait; I needed a hot shower. My skin prickled with dried sweat and I felt dirty. People had been touching my body. Twenty minutes later, I flopped down on the couch and reached for the remote. It was gone.

Can this day get any worse? In a fit of frustration, I clawed at the old wool blanket thrown over the back of the couch and yanked out the soft leather cushions. I finally found the remote wedged between two of the moving boxes. I slammed it down on top of the closest box before putting the couch back together and folding the threadbare blanket so its broad stripes lined up again. The red and blue stripes reminded me of the tiles in the Ellery Cancer Center that morning. Dr. Lander's voice echoed in my head. *Cancer. Cervical cancer.*

I grabbed the remote and turned on the TV as loud as

possible. I went around the channels three times before settling on a *Law & Order* rerun. Every other channel seemed to be showing stories of miracle diagnoses and bizarre surgeries. Before opening the bags of Chinese food, I laid an old towel over my lap in case I dropped any food. The brown leather couch and big screen TV were the only pieces of real furniture in the three-bedroom condominium. And, I bought those begrudgingly.

I considered furniture an impediment. Material things weren't worth their high cost. For much of my life, my mother had shuttled me from one roach infested trailer park to another. Any toys or treasures I accumulated along the way were either sold or left behind when Mama lost yet another waitressing job. We eventually stopped living out of suitcases the year I turned fourteen and we moved to Hawthorne, New Hampshire. That was the year Mama married Dale Clemmons. Mama was happy she finally found a man willing to take her. She didn't care that Dale considered us a package deal. She wanted the security of Dale's 300-acre dairy farm and the promise of a full wallet. Dale wanted Mama to cook and clean and pump up his ego. No one cared what I wanted. Mama decorated the drafty back bedroom in the crumbling addition to Dale's rambling farmhouse with flowered wallpaper and a fussy white canopy bed, as if ruffles and bows could hide what Dale did to me there.

Sometime during the second episode of *Law & Order*, my eyelids grew heavy. My apartment fell away. I was back in the Ellery Cancer Center following the tiles in the floor. I never lifted my eyes from the floor yet I kept losing my way. Then, I bounced off a Pepto-Bismol membrane and landed with a splat in a puddle of sticky jelly. On the other side of the translucent membrane, green cancer cells were hacking off pieces of the membrane and devouring them with glee. I pushed at the surface of the membrane, desperate to find an opening, when one of the cancer cells stopped and looked up. It was Dale.

I gasped awake. My eyes were open in the blue glow of the television, yet I could still see Dale's smirking face, pink flesh hanging from his lips.

This is Dale. He gave me cancer.

That can't be right. You don't catch cancer. Do you? I vaguely remembered reading something about vaccinating kids against a virus that caused gynecological cancers. *GVB? HPH? HPV?*

Okay, calm down. Use your brain. Learn what you need to know. Knowledge is power. I found the packet of information the nurse gave me and started reading.

For the first time in my life, the pursuit of information failed me. I learned that cervical cancer is caused by the sexually transmitted Human Papillomavirus. Since Dale was the only person I'd ever had sexual contact with, he had definitely given me the virus that led to the cancer. He really was devouring me from the inside out.

3
Unexpected Fears

A salmon glow oozed through the blinds as my alarm clock radio clicked on Thursday morning. I rolled off my futon, still in my workout clothes from the night before and tried to focus on the numbers on the clock. I had been up most of the night researching CT scans and LEEP procedures and had finally fallen asleep less than an hour before. The silky-voiced newscaster said Hurricane Mavis had gained strength off Cuba. Despite a mild hurricane season thus far, the newscaster pointed out that early September storms could be some of the worst. I knew from my research that was due to the warm Gulf Stream swinging north in late August. I staggered into the bathroom. I wanted to go to work and study the possible market effects of a direct hit to the Carolinas rather than drive to the hospital that morning to get a CT scan before my "procedure" that afternoon.

I twisted the shower handle to the limit and waited until

the room filled with bleach-scented steam. I was tempted to bathe myself in the bleach I scoured the bathroom with every Sunday. I felt dirty just thinking about people touching my body later that day. I climbed into the tub and scrubbed every inch of my body with a bar of deodorant soap and a stiff brush. When my skin was good and raw, I turned off the water. I wrapped a threadbare, yet clean, towel around my long hair and looked at myself in the mirror while I brushed my teeth. I looked like a healthy 29-year-old woman with finely freckled skin and good muscle tone. I was a little on the short side and kind of skinny, but I looked okay. I didn't look like a woman being slowly devoured by rogue cells.

I didn't see any point in ironing chinos and a work shirt to wear to the hospital. They would make me strip as soon as I got there. An old pair of jeans and a T-shirt would do fine. I didn't have the energy to blow my hair dry or even thoroughly brush it that morning, so I pulled it back in a low ponytail. When I left for the hospital, I looked more like a coed than a young woman going to have a piece of her cervix removed.

✳✳✳

The Ellery Cancer Center was already bustling with activity at half past the crack of dawn. I was not the only person with a full day of tests and treatments that morning. I joined the inchworm of cars winding their way through the parking garage and found a parking space on the roof of the concrete parking structure. Now that I had solved the hospital's code, I knew to follow the orange dots at the bank of elevators to the orange tile path leading to the radiology department. A cherubic lady, wearing a coral sweater against the clinical chill, took my name. Her kindly smile seemed more suited to sitting behind a table selling Bingo tickets than coordinating a room full of patients waiting to have radioactive fluids pumped through their bodies. "Did you already drink the contrast, dear?" she asked.

"No! Should I have?" I squawked. None of my research said anything about drinking contrast ahead of time. I gripped the counter to keep my hands from shaking. "I didn't know. Did I mess up the timing? Can I still get the test?"

"It's fine, dear. Just relax. I'll buzz them in the back and they'll be right out to talk to you." The receptionist peeled my white knuckled fingers from the counter and patted my hand. "You're fine, dear. It takes about an hour to drink the contrast but you've got plenty of time." I stared dumbly at the receptionist for another moment. "You can sit anywhere you'd like dear. Did you bring something to read? We have some nice magazines over there."

I realized the entire line of people behind me were watching me freak out and felt my face redden. I found a chair far away from everyone else and pulled out *Jane Eyre*. I liked the way the pages of my worn copy opened to my favorite parts. No matter how terrifying my reality, I had always been able to lose myself in Jane and Rochester's yearning for each other. However, when I opened the pages that morning the words swam in front of my eyes.

Why didn't anyone tell me that I needed to prepare for the test?

Maybe they told me on Tuesday. There was so much talking. I didn't catch half of it. Oh shit, maybe the cancer has spread to my brain. What if my brain is turning to mush? Come on, think. I read about this. What does it mean?

Suddenly a woman in orange scrubs squatted down in front of me. *Holy crap, where'd she come from?* Orange Scrubs held two tall foam cups with my name, my doctor's name and a series of numbers written on the sides in her gloved hands. *What exactly is in those cups that she has to wear heavy gloves to protect her skins from it?*

"Are you Lara Blaine?"

Can I say no?

I nodded. The woman set the cups on the table next to me. "Good morning, Ms. Blaine. Could you verify your date of birth?"

"April 21, 1984."

"Your address?"

"9E Crepe Myrtle Terrace."

"You are having a CT scan this morning. Correct?" We both nodded mechanically as the woman continued, "I have one of our special contrast drinks for you."

Special? Yummy special? Or special it-could-kill-you?

"We need you to slowly drink these over the next hour." The woman continued to nod like the little velvet dog with the weighted head that the Lee's kept beside the cash register. "When you're finished, tell the desk and they'll bring you back. Okay?" She stood up. "Do you need anything?"

"No, I'm fine," I replied. I had done my research. I understood how the contrast worked, in theory. I waited for the woman to disappear back into the bowels of the building before picking up one of the cups and sniffed it. *Smells like Coke. I wonder why they have to make sure the wrong person doesn't drink it? Is it poisonous to some people? I know I need to drink it slowly so it evenly fills my intestines. Will it kill me if I drink it too fast?* I noted the time, 7:09. I was already behind schedule. I took a tentative sip. It tasted like an amalgamation of Coke, skunked beer and pickle juice. *How am I ever going to drink all of this?* I rubbed my forehead. *Okay, think. You have an hour. You can do this. Just split it up.* I reached into my backpack for a pen and drew a horizontal line across the center of each cup, pinched my nose, and took another sip.

A middle-aged man watched me from a tangerine armchair on the other side of the room. I assumed he was ogling my breasts and regretted not wearing something less revealing than a thin T-shirt. I glared at him but he didn't look away. He raised his matching foam cup in a toast and smiled. *Isn't a girl safe anywhere? Do men have to be pigs even in a hospital?* I pretended to be concentrating on my book and studied him in my peripheral vision as I continued to take sips of the foul drink. The man's suit pants were worn at the cuffs, but his coat was pristine as if it spent more time on a hanger than his back. He reached deep into his sleeve to check his watch, which had slipped nearly to his elbow, then quickly slugged down the rest of his drink. On his way to the desk, he paused in front of me and pointed to my cup.

"You're doing that the hard way, you know."

"Excuse me?" I scoffed.

"I said, you're doing it the hard way. The gunk sinks to the bottom. You need to shake it up real good, and then slug it down like a whiskey. Don't sip at it like a fruity cocktail."

"Really?" I looked from my cup to the cup in the man's hand. His sticker said Norman, T. He had a Band-Aid wrapped around his wedding band to keep it from slipping off his finger. "No one told me."

"Of course they didn't." He rolled his dull eyes. "They never tell you important stuff like that."

"Why wouldn't they tell me?"

"Don't worry, you'll get it down after you do it a few times. This is my ninth CT. I think."

The contrast solution sloshed in my stomach. *Ninth? I thought this was a one-time thing.*

"Yup, get one every six months. Colon cancer." The man looked around the room. "Well, it's not too crowded in here today. Maybe we won't have to spend all day waiting around in the hall with our butts hanging out."

My breath caught in my chest. My research the night before taught me to be afraid of what the doctor would be doing to me later that afternoon, I didn't know to be afraid of drinking the solution incorrectly or being left in a hallway half-naked. As he shuffled away, I could see the seat of the man's pants hung off his body like shed skin.

I vigorously swirled the cup in my hand and took a big gulp. It was not nearly as disgusting as the first sips had been. *That was really helpful. Why didn't Orange Scrubs tell me to stir it? She should have told me.* I contemplated the chair where the man had been sitting. *Wow, colon cancer. Yuck! Gosh, I hope my cancer hasn't spread to my rear end.* I stared into my cup.

This keeps getting worse and worse.

✳✳✳

As 8:00 approached, a long line of people carrying cups identical to mine formed at the reception desk. *They knew to start drinking at home. How hard would it have been for Dr. Lander's office to tell me to start drinking the stuff ahead of time?* The pumpkin-colored chairs and cantaloupe sofas slowly filled. People were soon spilling out into the hallway like a toppled fruit display. I moved to a tiny settee in the corner and put my backpack and book on the seat beside me. I only had half a cup of solution left when a woman in a cherry red tracksuit pranced in and greeted the receptionist as if they were old friends. The receptionist said something to her before they turned in unison and looked at me. I cringed as she made a beeline for me and sat down. The woman would have sat on *Jane Eyre* had I not snatched her out of the way just in time.

"Oh my goodness, I am so sorry!" the woman drawled. "I just had to nab this spot before someone took it. This place gets so darn crowded at this time of day." She shoved a rolling suitcase under the settee then examined me. "I see you're drinking one of their delicious cocktails this morning."

I glanced into her cup. "Why is yours red?"

"It's red Gatorade," she tittered.

This woman is way too happy. Maybe she's been drugged.

"One of the nurses back home gave me a tip that you can drink the contrast in almost anything. I like Gatorade. You got Coke?"

"That's what they gave me. Should I have something else?"

"I have trouble getting it down in Coke. One time I had some Gatorade with me, you know just to have, and the nurses suggested I try it. Now, I always take it in Gatorade. Of course, I'll never be able to drink red Gatorade again, but it's not like I'm an athlete or anything." The woman laughed, a bit too loud. "It tastes just awful, but I can gulp it down right quick."

I peered down into my still half-full cup. This whole process was so much more complicated than I thought it would be, and I was just beginning.

"It really helps to know some tricks of the trade, but you'll get the hang of it, honey. For instance, I always wear just a cami under my clothes when I come up here. If you don't have any metal on, they don't make you wear one of those nasty gowns." I considered my clothes—I had metal closures on my bra and a metal zipper on my jeans. There was so much I still didn't know after doing hours of research.

The woman's bag had a luggage tag on the handle and an

airline ticket sticking out of the outside pocket. "You said a nurse from back home gave you the tip about the Gatorade?"

"I live in St. Augustine, that's in the northern part of Florida," the woman replied. I didn't need to prompt her. She seemed more than happy to tell me all about herself. "I started treatment at home, but once they figured out that I have this unusual kind of breast cancer, my doctors sent me up here to Dr. Bishop and his team. He's doing research on my kind of cancer, so I came up to be part of that. I can take a flight up early in the morning and be home the same day. It's a long day, but I'd rather not stay overnight." She finally took a breath. "Where are you from?"

"I live right here in Magnuson."

"You're lucky to live so close to such a good hospital. That would have made my life a lot easier over the last few years."

"Did you travel back and forth all the time? Didn't your boss get mad?"

"Oh, bless your heart. I had to go on disability. I stayed here for a few months while I was in treatment. Now I come back twice a year to get checked and talk to the doctors. If I have time today, I'm going to try to go see some of the research people to catch up with what they're doing."

"That sounds nice." *That sounds terrible! This lady has some rare awful cancer that could only be treated by the super-specialists here and she's all happy about it? I think the cancer ate away part of her brain.*

I gulped down the last of my drink and said, "Well, nice meeting you. Have a safe flight home."

"Have a blessed day!" the woman replied.

Oh yeah, I'm just so blessed.

I stood up, marched over to the reception desk, and declared myself ready for my scan.

The CT scan itself proved uneventful. The technicians asked me to take off my jeans, T-shirt and bra but let me keep my panties on under the roomy gown. I didn't feel as exposed as the man in the waiting room implied I would. Once inside, I compliantly lay there and let it happen. It was over quickly and then they were sending me on my way. No one even touched me.

✳✳✳

I had three hours of unscheduled time before my procedure. I followed the orange tiles back to the reception lobby and stood outside the Starbucks where Jane Babcock Roberts and I had shared the initial shock of our diagnoses. I wondered what she was doing at that moment. Was she running her business like it was any other day? Did she feel stymied by her diagnosis?

People pity young women. I didn't want people pitying me for sitting alone in a hospital coffee shop, so I walked outside and wandered across the brick courtyard between the Cancer Center's most recent additions. The humid air told of the coming storm. High thin clouds lined the eastern sky, but the actual storm clouds were still hundreds of miles offshore. I wondered if any oil tankers had been re-routed yet. I considered calling Letitia and telling her to check the tanker movement feeds, but I didn't want to risk her asking too many questions.

The set of doors at the far end of the courtyard led to a section of the Cancer Center the colored tiles hadn't taken me before. I explored the paths to the blue pulmonary clinics and purple hematology clinics until I came to a set of frosted glass doors with etched pictures of books.

A library. Exactly what I needed.

In the years I lived in New Hampshire, the Hawthorne

Public Library was my refuge from the awful realities of the farm. My grandfather was a geologist, so reading about minerals made me feel like he was still with me somehow. I spent my afternoons doing homework at one of the oak library tables in the nineteenth-century reading room or poking through the stacks. In the first years I lived there, I slowly worked my way through the Earth science section until I knew everything I could about rocks and elements.

Behind the frosted glass doors, I discovered an extensive collection of books on cancer and its treatment. Off to the side was a bookshelf where people could take books they wanted and leave books they were finished with. I sat in one of the overstuffed chairs scattered around the room and crossed my legs under me. The library was empty but I didn't feel alone at all. I pulled a leather bound copy of *The Heart of Darkness* from the shelves and inhaled the moldering scent of its yellowing pages. It was like going home.

When the Hawthorne Public Library closed at eight, I would walk the four miles out Clemmons Road to Dale's farm, quietly eat the plate of food Mama had left on the counter for me, and go to my room to read some more. Weekends were spent hiding in the loft of the barn. The cows didn't seem to mind my being there. Perhaps they sensed Dale had branded me as well.

One afternoon during my sophomore year, Susan Patterson, Hawthorne's head librarian and local fallen woman, came up behind me and draped a white cotton cardigan over my shoulders. "It's chilly in here today, hmm? This will cover up those bare arms." She ran her hand over my upper arm and inclined her head a little closer. "If I can see those bruises on your arms from way over there at my desk, so can those upstanding citizens in the meeting room.

You wouldn't want to give them any more grist for the mill." She raised her voice so everyone in the library would hear her. "Yes, that's so true. It is a shame we can't turn the heat on until next week. Research project going okay?" She winked at me and glided back to her desk.

I was ashamed that the librarian had seen the black and blues left by Dale's fingers as he held me down. I cringed to think how appalled she would be to see the bruises on my side where he had kicked me the night before. On my way out, I placed the folded sweater on the returns desk. "Thanks for the sweater, ma'am," I mumbled.

"That's okay, dear. You can borrow it any time. I keep it on a peg in the staff room."

When I turned to leave, Miss Patterson called after me. "Hey, wait up a minute." She hurriedly locked the library door and followed me out to the sidewalk. "I don't want you to miss your ride."

"Huh?"

"Doesn't your mother pick you up?"

"No. I walk."

"But it's got to be—" I stepped out of the puddle of light near the library door making Miss Patterson rush on. "I was wondering, would you like a job here at the library? We have an opening for a shelving assistant. It only pays minimum wage but you're here most days anyway, and I'm pretty sure that research project is long finished." I stretched the sleeves of my T-shirt down to my elbows. "You can do some dusting and re-shelving for a few hours then do your homework. What do you say? You'd really be helping me out."

Thus, my love of research was born. I worked at the library part-time after school and three full days a week during the summer. I did shelve books and clean, but I truly excelled when Miss Patterson asked me to help a patron research something. I learned all about the native birds of the Mississippi delta for old Mr. Shaw in anticipation of one of his birding trips and about the cathedrals of Spain for the Rotary Club's trip to Barcelona. On slow days, Miss Patterson and I would take our breaks on the cool granite steps at the front of the building. Over cups of Lady Grey tea, Miss Patterson taught me all about Charlemagne and the Hapsburgs. She'd been within months of earning her Ph.D. when she had returned to care for her terminally ill father and missed talking about history. Susan Patterson helped make my days in Hawthorne tolerable. No one could make the nights at the farm bearable.

***

Thirty minutes before my scheduled appointment, I left the solace of the library to make my way to the green waiting room. Perched on the edge of an avocado colored chair, I flipped through the account of a woman hemorrhaging to death after the simple procedure, but the words moved on the paper like a line of ants. The words began to consume the edges of the paper like leaf cutting ants devouring a banana leaf. I dropped the piece of paper with a shudder. When I looked again, it was just a piece of notebook paper covered with my own handwriting. No ants. No leaves.

I picked up the piece of paper and held it on my lap. The description of the woman who died was the same as it was when I copied it down from the deep recesses of the Internet the night before. As I read the terrifying account over a few times, the green walls seemed to lean over my shoulder as if reading along with me. The empty couches felt like they were creeping toward me on their dented wooden legs. I could feel the snake of anxiety creeping up my spine. For the next few minutes, I clung to the worn arm of the avocado colored couch, fighting to keep a hold on reality.

Eventually, Dr. Lander's nurse came and led me through the maze of hallways. I must have been holding it together okay because she didn't seem to notice my anxiety. The procedure room was three times the size of the one I had been in on Tuesday. One wall housed equipment panels and monitors. The nurse said, "I'm Cindy. I'll be assisting the doctor today."

"I know who you are. We met the other day."

"Great! Do you have any questions about what we are doing today?"

Don't use that supercilious tone with me, girlie. Like you give a damn about my questions. You don't even know who I am.

"No," I barked. I plopped down in the pink plastic patient chair and prepared for another long wait. "I understand what they're going to do to me. Just leave me alone."

The nurse stopped in the middle of pulling a paper gown from a drawer and looked at me. "Okay then," she responded, dropping the gown on the examination table like a used rag. "Take everything off from the waist down. The doctor will be ready for you in a few minutes." She exited the room, shaking her head.

Once half-naked on the examination table, I securely tucked the gown under my thighs on both sides. I read over my crumpled sheet of notes yet another time as I fiddled with the edge of the paper table covering. *Perhaps I should be lying down so I'm ready for the procedure.* I swung my legs up and reclined like a corpse. Muffled voices passed in the hall. They sounded like curses. I stared up at the yellowing ceiling for several moments imagining the doctor using long scissors to slowly cut out my organs one by one until my head felt like it was going to burst through my chest.

No. I shouldn't be lying down when they come in. That puts me in a submissive position. I popped up to sit on the edge of the table. *I need to be ready for it. I should be facing the door when they come in. Or, maybe I should sit over there in the chair.*

No, that won't work. Then I'd need to move over to the table after a while. I don't have any bottoms on. I hunkered down against the wall with my legs again swaddled in the sheet. *No. I'll stay here.*

Finally, after what felt like hours, the door opened. Dr. Lander and the nurse filed in without making eye contact. "Ms. Blaine? Sorry to keep you waiting." Dr. Lander sat down with her back to me while Cindy prepared a tray of instruments. "How did you tolerate the CT scan?"

"You should have told me to drink the contrast at home. I had to wait around for a whole hour in a room full of sick people." The doctor and Nurse Cindy exchanged startled looks.

"I'm sorry for any inconvenience," Dr. Lander replied. She didn't sound sorry. She moved to the sink to wash her hands. "Did you have a reaction to the contrast? Do you feel unwell?"

"I feel fine," I mumbled. I felt stupid. I felt afraid. I felt alone.

"Well then, I have the results here from the scans this morning and it looks like the cancerous cells are confined to a small area." The doctor turned to me for the first time and smiled. "That's good news!"

How can anything about this situation be good news?

Dr. Lander put on some latex gloves and started to collect

her tools. "So, do you have any questions before we begin?"

I whipped my list of questions out from under my leg and stormed ahead. "Yes. Yes, I do," I snapped. "How can I tell if you're cutting out my bladder? What if you perforate my bowel? I won't let you do a full hysterectomy!"

Dr. Lander blinked in astonishment and stepped back a few feet with her palms raised in surrender. "Whoa, Ms. Blaine. Where is that coming from?" She placed her tools on the small counter and peeled off her latex gloves. Dr. Lander perched her glasses on top of her short blond spikes. She rubbed her eyes for a moment before she turned to the nurse and said, "Cindy, I think Ms. Blaine and I are going to need a few minutes to talk. I'll buzz you when we're ready to proceed. Could you have Dr. Rosen check in with the patient in four?" Cindy glanced at me as if I were a lunatic and rushed out of the room.

"Okay, Ms. Blaine, what's going on?"

"You can't fool me!" I screeched. "I read all about it on the Internet. You tell women it's just going to be a little part of their cervix but you take everything. Everything!" *Oh my god, I sound like a crazy person.* I caught a glimpse of my face reflected in the paper towel dispenser. My eyes looked mad and pink blotches stained my pale cheeks.

Dr. Lander stepped forward and looked me squarely in the eye. I blinked back desperate tears. "Where is this coming from?"

"I read all about what people like you do to girls like me." I wanted to sound fierce, but my resolve had petered out. I was tired, and this conversation wasn't going the way I planned.

Dr. Lander stepped back again and started pacing. As harsh as her touch had been, I preferred it to her letting go. "Now, it sounds like you found some real horror stories on the Internet but—" She stopped pacing and picked up my file from the desk and held it in front of her. The doctor placed her glasses back on her nose. "Perhaps we should go over your treatment plan now. Okay?"

I glared at the doctor but didn't say anything. I knew when I was beaten. "Firstly, we can remove all the affected area today. In a twenty-nine-year-old woman, I feel it is better to aggressively treat the cancer now so we don't have to treat it ever again in the future, so I recommend you undergo a course of radiation as well. Do you understand what is involved in radiation treatment?"

I nodded. I had no idea what radiation entailed, but I wouldn't give Dr. Lander the satisfaction of admitting my ignorance. Not now.

"Now back to today. Do you have any questions about the LEEP procedure itself?"

I bit the inside of my cheek. *Why did this happen? Why am I here?*

"No, let's just get this over with."

4
Hurricane Lara

wanted Hurricane Mavis to bear down on North Carolina, yet Friday dawned an ordinary day. High thin clouds licked at the edges of a clear sky. The radio said Mavis was gaining strength off the coast of Florida. It wasn't enough. I needed more. I needed that day to be different. I was different. A piece of my flesh had been burned out with a piece of hot wire. Some spotting and a few abdominal twinges just weren't enough. I needed gushing blood and excruciating pain.

I needed to keep track of Mavis. She was important, not the cancer. Before I settled into my cubicle for the day, I slipped into Garlic Breath's cubicle. He kept an extra monitor under his desk so he could watch sports instead of working. I set it up on a file box beside my desk so I could track the storms progression on the NOAA website while I compiled data and built flowcharts on how shipping routes, fishing, and tourism would be affected by a direct hit to Charleston, versus Wilmington.

Just before lunchtime, Garlic Breath stood up and bellowed over our joint cubicle wall. "Hey, that's my monitor. Give it back!"

I glanced up at him while I pointed to the company logo on the side of the monitor. He had muffin crumbs in his short beard. "It's not yours. It says right here, 'property of Bettel Occidental.'"

"It's mine."

"No, it's not," Letitia said from the passageway. She had crept up on us without a sound. She held a frappuccino in one hand and a golf umbrella in the other. "What's going on over here?"

"Blaine stole my monitor."

I stood up to face my accuser. "I didn't steal anything. It's not his personal property."

"Calm down, Lara. He's not really accusing you of stealing." She hooked the umbrella over the top of my cubicle and took a sip of her drink. "What's with the radar maps?"

"If the hurricane hits Charleston, shipping lanes will be shut down for at least a day or so. But, if the storm swings north, Virginia Beach—"

"Okay, okay, okay. I don't need the details right now. Type that all up and I'll look at it later." Letitia turned to Garlic Breath with a rapacious smile. "It appears that Blaine over here is using the extra monitor to do actual work. You will just will have to watch the Marlins game on your phone."

"The game was cancelled," I mumbled as I sat back down at my desk. "Heavy rains over Florida and Georgia."

"But," Garlic Breath protested, "she keeps hogging all the supplies around here. Look at all the file boxes she uses." He gestured to the stacks of color-coded, neatly labeled file boxes stacked along the wall outside my cubicle.

Letitia picked up her umbrella and started to walk away. "You know the deal. Blaine took this funky cubicle at the end so she can have more storage space. If you want a place to store your projects while they're in progress, I suggest you actually work on some projects." Letitia stalked away on her tiny stiletto heels and disappeared into the elevator. When she was gone, Garlic Breath kicked over the closest stack of boxes. My notes on bauxite futures mingled with my notes on tea crop projections. I left them on the floor; I needed to concentrate on the hurricane.

I secured my hair on top of my head with a sharpened pencil and prepared to immerse myself in the world of shipping until I realized I would need Pathetic Dog Owner's help with the data on crude oil tankers. Letitia had hired him because he was an expert on the price of crude oil. Like me, he had degrees in both geology and finance; unlike me, the guy couldn't string a sentence together. I had to rewrite his reports every month before I could aggregate them with the rest of the department's. Our similar backgrounds made Letitia compare him to me even more than the rest of the people on the eighth floor. Pathetic Dog Owner came up lacking every time. I guess he resented me for that. He always skipped over my cubicle when he walked around hawking Girl Scout cookies and made snide comments to Garlic Breath about how I was too much of a skinny bitch to enjoy a good cookie. He somehow managed to make eating Thin Mints feel tawdry.

As much as I didn't want to talk to him, I needed Pathetic Dog Owner's information. He was talking on the phone with his back to me when I walked across the office to his cube. The pictures of a shaggy German shephard seemed to have multiplied on the cubicle walls since I had last looked in. A scratched dog crate crouched under the desk. Pathetic Dog Owner had his work calendar open on his laptop and flipped through another calendar on his phone as he seemed to be scheduling a series of appointments. I craned my neck to see if a sick dog was napping in the carrier.

"Can I help you?" Pathetic Dog Owner demanded as he hung up.

I pointed to the carrier. "Is your dog in there?"

"She's at the vet today, as if it's any business of yours." He pushed the carrier further under the desk with his toe and tossed a Diet Pepsi can into the trashcan.

"That should be recycled."

"What do you want?"

"I need to know how many tankers are off the southeast coast right now," I said as I pulled three cans out of the trash and held them against my chest.

"I don't know," Pathetic Dog Owner barked. He gestured to the teetering piles of file folders and printouts scattered across the desk. "I have enough on my plate today without you wanting me to help you. Go away."

I dropped the cans in the tall blue container next to the restroom and slunk back to my desk. *That was a colossal waste of time. These people all hate me.* It took me four hours, but I managed to get a handle on what I needed to know. When I finally looked up, the hurricane had gained speed, the office had fallen quiet, and I was late for spin class.

I rushed into the lobby of Silver Star Fitness and groaned when I saw the class was already in full swing. A Stepford wife in red bike shorts pedaled my favorite stationary bike on the other side of the glass wall.

"You're too late," the bouncy babe behind the counter blathered. "There's a storm coming. Everyone from the

Saturday morning class came tonight."

"But it's Friday night," I said as I signed in. "I always take spin class on Fridays."

"Sorry," Bouncy Babe replied. "There's a Zumba class in a few minutes."

Yeah, that's gonna happen. My mind raced as I turned toward the locker room. It was a Friday, I was supposed to be riding to nowhere beside a room full of people unable to communicate over the loud music and barking instructor. My body shuddered with pent-up energy. Spin class or no spin class, I needed a workout. Once in my bike shorts and oversized T-shirt, I slipped into the cardio room. If I could find an open stationary bike, I could maintain a shadow of my routine.

There were no open stationary bikes. I wasn't about to stand there and wait until one opened up; someone might try to talk to me. There was an open treadmill in the center of the room. Thursday was treadmill day, but it would have to do. I stepped onto the treadmill and ran at a moderate pace to warm up. It felt good to move my muscles after being folded up at my desk all day. The digital display said I had run two miles when the man to my left finished his workout and a woman a few years younger than me took his place. She placed her trendy imported water bottle down between the machines and popped a set of ear buds in her ears.

She's probably not even listening to music. I bet she just puts those on to look cute. Look at that smirk. I bet she's making fun of me in her head right now. She's just like the people at work, always mocking me. They all hate me.

I had to run faster to outrun my thoughts. I increased the speed and incline on the machine and turned my head to watch the hurricane coverage on the large television hanging from the ceiling. A blast of sweat and cheap cologne hit me as if I'd run through a patch of skunk cabbage. The middle-aged man haphazardly jogging on the next treadmill grinned like a hyena watching a springbuck at the watering hole. I knew that look; I had seen it on Dale's face far too many times. I glared at him, but the man looked right through me. He was looking at the girl bobbing along in her tiny spandex shorts and red jog bra.

What a pig! That girl is young enough to be his daughter.

I adjusted my pace to block his view. The man stepped back to the end of his treadmill to see around me. I stepped back too. "Hey!" The man said with a shake of his head. A drop of sweat flew into my face. The people on the treadmills around us stopped watching the hurricane swirling on the Weather Channel to watch us.

I stepped off the treadmill belt and blurted out, "Stop staring at her!" Spandex Girl slipped her ear buds out of her ears. I whirled around and yelled, "Yeah, I'm talking about you. I caught this creep watching you bounce."

The girl shot me a confused look, jumped off her machine, and stormed off in disgust. Before she disappeared into the locker room, she winked coquettishly at the man over her shoulder. The man punched the controls of his treadmill and the machine thumped to a stop.

"See what you did?" the man yelled, wiping his forehead with his already drenched T-shirt. Rivulets of sweat stuck the hair on his stomach to his skin. "Why don't you mind your own business? She didn't seem offended." The people around us all stopped their machines to hear what was going on. "Why would she wear that get up if she wasn't asking for guys to look at her?"

"Oh yeah?" My heartbeat was pounding in my ears. "She

was asking for it, huh? Right!"

I was so done being a sexual object. Men, and sex, had given me cancer. Before my brain could catch up with what my body was doing, I vaulted off the treadmill. Every time my stepfather said I was "asking for it" by being young and pretty came back to me. That memory was behind each punch to the man's fleshy face. I kept yelling, "Oh yeah? Oh yeah?" as another gym member pulled me off him. "Get off me!" I yelled.

I fought against the hands holding me while another man grabbed my legs and they pushed me through the locker room doors. I fell on the floor in a heap.

Felicity, the manager, ran in behind me. "What the hell is going on? Someone said you punched Ronny?" My breath hitched in my chest. I couldn't form words for a moment. Pointing at the young woman still standing there naked despite the small crowd forming in the locker room, I stammered, "Her... He was watching that girl run!"

The gym manager draped a towel over the naked girl. "Look, Ronny may be a dirty old man but you can't just haul off and punch the guy." She waved the remaining people out of the locker room while saying, "Okay, okay, show's over." She handed me a towel to wipe my face and sat down on a bench. "Look, we have really strict rules about violence in the gym. I don't have a choice. I'm going to have to revoke your membership."

I was stunned. Ronny had acted like a pig and I was the one getting kicked out? Felicity left me sitting on the locker room floor. "Just get your stuff and go. Hopefully he won't press charges." I wandered out to my car in a daze without even picking up my food from Lucky Lee's.

I've spent every weeknight for the last six years in that gym.

Where am I going to go now?

✱✱✱

A crash jolted me awake. I had fallen asleep, still in my workout clothes, face down on the couch. Heavy rain and hail lashed the windows but the power was still on. Blue light from the television bathed the room. I squinted at the whirling clouds on the screen. The Weather Channel showed the eye of the hurricane passing over Goldsboro, NC. *But where did it come ashore? Did I miss it? Was there damage?*

I lifted my head. Something wasn't right. A yellow glow shone from the kitchen. *Did I leave the refrigerator open? When did I even open the refrigerator?* I hadn't eaten anything when I came in from the gym. My stomach, empty since a few bites of peanut butter and jelly sandwich at lunch, grumbled to be satisfied. I stood up and walked toward the kitchen just as a particularly strong gust of rain slapped against the transom windows above the television.

My sweaty T-shirt had dried while I slept. It made a ripping sound as I peeled it off like a bandage. In the kitchen, the refrigerator was secure. The yellow light came from a halogen streetlight shining through the sliding glass door leading out to my postage stamp of a back yard. A section of the twelve-foot stockade fence that separated my yard from the neighbor's had blown down.

Another gust of wind blew a child's plastic chair through the gap in the fence. I slid the door open and jumped through the sheet of water tumbling over the edge of the gutter. I was instantly soaked. Tiny pellets of hail stung my skin as I rescued the tiny chair. I had seen, but never spoken to, my neighbor on the other side of the fence. I knew he was older than me, somewhere in his early forties, with a ponytail and a motorcycle. He played video games late into the night and had a little girl with a red jacket that spent weekends in the front bedroom. The toys littering the backyard obviously belonged to her.

I reached through the opening and picked up a Barbie doll that had blown under a bush. I pulled a piece of mulch from the doll's hair and straightened the muddy ball gown. I tried to remember if I had ever owned such a doll. The various church daycare centers I attended as a little girl had bald, naked Barbies and a few armless Skippers, but I didn't remember having one of my own.

Then, I did remember. The girlie-pink room Mama set up at the back of Dale's sprawling farmhouse had a shelf of Barbie dolls in spangled gowns as if a bunch of little girl's toys could make up for Dale stealing my childhood. With a force that rivaled the storm, I threw the doll and the tiny chair back through the gap with a massive yawp.

∗∗∗

After the first night Dale came into my room, I lay naked on the floor in shock. My knees and hips had rug burns from when I tried to get away from him. My throat was raw from screaming and my ears still rang from Dale slamming my head against the canopy bedpost. My jaw ached from where he had punched me when I bit his shoulder. Depleted, I waited to hear Dale snoring from the TV room before wiping the blood off my thighs. I pulled on a pair of jeans, gathered a few books in a suitcase, and crept into the master bedroom.

"Mama!" I whispered. "We've got to go!"

Mama sat up against the velvet-upholstered headboard in a black satin robe. "Hush up, girl!" She pushed me off the bed. "And stop that caterwauling. You want to wake up Dale?"

"Mama," I cried. "Mama, he… he…"

"Shut up!" Mama shoved a pillow into my face. "You think I'm deaf? I could hear what was going on back there."

"You heard?" I gulped in the perfumed air trying to stop crying. "But..."

"You shouldn't fight so much. You'll get your pretty face all ruined. You're gonna be all black and blue tomorrow."

"Why didn't you stop him?" I started to sob in earnest. It had been horrific enough to be beaten and raped but I had been able to hang on thinking we would escape by morning. Some of my mother's ex-boyfriends had tried to touch me in the past and Mama had always kicked them out the next day.

Mama slapped me across the face with the television remote. I saw stars. "You stop that bawling. Look, it isn't easy landing a man like Dale when you've got a kid. Especially one like you. Now Dale has fixed us up pretty nice here. Don't you like your new room?" Mama whined. "All you got to do is be nice to old Dale every once in a while and everything'll be fine. You've got a pretty face and nice little bod, so I suggest you use it and get as much as you can out of him. If you play your cards right, I bet he'd buy you a car for your birthday."

Mama pulled at the skin around her eyes. "'Cause let me tell you, baby, it won't last. I was a real looker when I ran away to Nashville. Look at me now. My boobs are sagging. My face is gone. I didn't have two pennies to rub together before I met Dale. Now we have more money than God. So keep your little trap shut."

Mama had never been an ideal mother—far from it. She had disappeared for days at a time leaving me alone with no food. She refused to buy me a winter coat until I was "done growing". She dragged me from place to place, but I never expected her to blithely sacrifice me for a little financial security. My childhood, as grim as it had been, ended that night. I went back to my room and tore the pink sheets off the bed. The dotted swiss curtains made a satisfying ripping sound as I pulled them off the windows. I ripped the fabric into shreds until I was spent and tossed the pile of rags in the closet. The next morning I spackled foundation over my bruises and went to school as usual. I was trapped. I had no money, nowhere to go, and no one that loved me.

I didn't speak to my mother in any real way after that night. From then on, my mother supplied me with food and water like she did the other livestock. It was clear to me that she had sold me, her only child, to Dale like a good milking cow.

5
Frayed Edges

osing my gym membership left a hole in my routine that sucked at my sanity. I couldn't sleep; the nightmares started as soon as I closed my eyes. I couldn't eat; everything I put in my mouth tasted bitter. My muscles twitched to run yet felt heavy on my bones. Work was my only relief.

A week after the unfortunate incident with the letch at Silver Star Fitness, I was tapping away at my keyboard when my screen froze. A message popped up alerting me that my laptop had lost its connection with the secure server. "What happened?" I yelped. I craned my neck to look over the top of the cubicles. The eighth floor was dark. Everyone else had gone home. The only puddle of light came from the articulated chrome lamp on Letitia's desk. Her normally flawless high ponytail had slipped behind her left ear, her starched shirt was a mass of wrinkles, and a pair of heavy black glasses were perched on her slender nose as she frantically banged on her keyboard. Piles of spreadsheets were strewn across her office floor. I couldn't remember the last time I had seen her using hard copies of anything.

I sprinted down the passageway and stormed into her office. "What's going on? Why can't I get on the server?"

"It should be back up in a few hours. They shut the servers down for maintenance," Letitia sighed. She rubbed the back of her neck and took a sip from the Starbucks cup in front of her. Black coffee, not a good sign. "Wait a minute—why are you still here? It's eight!"

I moved a tower of pizza boxes off the chair in front of her desk and sat down. I suddenly felt woozy. I hadn't had anything to eat or drink all day. Letitia tossed her coffee cup into the trash and licked her lips. "Actually, since you're here. I need to talk to you. A little birdie told me you asked about the crude oil tanker exchanges. What are you working on? Did Robertson down on five ask you to do something for his department?"

"No, but I would be happy to help out Robertson's team if they want me."

"No, I don't want Robertson poaching my best worker bee." Letitia twirled a freshly sharpened pencil between her red talons and looked at me through narrowed eyes. "Are you all right? You're blinking an awful lot. And, you look like you're about to explode out of that chair. How do you have so much energy? You were here late last night, too."

"I was just finishing up some research."

"Whatever." Letitia rubbed the bridge of her nose under her glasses. "I got a call this morning from the cleaning crew supervisor. She said you were here until after midnight harassing their people?"

"I merely pointed out that they should vacuum

everywhere, not just the main walkways. If they can't do an adequate job I am more than willing to use their vacuums to—"

"Yeah, okay." Letitia rolled her eyes and stretched her long legs under her desk. "Just don't talk to the cleaning people, okay? And you shouldn't be in the building after six. Work from home if you need to."

Going home was not an option; that was where the nightmares were. I looked around at the stacks of paper. My latest report was on top of the stack next to my feet. "You're never here late either. Why are you here after hours looking at my reports?"

"Don't be so paranoid, Lara." Letitia waved at the stacks of paper. "I'm looking at everyone's files. Year-end is coming up and the numbers aren't reconciling. Peter and I have been at this all day. I even had the IT group up here at lunch helping. Didn't you notice the three guys sitting in here all afternoon?"

"But—"

"Are you sure you're feeling okay? You look a little green."

I got up to leave. "I'm fine. Absolutely fine. There's nothing wrong with me."

"Why don't you go home and get some rest. The servers will be back up by morning. Unless," Letitia laughed under her breath, "you want to stick around and figure this out for me?"

"No. I'll leave you to it." I backed out of the door and went back to my desk to gather my things. I didn't want to be anywhere near Letitia when she discovered that Garlic Breath had fudged the numbers on his pork belly forecast. I had overheard him telling Pathetic Dog Owner about it at lunch a few days before.

***

I swung by Lucky Lee's and picked up my food even though it was already cold. Susan asked me if she should start preparing my order for a later pick-up. I didn't know what to say. My schedule had been ripped apart, just like my cervix. When I got home, I threw the bag of food in the trash and ate a spoonful of peanut butter in front of the television. I couldn't be bothered to reheat the Moo Goo Gai Pan.

As much as I resisted, I eventually succumbed to sleep. The nightmares were worse than ever. This time, a giant spider with red pincers and bright red lipstick around its sharp mandibles chased me through the darkened office hallways. The fire exit was yards away when a computer keyboard jumped up and bit my leg. A computer mouse scampered over the keyboard and hogtied me with its cord.

The next thing I knew, the dream changed. I lay splayed out on an icy examination table. Instead of metal stirrups, human hands emerged from the sides of the slab to hold me down. At first, a bright white light blocked out any sensation except a faint heartbeat within the fingers grasping my arms and legs. The light dimmed to reveal grotesque man-beasts, covered with stubble and reeking of whiskey, surrounding me. They each held a glowing electrode. Suddenly, a woman with enormous purple eyes that wept tears of blood appeared beside my head. The woman's eyes grew until they were larger than her face itself. The room slowly flooded with her bloody tears. When the tears licked at my skin, she raised her long speculum fingers above my body and snapped them together. In unison, the man-beasts stabbed me with their burning electrodes. Wherever they penetrated my body, purple goo ran out in hot rivulets that swirled into the bloody tears. The nightmare went on and on for hours, yet I didn't die.

I reeled awake, shaken and breathless, to the sound of my cell phone ringing next to my head. It switched over to voicemail and I heard Letitia's voice blast through my apartment. "It's 10:00, Blaine. Where the hell are you? You missed the staff meeting. I even had to aggregate the department's reports myself." My arms and legs felt like they were filled with sand. There was no way I could go into the office. For the first time ever, I rolled over and blew off work.

✳✳✳

Hours later, I rolled off the couch determined to find a new place to work out. I couldn't go through another night of nightmares. My body needed sleep. The three private gyms within a few minutes of my condo were all filled with a bunch of Chatty Cathies who asked way too many questions and had moldy locker rooms. I ended up at the Y. It was the only place with clean showers that had the German equipment I liked. I'd missed climbing the Eiffel Tower every Tuesday. When I saw the Schlein TdF99 stationary bike tucked in the corner of the busy cardio room next to a Schlein TE1889 stair stepper, I bought a membership. I was excited to use the stationary bike, until I saw the note attached to the handlebars saying to see Liam before trying to use it. I didn't want to talk to anyone, especially not someone named Liam. I considered just using a treadmill, but couldn't resist the lure of the Tour de France course programmed into the machine. I went looking for a muscle bound leprechaun.

Liam ended up being the goofy redhead with spindly arms and legs at the front desk. When I asked him about the stationary bike, he said, "You want to use the Schlein TdF99? Really? It's a complicated machine."

"I'm a smart girl. I can handle it," I snarled. An urge to punch the guy in the face made me take a step back. I couldn't do that again. "I've used the TE1889 stair stepper by the same manufacturer," I said demurely.

Liam jumped over the low counter and started walking toward the cardio room. "Do you like to climb the pyramids or the Eiffel Tower?"

"The Eiffel Tower. The pyramids are too easy," I replied and hurried after him. "So can I use the machine?"

"Oh sure," Liam said. "We just keep it locked. A week after the machine was donated, some bozo pushed all the buttons at once and jammed it all up. I'll run you through the operating instructions and give you a code. This way we know who uses the machine in case anything goes wrong."

"Very prudent," I replied. "I'm all for security measures."

"Well, jump on," Liam said. "Let's get this thing adjusted." The Schlein TdF99 could be customized to each user, so Liam programmed in the proper settings for my leg length and arm length. I appreciated having proper body mechanics while exercising, but it unnerved me to have this kid putting his hands so close to my thighs while he adjusted the controls. I held on tight to the handlebars to keep from reacting to his close proximity and regretted wearing spandex bike shorts under my oversized T-shirt instead of baggy sweatpants.

"Did you know that this is made by a German company?" I asked. "The Germans are a very efficient people. It makes sense that they would design exercise equipment that allows you to climb a specific hill rather than just climbing to nowhere."

"What does that say about our American machines?" Liam chuckled. "Are we all fat, dumb, and happy to be going nowhere fast?"

"Americans prefer recumbent exercise bikes to upright models because they are easier for obese people to ride."

"Hey," Liam said, swatting my arm. "Don't knock the obese. Some of my best clients are obese."

I resisted swatting him back. *It's okay, it's okay. He's just being friendly. He didn't mean anything by touching you.*

"What is the Tour de France setting all about?" I blurted out.

"You can do the course Lance Armstrong rode in 1999. That's why we have the machine. The guy who donated it didn't want it anymore after the doping scandal."

"Show me how it works so I can climb the Pyrenees next time."

Liam shot me a look that could have been leering or could have been envious. "Well, all right then. Let's go."

6

Bright Blinking Beacon

E llery Hospital sent me an automated reminder call that essentially said: press one if you're completely brain dead and have to be reminded you have an appointment to verify they cut all the cancer out of your body, press two if your appointment is a bright yellow blinking beacon on your calendar that obliterates everything else on the page, or press three if you were trying to put your appointment out of your mind and this message just wrecked your day. I pressed three.

Three weeks had passed. Another full day at the Cancer Center was in order. First they wanted to peer inside me again with a CT scanner. Then, I had an appointment with billing to pay my $1000 out-of-pocket fees, then see Dr. Lander in the afternoon. Letitia wasn't happy that I was missing another staff meeting, yet she couldn't argue with my work product. The executive committee was bowled over by the presentation I prepared for her on copper trends just the day before.

I considered swinging by the hospital the night before to pick up the contrast solution, but the idea of having that stuff in my house creeped me out more than the idea of sitting in the orange waiting room drinking it. I did step into a convenience store after picking up my food at Lucky Lee's for a bottle of red Gatorade. As I waited to check out, I thought about Cherry Red Tracksuit Woman and mentally thanked her for giving me the Gatorade tip.

The CT scan went well enough. I got there on time, the red Gatorade masked the taste of the contrast as promised, and I chugged down the Gatorade-contrast mixture without any trouble. The people in billing were pleasant. They even gave me a handful of Halloween candy on my way out. The whole morning was remarkably painless. It was a bit disconcerting.

My appointment with Dr. Lander was over before my clothes had lost my body's warmth. She checked my cervix, said my scans were clear, and proclaimed me healed. I wandered over to the checkout lobby feeling like I had missed a step.

I moved forward in the line snaking down the hallway a few times when I heard my name rumble behind me. Immediately, an icy hand of fear traced a finger down the length of my spine. *Dale! He's found me. The hospital must have tracked down Mama for some reason and told them where I am. No, that can't be. There's that whole HIPPA thing.*

"Lara," the voice croaked again, slightly louder this time. I set my jaw and slowly turned my head, afraid but prepared to feel Dale's hot breath in my face. I didn't expect to see Jane waving at me from the back of the lobby.

I jumped out of my place in line and went over to where she clutched the low railing skirting the checkout lobby.

"It's nice to see a friendly face," Jane crackled. She had metamorphosed into a cancer patient in the past month. Jeans and a loose silk caftan had replaced the black power suit and red heels. Her long silver hair was twisted on top of her head with a lacquered clip. She looked pale and grim.

"Do you need some help?"

"Thanks. I'm feeling pretty wonky all of a sudden. It's this god awful place." Jane placed a hand on my shoulder and leaned ever so slightly on me as we joined the back of the line. Her loose grey tunic was as soft and cool as fog against my palm when I took her elbow. "So, how are you?" she asked.

"Okay, well, you know, not good." My breath caught in my chest as I realized Jane was the only person on the entire planet that knew I had cancer. I hadn't told anyone about the diagnosis or procedure; there was no one to tell. Jane squeezed my shoulder slightly, even though I propped her up. I took a deep breath before going on, "I'm fine. The doctor just told me I'm healing fine."

A man behind us harrumphed as the line moved forward. Without thinking about it, I grasped Jane around the waist to help her step forward. Her vertebrae felt like knots in a birch limb.

"So, are you?" Jane asked.

"Am I what?"

"Healing."

"The doctor says I am." I bit my lip. I would never fully heal. A vital piece of me had been cut out forever, but I couldn't tell Jane, right there in the checkout line, that I would never be the same. Never be whole. Jane had her own cancer to worry about. Why would she care? "It's only been a few weeks… I guess I don't really know yet."

We jerked forward again along the well-worn path in the carpeting. "Is this it?" Jane asked. "Do you have to have any further treatment?"

"Radiation, in a few weeks." I didn't want to think about radiation. I wanted to enjoy talking to Jane. "You?"

"Chemo," Jane said. Her manicured nails dug into my skin as she grabbed my arm with a surprisingly strong grip. The smell of fear mingled with her Chanel No. 5. "They told me about it just now. Right before they put this... thing... in my chest."

Jane reached inside the slit of her caftan to scratch at a large bandage covering her collarbone. Apprehension as bitter as day old coffee trickled down my throat. I knew from my reading that a Hickman catheter could be permanently implanted in a cancer patient's chest to protect their veins from the caustic chemotherapy drugs.

"I start next Monday," Jane rasped.

"So soon?" I didn't know that much about chemotherapy, but I associated it with uncontrollable vomiting and pain. I didn't want that for Jane.

"Yeah," Jane replied. "No surgery. I thought I was going to have surgery. They told me I would have surgery." She squeezed my arm even harder and growled. "He told me I couldn't have the surgery because the tumor is too big. Can you believe that? There is a committee somewhere that decides which tumors are too big to be removed." Jane pursed her lips and blinked rapidly as if to hold back tears.

The line moved forward another step and Jane finally released my arm to steady herself on my shoulder. I flexed my fingers behind her back to get the feeling to return to my hand.

"You know," Jane said, "I keep coming back to the same

thing. He said that 'chemotherapy would yield the best outcome.' Not preserve my life. Not eradicate the cancer. Yield the best outcome.'" Jane's body pulsated with emotion making the stray tendrils that had escaped her topknot tremble around her long neck. "I... I don't know what to do with that."

Jane had articulated exactly how I had been feeling since my procedure—I don't know what to do with that. I could stare at the books I borrowed from the library until my eyes were as dry and fuzzy as the text, but I still didn't know what to do with my feelings. My brain understood the facts but my heart still told me the cancer was a mark of my shame.

Jane pulled her shoulders back and thrust out her quivering chin. "This is not who I am, Lara. I am not just another woman in her sixties diagnosed with cancer." She stared at a woman approximately her own age in a pink ribbon bejeweled tracksuit and pink ball cap covering her bald head.

"I am not one of these people," Jane spat. "I will not be at the mercy of microscopic terrorists nor will I be beholden to nameless, faceless medical boards." Anger made Jane's breathing even shallower. Beads of sweat formed on her upper lip and neck. Her voice was shrill as she tossed her head back to examine the full expanse of the checkout lobby. "Can you believe this place? Look at the inefficiency in this system. This is not the way it would be if I were in charge. What's the point of this line? Why don't they have a few computer kiosks out here so we could simply use a touch screen to schedule our next appointment and then drop our forms in a slot? It would be so much more efficient to coordinate schedules with a machine than have to wait in this stupid line to talk to one of those chipper little ninnies up there. They have no added value."

Jane's eyes were beginning to roll back in her head and her breathing sounded like a clogged drain. The people around us were staring and giving us extra room. Frightened Jane would faint, I placed my palm against the center of her back and said, "You start chemo next week?" This seemed to pull Jane back from a precipice.

She blinked a few times then pointed to a plastic folder in the tooled leather bag slung over her arm. "They gave me another pile of pamphlets. My son can read them." Silver bangles trickled down Jane's arm as she pressed her left hand against her chest and tried to take a deep breath. I could feel a gurgling sensation through Jane's slender back. "They tried to tell me what to expect. I didn't absorb any of it. A sweet little nurse even gave me a tour of the chemotherapy room after they put this thing in my chest."

There was horror in Jane's eyes as she turned to face me. "They were ghouls in barcaloungers, Lara. People were watching television and knitting with tubes hanging out of their arms. It's not right. They try to make it homey, but there is no hiding the fact that they are pumping poison into those people." Jane's lips began to tremble again. "No... I don't want to do it. They can't make me do it."

Neither of us noticed that it was finally Jane's turn to pass in her encounter form until the man behind us poked me in the back and grunted, "Hey Lady, I don't have all day here."

I reared on him and snapped, "Back off! Can't you see she's really sick?" The room stood in stunned silence as I helped Jane to the counter. I had committed the cardinal sin of speaking the truth. We were all sick. None of us had time to wait in line.

We stepped to the counter arm in arm. The receptionist

mechanically took both of our encounter forms and handed me both of our insurance receipts. I felt a flush of pride to have Jane clinging to my arm as the room full of people watched us walk out into the busy corridor.

"Thank you," Jane said when we were a few yards away. "I hate a bully."

We walked companionably to the bank of elevators. "Are you parked in the garage?" I asked.

"I called my son a while ago," Jane said, resentment deepening her already gruff voice. "He said he would pull the car up in front of the main lobby." I pushed the button for the ground floor. When the doors closed, Jane squeezed my arm again. "No laughing, okay? I don't think I could take that again." I blushed at the memory of our last elevator ride together and stared at the safety instructions on the inside of the doors. "Oh, I'm just kidding, Lara. Fall apart all you want. What the hell."

In the vast, sunny reception lobby, I spotted Jane's son through the windows—the same blonde hair, the same angular build, the same fierce expression. He was pacing in front of a sleek grey Jaguar and shouting into his cell phone. We stepped through the automatic revolving doors, stopped beside the car, and listened to him yelling about appliances needing to all be the same color.

"Tom!" Jane banged on the roof of the car. "Unlock the doors."

Tom jumped, finally noticing us standing there beside the car, and quickly ended his phone call. He ran around the front of the car and took his mother's elbow. "Thank you, nurse. I can take it from here," he said dismissively.

Jane gently elbowed him in the ribs as she transferred her grip from me to her son. "They don't send out a nurse with me, silly. This is my friend, Lara."

Friend? I don't have friends.

"Okay, Mom," Tom said without giving me more than a cursory glance. "Let's get you out of here. You should be home resting." Tom unlocked the passenger side door and helped his mother slide into the low car before running around to the driver's side. Before pulling the door closed, Jane pressed one of her business cards into my hand. "Thank you, Lara. I'm sorry I'm such a mess today. I hardly asked you about yourself."

I gripped the rectangle of paper like a prize. "I'm fine, really."

"We should meet for coffee sometime. I don't know how much I'll be working for a while, but you can always get a message to me at that number. I'd like to know how things work out for you." I was stunned that Jane would want to see me again. "Do you have a card?"

"No, they don't give people like me business cards. But, here." I pulled a piece of chocolate out of my pocket, ripped the paper wrapper off, and wrote my cell phone number and email addresses on the inside. We said a hurried goodbye before Tom pulled away from the curb. I opened the foil inner wrapper and licked off the melted chocolate as they drove away.

7
Cheshire Cat

Two days after Dr. Lander gave me the kiss off, I received a call from the offices of a Dr. Obatu. Not an automated call from a computer, an actual phone call from a live human being. A woman with a charming lisp asked when it would fit into my schedule to come in for an initial consultation. I chose to go later that same day. If I put it off, the idea of radiation would blot out everything else. Better to get it over with so I could get on with my life sooner. A few minutes later, I received a surprisingly thorough and welcoming confirmation email from Dr. Obatu's staff. The email also included a list of questions the doctor would be asking along with pictures and short bios of the staff.

The women behind the desk were filing away the day's activity when I arrived at 5:43. "I'm Lara Blaine," I panted. It had been a longer walk to the basement level department than I anticipated. I should have given myself an hour to get there rather than fifteen minutes. "I had a 5:30 with Dr.

Obatu. I hope I'm not too late."

An extremely pregnant woman with a ready smile said, "No, you're okay. Dr. Obatu is actually running late this afternoon. We had an emergency right after lunch and he never caught up."

"One thing out of place can mess up the whole day, huh?"

The receptionist nodded distractedly while searching through the forms on her desk. "What did you say your last name is? Blare?"

"No, Blaine. Lara Blaine."

"There must be a mistake somewhere," the receptionist said looking down at the blue folder in her hand. "Was your maiden name Larissa Scott?"

An icy fist gripped my heart when I heard that name. I reached across the desk and snatched the file out of her hand. "How did you get that name? I changed that!"

She took the file back. "Excuse me," the woman said with a tone that only a mother of little boys would have. "That is hospital property." She put the file down on the desk out of my reach and opened it up. "I see now. Yes. I am sorry. It says Lara Blaine right here. Just the pediatric files that came from microfiche have the other name."

The woman asked me to verify my date of birth and address but I couldn't speak. I felt like my throat had been stuffed with dry leaves. All I could do was stare at a brown spot on the tip of her nose and nod at her questions. "For future reference, you are file number BL2911. It would be good to know your number in case there's ever any question about your name. Knowledge is power, you know." I stood there staring at her nose until she handed me a clipboard. "We'll need you to fill out these forms before you go in to see the doctor. You've got plenty of time."

I drifted over to a grouping of couches and chairs. The yellow and blue plaid couches were newer than the furniture in the succession of waiting rooms upstairs. There was the requisite television and magazines but someone had also taken care to place soft throws over the backs of the couches. The area seemed more like a living room than a waiting room. On a side table, there was a large basket filled with packets of cookies and crackers and a tray of miniature water bottles.

I poured a bottle of water down my throat and tried to calm down. *That name. How did they get that awful name?* I vaguely remembered filling out a form authorizing the hospital to access all my medical records and putting that name down as "other names," but I never thought they would bother to actually get my records.

After I left Hawthorne, I legally changed my name to keep Dale off my trail. My grandmother thought Larissa was a silly sounding name, so my grandparents always called me Little Lara. Blaine was my grandfather's middle name. I never knew who Mr. Scott was or if there even was a Mr. Scott. Scott could have been some guy Mama met in a bar.

I filled out the straightforward forms and wondered what else was in the file folder behind the desk. What kind of details would the doctors look for? Old Doc Babbitt prescribed me antibiotics for my recurrent "infections" like the vet shot up the milking cows for recurrent mastitis. He must have known what Dale was doing to me. He probably didn't write anything incriminating in my records though. He owed Dale way too much money in poker debts. Babbitt probably only sent my immunization records.

I nibbled on an oatmeal cookie as a new sense of panic washed over me. *What if someone from Babbitt's office mentions that Ellery Hospital requested my files to Dale or Mama? Everyone probably knows that Dale is looking for me. What if they find out where I am? What if he's coming to get me right now?*

I was still lost deep in my thoughts when someone touched my arm. I flinched, but the petite woman standing over me had already encircled my wrist with her small warm fingers. "Ms. Blaine?"

"Yes?"

"I am Rosaria. We can see you now," she said. She spoke just above a whisper forcing me to concentrate on each heavily accented word. Unlike the other nurses I'd met, she wasn't wearing scrubs. Nurse Rosaria wore a navy blue cardigan over crisp white trousers and a starched white shirt. An enameled pin with snakes wound around a winged pole adorned the Peter Pan collar of her shirt. She exuded competent efficiency. Rosaria scanned the waiting area. "Is your person in the bathroom?"

"I have a person?"

Rosaria sighed and tried again. "Are you alone?"

You have no idea how alone.

"You did not bring anyone with you? Someone to take notes?"

I shook my head and picked up my backpack. Rosaria mumbled something in Spanish and walked away. "Come then, let's get you in a room."

I trotted after her down the dark hallway. The department was clean and neat with supplies neatly stacked in locked glass cases. It didn't smell of the disinfectant that pervaded the rest of the hospital; it smelled of lavender. Our footsteps echoed in the quiet as we turned left and then right, then left again and ended in a large room dominated by a gynecological examination table.

Can't they just talk to me? Why do I always have to be on my back with my feet up in the air? I stepped inside and put my backpack down on one of the three upholstered chairs surrounding a small table. I expected Rosaria to shove a gown at me and leave me alone again, but she stepped inside with me and closed the door behind her. She sat on the arm of one of the chairs, sizing me up. "So, you have been diagnosed with cervical cancer," she stated matter-of-factly. "How are you adjusting?"

Why is she asking me how I'm adjusting? They're only supposed to ask about my cervix. I backed away until I bumped into the wall. "Adjusting?"

Rosaria slid into the chair and signaled for me to sit across from her. "Now dear, do you understand what is happening today? You are here to talk to the doctor about receiving radiation to the pelvic region. Do you understand what that means?"

I was embarrassed to admit that although I'd read extensively about radiation, I still didn't understand it. It seemed like a bad idea no matter how much the literature explained its therapeutic benefits. On some level, I had to believe the treatments would be painful and leave me scarred.

I sat down on the edge of the chair next to Rosaria and mumbled, "No. Not really."

"That's okay, I'll tell you." Rosaria gently took my hand in hers. Her skin was warm, but her fingers were covered with rough calluses. I recalled how my grandmother's fingers were similarly rough from pruning her roses and endlessly pulling weeds. I cast a sidelong glance at Rosaria's face. Her skin was the color and texture of a banana nut muffin. Deep-set brown eyes met my gaze without any hint of judgment or impatience.

Why is this woman being nice to me? They're not supposed to be nice. I had this all figured out—they treat us like cattle and we're just supposed to take it.

Rosaria gently patted the back of my hand as she slowly spoke. She told me in clear, easy-to-understand terms how the treatments would work and what to do if I had any problems. Before letting go of my hand and reaching for a slim binder, she gave my fingers a quick squeeze. "Everything I just told you is in here." Rosaria placed the binder on my knees. "My phone number is printed inside the front cover along with Dr. Obatu's information and how to reach us after hours. If you have any questions at all, you may call me at any time. Do you understand?"

I didn't understand any of it really. *Why was I there? Why did I get cancer? Why was this little woman acting so nice to me? Why wasn't she like Dr. Lander's nurse? Were they trying to trick me?*

"Yes," I replied.

"Now then, we have some other issues to address," Rosaria stood up and slipped back into a more professional tone. "Do you have any children?" She began gathering supplies and equipment.

I was taken aback by the irrelevant question. Nurse Rosaria didn't strike me as the type of woman to make idle chitchat about her children. "No, I don't have any kids."

"Do you think you might like to have children?" Rosaria turned and looked right into my face with those big brown eyes. I didn't like that at all.

"No, no kids," I snapped.

"Are you certain?" Rosaria pulled a gown out of a low

drawer and placed it on the examination table. "Because if you ever do want to have children of your own, we should discuss referring you to a fertility specialist."

I slumped back in the soft chair and stared at Rosaria. "What?"

Rosaria's hand flew to her mouth. She dropped the pair of gloves in her hand and scurried over to me. "I'm so sorry, dear. Didn't Dr. Lander discuss the implications of your diagnosis?"

"No! Maybe…" My head swam. I tried to remember what Dr. Lander said. "I don't know. She said a lot of stuff, but I don't remember her saying anything about babies!" I felt stupid. Dr. Lander had probably told me something about infertility issues, but I heard so little of what she said. Dr. Lander could have said my arms would fall off the next week and I would have just nodded and waited for her to finish.

"I'm sorry, Miss Blaine. I did not intend to frighten you, but you do need to consider all the possible outcomes. If you think you might want to have children in the future, we suggest you have some eggs harvested before the radiation treatments, just in case."

I didn't plan to have children, but I didn't like that possibility taken away from me either. Then again, no man would ever want me now. I was damaged goods.

"No. That won't be necessary."

Rosaria studied me for a moment then turned back to the examination table. She pulled a blanket out of a warming drawer. "Dr. Obatu will want to take a look to make sure all the tissue is healed before we start a course of radiation. Put this gown on and lay the blanket over your legs. We'll be back in a moment." I stood up to strip as Rosaria slipped out of the room.

Even though my thoughts were still racing, I noticed the gown was much softer than the paper napkin I'd worn in Dr. Lander's office. This gown was white cotton with soft knit trim and designed so the fabric modestly overlapped in the front. I wrapped the soft warm blanket around my bare thighs while I sat on the examination table looking around the room. There were no glib posters encouraging patients to look at the bright side of cancer here. The walls were painted a sunny yellow and had diagrams of the reproductive system taped up on them. I studied one poster that detailed the cervix from different views and levels of magnification. There was a certain beauty in the body's complexity. Pamphlets had been pinned to the wall beside the table. I perused a pamphlet detailing the services available from the hospital's counseling department, one on healthy eating habits during radiation, and one on tango lessons. I read a pamphlet on side effects until Rosaria re-entered the room, leaving the door open behind her. In the dark hall, I could barely make out the form of a tall slender man. The man's skin was so dark that he looked like a lab coat with a broad white smile floating above it.

Oh my goodness, my doctor is the Cheshire cat.

"Good evening, Ms. Blaine," the doctor said in a rich French accent. He reached out and shook my hand. My hand disappeared inside his large hand. "I am so very sorry to keep you waiting. I am Reginald Obatu."

He sat down in one of the upholstered chairs and opened my file on the small coffee table. "Before we examine you, let's talk for a moment." He crossed his long legs and studied my face for a moment. "I have spoken with Karen Lander about your case. She asked me to reassure you that she is very confident that she was able to remove all the cancerous cells.

We both agree that, with radiation, your long-term prognosis is very positive." Dr. Obatu glanced down at his notes and continued, "Before we proceed with your treatment plan, what are your concerns about radiation therapy?"

Why do I have to do this? Will the radiation beams melt my insides? Will I glow?

"Nothing, I'm all set," I replied.

The doctor seemed taken aback by my curt response. "Well, if you think of anything you would like to discuss with me or Rosaria, we are at your disposal." The doctor slowly flipped through my file and made some notes as if giving me time to formulate a question. After a few minutes, he looked back up and continued, "I am ordering fifteen external beam treatments and then one final all day brachytherapy treatment some time after that. If you are sure you don't have any questions, why don't we take a look at your cervix now?"

I slid my body to the end of the table and lay back in the examination position. Unlike in Dr. Lander's office, I couldn't completely divorce my mind from my body this time. I watched Rosaria's face as she assisted the doctor and was aware of Dr. Obatu's warm instruments and gentle hands on my skin. When the examination was over, I sat up and stared at the floor waiting for the doctor to give me the bad news. So far, every time someone had looked inside me, it had been bad news. Dr. Obatu rolled the examination stool over and leaned forward to look up into my face. He smiled warmly and said, "You have healed very well."

I didn't know what to say to that. I fiddled with the gown over my knees and turned away. Out of the corner of my eye, I saw the doctor sit up and exchange worried glances with his nurse. He put a large hand over mine and gave it a slight squeeze. "Well, I'll say goodbye for now then. Rosaria will go over what to do before the simulation." I was tempted to grab his hand and force him to stay, to tell me everything was going to be all right.

Before I left, Rosaria went over the simulation process and gave me a parking pass to the restricted Yellow lot. She asked several more times if I had any questions but I shook my head every time. This Dr. Obatu and his astute nurse confounded me. Doctors in my universe were not compassionate. I had been able to tolerate my interactions with Dr. Lander because, to Dr. Lander, I was just a diseased cervix inconveniently attached to a difficult woman. With Dr. Obatu, I felt laid bare. I didn't like feeling so exposed. I was comfortable in the emotional fortress I had built myself. Not necessarily happy, but comfortable.

8

Exotic Birds

Meeting Dr. Obatu left me discombobulated. Climbing Alpe d'Huez on the Schlein TdF99 didn't help. Adhering to my routine of Chinese food and a long shower after my workout didn't help. Reading *Pride and Prejudice* didn't help. As soon as I closed my eyes, I was back on the metal slab being tortured by the woman with speculum fingers. Then, instead of stabbing me with probes, the man-beasts branded me with glowing metal flowers until my skin bloomed like a garden of weeping welts. The sensation of drowning in a sea of bloody tears made me wake up breathless and sweaty. I couldn't close my eyes again. The memory of the faceless woman whispering, "You're all alone. You're all alone," over and over in my ear still echoed in my head.

I dragged my body downstairs and booted up my laptop. By dawn, I had emailed Letitia my analysis of the copper and manganese markets and thrown in a forecast of how plumbing supply prices might affect housing starts in the northern states for good measure. I went ahead and converted my report into a PowerPoint for her and rewrote my analysis in plainer language. I knew she would ask me to do that before her next meeting with the executives on the ninth floor anyway.

At 6:00, fingers of fog crept over Ruby's hood as I resigned myself to a long, slow commute to work. I looked east and saw the sun struggling to burn through the mist above a line of big box stores. Blue flashing lights emerged from the fog bank ahead just as a line of cars broke off and took the first exit. I joined the line and hoped they knew where they were going; I only knew one way to get to the office from my house. The green sedan in front of me had a Bettel Occidental Commodities parking permit on its rear window and a bumper sticker that said, "God is talking. Are you listening?" When it turned its blinker on and headed east, I followed. Twenty minutes into the drive, I was still behind the same green sedan. I followed them until they pulled into the Bettel Occidental Commodities parking lot. I wasn't clear how we got there, but we did. As I pulled into my usual spot, a round balding man got out of the green sedan. He took a hard look at me before walking into the building. *Observant. Good. I could be a stalker or something. I did follow him the whole way here all on side streets.*

Later that morning, I was checking Red Headed Woman's report on coffee futures when I received an email message from Human Resources telling me to come down to their department as soon as possible.

What now? I was just getting a handle on how the wars in Central Africa will affect Arabica prices this winter. I bet Pathetic Dog Owner reported me to HR for asking him about those crude oil tankers after Letitia didn't punish me. What a crybaby!

I grabbed my backpack and stormed toward the elevator. *Might as well go face the music; I'll never be able to concentrate now.* I gave the wall of Pathetic Dog Owner's empty cubicle a swift kick on my way by. Several photographs fluttered to the dusty carpet.

The Human Resources department didn't feel like it belonged with the rest of Bettel Occidental Commodities. The lobby alone was the size of half my department. I wasn't certain how to proceed when I initially got off the elevator. I stood in front of a monumental reception desk for a second until I saw two young women collating stacks of papers around a table in one of the three glass walled conference rooms. I waved to them; they just blinked at me like goldfish endlessly circling their bowl. I set off down the wide central corridor to find the person who sent me the email before they sucked me into their zombie-like task. Brass nameplates graced each of the glass office doors. There was no warren of anonymous cubicles here. Then again, I wondered if the offices had glass doors so the other people could see if an employee went postal inside.

Vanessa Klaitner was on the phone when I found her. Her unnaturally orange hair blossomed out of a hot pink scrunchie atop her head and framed her round face like a Gerbera daisy. She wore a violet silk blouse with an intricate ruffled neckline and a bright yellow jacket. Vanessa was the type of person who used all the crayons in the box. When she saw me, she quickly hung up and waved me in.

"Ms. Klaitner?" I said. "I'm Lara Blaine. You sent me an email?"

Vanessa slowly massaged a file folder with my name

written on the cover. "Yes, please come in. And, close the door."

Oh boy, here it comes. I knew Letitia was pissed at me for missing two staff meetings in a row, but I didn't think it would get me fired.

She cleared her throat and focused on the wall behind my head. "Ms. Blaine, I asked you to come down because... well, we have a little problem."

I stepped across the plush carpet to the edge of her desk. "A little problem?"

Vanessa bit the bright pink lipstick off her lower lip as she fiddled with the silk flower attached to her ballpoint pen. "You see, Letitia came down here first thing this morning... and, uh, said that she was, you know... worried about you." I started to protest but Vanessa put her hand up to stop me. "Let me cut to the chase. Letitia says you've been acting weird. She told me you sometimes have way too much energy and at other times seem to be out of it. You've been getting into arguments with your co-workers. Missing meetings. Working crazy hours. Writing reports in the middle of the night... You do look a little pale."

"I'm fair!" I pointed at the file folder in front of Vanessa. "Are you firing me?"

"No, not today." Vanessa nervously tugged at her ponytail. "Bettel Occidental Brokerage is committed to supporting our people as both individuals and employees."

What the hell does that mean?

Vanessa tapped her long vermillion nails on the edge of a stack of sticky notes. "We understand that our line of work can be very stressful so when one of our team members gets themselves in a pickle, it's Bettel policy to provide you with whatever treatment you need."

"A pickle? You call cancer 'getting into a pickle'?"

Vanessa slammed her hand on the desktop. An acrylic nail bulleted past my face. "Cancer? Letitia said you have a drug problem."

"No way! Me? Drugs?" I sat down hard in the chair in front of the desk. "She thinks I'm a drug addict?"

"My God," Vanessa scoffed. She swiveled in her ergonomic chair and tossed the file folder onto the low cabinet behind her. "That Letitia. She can't tell the difference between someone who's sick and a drug addict? Makes you wonder."

She shook her head as if it was an Etch-A-Sketch before swiveling back to me. "I'm sorry, Ms. Blaine. What can I do to help?"

"Help?" I covered my face with my hands. *Letitia thinks I'm a druggie. I can't believe I just told a complete stranger that I have cancer and she wants to know how she can help?*

"I'm sorry. Of course. Your condition is none of my business. And it certainly has no bearing on your tenure here at Bettel. If you don't want to talk about it, that's absolutely fine." I started to get up to leave when Vanessa went on, "On the other hand, now that I do know that you're having… health issues. I really would like to help."

I turned to look back at her. "Can you cure cancer?"

Vanessa got up and stepped between me and the door. "I'm sorry, I wish I could do that for you." She put a hand on the door to keep me from leaving. "I can deal with Letitia for you though."

"She really said I'm a druggie?"

"She really did." Vanessa gestured to the chair in front of her desk. "Please sit down. I'm sure there's something I can do to make things easier for you around here."

"I don't get it. Why would you want to help me?"

A wide smile spread across Vanessa's face as I sat back down. She pulled two Diet Cokes from a mini-fridge behind her desk and pushed one toward me. "Look Lara. Can I call you Lara? I really do want to help you. But I also really need to know what the deal is up on the eighth floor."

"What do you mean?"

"Letitia goes through team members like paper towels. She fires people without cause all the time, so she's killing us with unemployment claims. Seventy percent of her team has been with her less than a year, yet you've been with her for more than six. Maybe you can tell me, how does she wow the executive committee every month with such an inexperienced staff?"

That's because I do all the work!

"Is the department over staffed? Are there redundancies? She says she needs all twenty-two desks, but I'm not so sure about that." Vanessa played with the tab on top of her soda can. "Look Lara, I don't know what kind of relationship you have with Letitia, but something tells me that if you weren't willing to share your illness with your her, it's not that great of a relationship."

"I was afraid she would fire me if I told her."

"She can't fire you for getting sick."

"I was worried about losing my health insurance."

"Okay." Vanessa bit her lip again. Poppy-colored lipstick floated on her front teeth as she asked, "Do you need to spend some time in the hospital? Do you need to take some time off? We could talk about going on short-term disability."

"I don't think that'll be necessary. I'll need to take next Tuesday off to go to an appointment. Then I'll have to either come in late or leave early for a few weeks." I felt disoriented. Why was I telling this woman any of this? I didn't know her.

"We can definitely arrange that. I pulled up your file earlier and you have tons of sick time. Did you know you have nine weeks of vacation accrued? You can take several weeks off if you want to."

"I think I'd rather work if it's okay with you guys."

"Okay, but you'll need to take it easy," Vanessa said. "I can ask Letitia to reassign some of your work to one of the other people in the department."

"No need," I replied. "I'm ten days ahead."

"You're ahead? Greg Blankenshipp was just down here the other day complaining about how much work Letitia piles on you guys."

"He's just lazy."

"Whatever works best for you. I just want to help."

"I appreciate that, but what do you want in return?"

"Just keep your eyes and ears open. I want to know how Letitia manages to get such good results out of the revolving door of people up there."

"I help her out a lot."

Vanessa popped her Diet Coke open and drank half of it down. "So what should I tell Letitia about this meeting?"

"I don't want her to know I have cancer."

"Okay." Vanessa took another sip from the can while studying me. "That makes things a little more difficult. How do you want to explain needing to take time off?"

"When I came in you alluded to drug treatment programs. Why can't we let Letitia think I'm going to one of those?"

Vanessa raised her eyebrows. "You want her to think you have a drug problem?"

"Not necessarily," I replied. "I just don't want to tell her the truth. Will you get in trouble if you lie?"

"Only if someone finds out," Vanessa snorted. "People

lie to me all the time about why they need time off when I know they are going on vacation or getting plastic surgery. It's about time I stretch the rules for someone who really deserves a few days off."

I shook my head as I thought about how angry Letitia would be if she found out HR had me spying on her. "I don't know. Letitia is going to be pissed if she finds out you're doing anything to help me."

"Honey, the woman reported you as a drug addict. I wouldn't worry about her feelings." Vanessa stood up and opened her office door. "Tell you what—you look tired. Why don't you take the rest of the day off? I'll tell Letitia you had to go. Don't you worry about a thing."

I didn't know what to say. I got up and walked out of the office without saying goodbye. The two women in the conference room stopped collating and watched me walk back to the elevator like cows watching a car pass their pasture.

9
Burning Blue Soul

Tuesday morning I sat at my desk trying out convenient emergencies that would allow me to take the afternoon off. I didn't have children or pets that could suddenly need me at home. I hadn't heard anything more from Vanessa Klaitner. I assumed she was lying when she said she wanted to help me.

"Blaine!" Garlic Breath hooted through our mutual cubicle wall. "Did you screw something up? 'Cuz Letitia's heading this way and she looks pissed." I swiveled in my chair to see Garlic Breath's bald spot disappear behind the wall and Letitia glaring at me.

A Venti Starbucks cup appeared about to crumple in her grip and shower me with black coffee. "HR called," she barked. "They want you to go to some ridiculous stress management seminar this afternoon."

I fought back a smile. "Oh, wow. I'll have to spend the whole afternoon down in HR?"

Garlic Breath's bald spot popped up over the cubicle wall again. I threw a pencil over my shoulder and he ducked back down.

"I'm watching you, Blaine," Letitia spit. "You better not come in tomorrow looking like you've been partying all night."

"Of course not, Letitia. I'll be here at the usual time, ready to go," I replied. "Well, better finish this analysis of how the upcoming elections in Bolivia might affect silver futures before I go."

Letitia turned to Garlic Breath and snapped, "What are you looking at? Get back to work!" before slinking back to her office. Before leaving, I sent Vanessa Klaitner an email thanking her for fabricating the stress management seminar to correspond with my appointment.

Later that day, I followed Rosaria's excellent directions to the Radiation-Oncology department for my simulation appointment. The prospect of being measured for radiation treatments made every muscle in my body twitch to run away. My voice sounded shrill in my head when I gave my name to the technician far down a dim hallway.

"Am I in the right place? I'm patient BL2911."

The technician looked at the encounter form I handed her. "BL2911, huh? How about I call you Lara? Are you alone?" I nodded. She led me to a large room filled with machines that appeared to be the spawn of cameras mating with x-ray equipment.

"What are all the machines for?" I had read the extensive description of the radiation treatment process that Rosaria had given me, but the literature didn't say there would be quite so much machinery involved. I envisioned something more along the lines of a firing squad.

"I'll be using this equipment to take very accurate measurements of your body so we can focus the radiation only where it needs to go and nowhere else. A little later we'll do your blocks, then we'll make your cradle."

"The blocks are the little shields?"

"Exactly." Emma pulled a stool out from beneath the table and helped me. "Someone's been doing her homework."

I blushed at the compliment. "I'll stay really still, I promise." I lay back without being asked to and didn't move as Emma put warm blankets over my chest and legs before sliding off my gown. I watched her in my peripheral vision as she pushed a series of buttons that brought the large machine hanging from the ceiling to life. It extended its mechanical arms, rotated, and hovered over me. My heart beat like a jackhammer in my ears. I tried to focus on the machine's controls as thin beams of light danced across my naked pelvis. I could feel my brain slipping away from my body.

For the next forty-five minutes, I was only tangentially aware of Emma humming a dance tune as she made notations in my chart and occasionally tapped on my skin with something damp. When the machine stopped moving, Emma turned up the lights in the room. I craned my neck to see what she'd been doing. There were a few lines snaking across my belly and trickling down my upper thighs but most of the bright purple lines of Sharpie marker pointed toward a large circle just above my pubic bone. There was a target drawn on my womb.

"Now don't try to wash these off. The radiation tech will need these to line you up in the machine. Eventually, we'll replace some of them with tiny permanent tattoos." Emma pulled the paper robe over the marks and helped me sit up.

"Now then, why don't you take a bathroom break while we set up for the next part?"

When I returned, the table was covered with a pillow-like mass filled with a foamy substance. After Emma helped me up on the membrane, the filling conformed to my thighs and lower back. Emma moved my body around the table like she was positioning a doll. She worked until the lines on my body lined up with the register marks on the table and the reference beams from the machine.

"Okay now, it's very important that you not move at all while the chemicals react and the medium sets up. It may get quite warm. If you get uncomfortable just holler. I've got cool cloths that we can put on your head and shoulders."

I'd had plenty of experience lying still and divorcing myself from what was happening to my body, but this was different. I couldn't ignore that the table beneath me was getting hotter by the second.

Oh my God, my skin is burning off! This must be what Hell will be like. I lay perfectly still while I imagined the skin on my buttocks and inner thighs cracking and peeling off in sheets. I saw my muscles falling off the bones like a roasted chicken thigh and being consumed by fire. I struggled to get ahead of the images inside my head.

Suddenly, I was no longer in the simulation suite. I was running through a dense rainforest. Flames licked at my heels. I dove inside the center of a Strangling Fig and climbed on top of the rotting carcass of the tree the vines had choked to death. Scorched book pages and leaves the size of dinner plates floated down from the canopy high above my head. The trees around me were quickly engulfed in a roar of flames. A wave of acrid smoke washed across the forest floor. I couldn't breathe or see my hands as I grabbed onto the closest vine and climbed up in search of fresh air. I needed to get out of the Strangling Fig before it caught fire. I spotted a giant bird's nest in the next tree and crawled over the lip. Although the outside was woven from branches and vines, the inside was striated and wet. I slid down the steep sides and landed waist deep in a puddle of bloody goop. Floating in the center of the nest was a wicker bassinet. A baby, my mutant never-to-be-born baby, extended a tiny pus covered hand over the edge of the cradle and gurgled, "Are you alone?"

✳✳✳

That night the nightmares turned in on themselves. Instead of fanciful beasts, Mama's smoke-ravaged voice filled my head. I heard a beeping and Mama saying, "The mason jars. He don't know you took the mason jars. It all burned… The cancer come. You're all alone. It all burned. He don't know." My eyes snapped open. The room was pitch black, yet I could sense Mama tracking me like a shark smelling blood in the water.

I rolled off the futon and kicked at the sheets until my legs were free.

She knows about the cancer. She knows they're going to burn me.

I sat up surprised to find my cell phone in my hand. Had I answered the phone in my sleep? The phone said I had one recent call. It had a 603 area code.

Did I dream about the mason jars?

Oh my god, they've found me. Or did Mama really call? Does she know about the mason jars?

A shelf of mason jars had been my ticket out of Hawthorne. Three weeks before graduation, I was in the hayloft working on my valedictorian speech when I saw the light come on in the room above my bedroom. The two rooms on the second floor of the addition hadn't been used for at least twenty years, not since Dale's mother died. An ice dam had damaged the roof during the blizzard of '78. Dale had never properly fixed it, so whenever there was a blowing storm, rain seeped between the siding and the walls. On the north wall, the faded plaid wallpaper was the only thing keeping the horsehair plaster attached to the rotten lathe. I had explored the two bedrooms not long after Mama and I moved to the farm but had not ventured up there since. The smell of mildew and grief were overpowering.

From my vantage point in the barn, I could see Dale waltzing a wardrobe away from the wall in the room that had once been a sewing room. His mother's dress form still stood in the corner with the beginnings of a wool holiday dress pinned to it. Moths and mice had eaten holes in the red fabric until it hung like a tattered flag. I flicked off my lantern and ducked below the windowsill, hoping he didn't see me watching him from across the yard. Dale took something out of the wardrobe, placed it on the floor, then pulled a wad of cash out of his jeans pocket. A greasy smile spread across his face as he thumbed through the bills in his hand. Then, he rolled them up, put them in a mason jar, and returned the wardrobe to its place against the wall.

I had wondered where Dale kept his money. I knew there was money. And, I knew Dale didn't believe in banks or taxes. I had heard enough of his drunken rants about how the government was trying to bilk him out of all his money. He also bragged incessantly about how stupid the drunks down at the Rusty Nail were and how easy it was to trick them into ridiculous loan agreements. He stole from people. I didn't think twice about stealing from him.

A week before graduation, I made my escape. Mama had

gone to Portsmouth to buy a dress to wear to the ceremony, and Dale was on his annual "fishing trip" with Doc. At first when I pulled the heavy wardrobe away from the wall, I thought Dale had moved his money. The jars in front were filled with grape jelly and pickles. I pushed those out of the way and found row after row of jars filled with money. I'd hoped to get enough cash to get out of town and tide me over until I could start college. I found more than I needed. All told, I stole $52,782 of beer soaked, slightly moldy greenbacks. The police found Dale's truck a few days later in a Wal-Mart parking lot near the Massachusetts border with the keys in the glove compartment.

10
Tea For Two

The whole weekend loomed in front of me like a vast ocean of shark-infested waters. I had nothing to do and I was afraid to close my eyes. By 11:00 on Saturday morning, I had already climbed the Eiffel Tower at the Y, bought a week's worth of cereal and bread, and balanced my checkbook.

My plan had been to spend a nice, quiet afternoon in the office where I could work in peace while everyone else did things with their families. I'd intended to get the security guard to let me into the conference room on the sixth floor where I could spread out my charts on the long table, at least until I listened to Letitia's voicemail from the night before. I heard traffic sounds in the background as she shouted, "I don't know what kind of sob story you gave HR, Blaine, but that Vanessa woman rained down some hell fire on me this afternoon. All I asked was for them to dock your pay for the time you were at their little stress management seminar. You don't seem any more relaxed, and I had to put together the report for Mariano all by myself. Which they hated!" Brakes squealed in the background. I heard Letitia swear under her breath about a spilled drink. Then, she was back, yelling at me. "You may be smart enough to have conned HR, but I'm not buying it. I know there's something going on. I'm not going through another Reynolds. Or even another Logan thing. You hear me? Take the weekend and get your act together!" I couldn't remember who Reynolds was. Logan may have been the tall guy who sat near the recycling bin. He missed a lot of work when his wife was sick. Letitia fired him the day after the funeral.

I was cursing my fate while scrubbing the kitchen floor when my cell phone rang from the living room. It rang three times before I wrestled off my rubber gloves to find the phone in my backpack.

"Lara?" a breathy voice crackled through the phone.

My stomach dropped. *Oh my God, Mama! They've found me!* I stabbed the off button. The phone immediately rang again in my hand. I tried to sound like a large dangerous man as I barked, "What?" into the phone. If Mama and Dale had tracked me down, I didn't want them to think I lived alone.

"Hello?" the voice said. "I'm trying to reach Lara Blaine. This is Jane Babcock-Roberts. I'm a friend of hers from the hospital?"

I dropped the phone. It bounced off the couch. "Hello? Is someone still there?" was muffled by the carpet. I seized the phone.

"Yes. Yes, I'm here." I raked my fingers through my tangled hair and pulled my T-shirt down straight. "I'm sorry, I thought it was a telemarketer."

"I hate those people, too," Jane scoffed. "How are you? I've looked for you at the hospital."

I slumped down on the couch. "I haven't been there much. Just twice since I saw you."

"Really? I seem to be there all the time lately."

"How's the chemotherapy going?"

"It's awful. But that's not why I called. I was just sitting here—that's about all I can manage these days—and something told me to call you." It made my heart skip a beat to hear that Jane had been thinking about me. "Are you busy today? Could you meet me for coffee later on?"

"Sure," I stammered. My blood felt like club soda in my veins. *Is this what people feel like when they are asked out on a date?* "I could do that today."

"Good. There's a teashop in East Lake Shopping Center called Annie's or Amy's. How about four o'clock? We'll do afternoon tea."

"Okay, I'm sure I can figure out how to get there. See you then." I jumped up and bolted up the stairs to get ready.

What does one wear to afternoon tea?

I wanted to look pretty for Jane. I found an old black dress in the back of the closet that, after running it through the dryer for a few minutes to get the dust out of the shoulders, I hoped would be passable. I felt like Elizabeth Bennet being summoned to Rosings Park in *Pride and Prejudice*.

In the end, the teashop wasn't as grand as I feared, or hoped. It was wedged between a children's second hand clothing store and an auto parts distributor in a half empty strip mall. The place was a riot of cabbage rose and ivy patterns only occasionally broken up by white lace doilies. I chose a table in the window with two chintz-covered wingback chairs separated by a pink linen draped table. The only other patrons on this Saturday afternoon were a mother having a tea party with three ruffle-and-bow-covered little girls and two elderly ladies thoroughly enjoying some lemon tarts. In my excitement, I had allowed myself far too much time to get lost and arrived twenty minutes early. I used the time to read up on tea.

Jane pulled up in the grey Jaguar and laboriously pulled herself out of the low car. I could see she was even thinner than the last time I saw her. Her long silk sweater couldn't hide how much her slinky knit pants drooped over her driving moccasins. The short walk from the parking lot visibly winded Jane. She slumped into the soft armchair and wiped away a thin layer of perspiration from her upper lip with the linen napkin. I was glad I had chosen that table instead of one of the ice cream parlor tables at the back of the shop.

Jane glanced around, taking in the hundreds of teapots and knick-knacks crammed into every available inch of wall space. "Wow, this place is something. I'm not sure if I love it or hate it. I've wanted to come here for ages and never had the time. Now I have the time and I can't go anywhere."

"It does make you think of the Mad Hatter and the March Hare."

Jane smiled awkwardly as if she had no idea what I was talking about. "So did you look at the menu? What exactly is afternoon tea?"

I sat up straight in my chair and smoothed my dress over my knees. "You can have an assortment of cakes and sweets or an assortment of little sandwiches. Or you can get the works, which is a little of everything. They have a long list of teas, or you can have coffee, or a cold drink. It's a tea shop, so I think we should get tea."

"I'm tempted to just have coffee, but I agree—we should go for the full experience." Jane patted her forehead with her napkin. Some makeup came off with her perspiration; her skin was grey under her mask. "You never know when we'll get the opportunity again," she said wistfully. "I'm exhausted from the walk in here. You order."

A bubble of proud satisfaction welled up in my chest as I signaled to a woman as short and round as a teapot. She rushed over to take our order. I suppressed a giggle as I ordered tea for two and pots of both Irish Breakfast and Earl Gray teas. When the woman disappeared into the back Jane asked, "What's so funny?"

"It's just that when she walked up I couldn't get the image of Mrs. Tiggy-winkle out of my head. I half expected her to ask me if I knew where the missing penny was."

"Mrs. Tiggy-winkle? From the children's book? Oh my goodness, that is funny." The woman quickly returned with rose strewn pots of tea. We both giggled behind our napkins. "Oh Lara, this is already the most fun I've had in weeks. I can't tell you how much I appreciate you meeting me today. It's nice just to get out of the house."

I blushed. "I was glad to get out, too."

"I escaped, actually. Tom went back to his apartment to take care of a few things and I snuck out. He is giving up his lease and moving into the house until I can go back to work." Jane arranged the collection of petite forks and spoons beside her plate. "He'll be angry that I've left the house."

"What do you mean?"

"My son has become my jailer as well as my usurper these days. I'm not supposed to be exposed to germs, so I've been under house arrest for the last few weeks. Tom won't even let me go the grocery store or go pick up a video. Would you believe he won't let me drive my own car anymore?"

I eyed the gorgeous little sports car gleaming in the

parking lot and understood Jane's indignation at being denied access to it. "He insists it's not safe for me to drive while I'm taking all these drugs."

"What did your doctor say about that?"

"Tom actually hid my keys from me." She proudly dangled a single key attached to a dealership's promotional fob from one long finger. "He didn't know I had a valet key in a drawer."

"What about your business?"

"I was keeping up pretty well for a while there, even though I felt weak. But once I started the chemo, it became very obvious, very fast that I'm going to have to step back for a while. Tom is pinch-hitting for me right now. He already knew the ropes. He worked for me several years after he got his MBA but it didn't work out. I'm afraid Tom and I are a bit too much alike. We can't both be the boss."

"So you're not working at all right now?"

"I tried to after the first chemo treatment." Jane shuddered and took a long slow sip of hot tea. "Oh, that feels good. After that first chemo treatment I was chomping at the bit to get back into the office. I was tired of laying in bed feeling like crap and worrying about Tom. I don't ever want him to feel I'm a burden. I don't want to be that kind of mother.

"Anyway, I was driving myself so crazy thinking about the mountain of things that needed to be done that I pushed myself to go back before I really should have. I kept telling myself that no one else was capable of doing the things I do." She rubbed her chest. "Well, at least I thought they weren't."

"I appreciate Tom staying at the house and keeping me company, but I don't like him interfering in my work life so much. At home, I'm his mother and I'm willing to indulge him, but at the office, I'm the boss. Or at least I used to be."

"What do you mean?"

Jane played with the sugar cubes in a small dish at the center of the table forming them into a series of pyramids. "He has completely taken over. I hired this girl, Candace, a year or so ago. She was supposed to hold the wives' hands when they can't seem to decide on counter tops and light fixtures. Tom's got her making major design decisions. The other day at dinner he let it slip that she is switching out the granite counters that I had ordered for the Riley job with poured concrete. Concrete!"

I tried to look incredulous even though I didn't know a counter top could be poured anything.

"Anyway, I was so excited to be back in the office, I forgot to bring any anti-nausea medicine. The morning went okay, but by noon I felt pretty queasy. I should have called Tom to bring the pills, but I didn't want him to make me go home. At one point, my assistant had to help me into the bathroom to be sick. Then, of course, getting sick made the coughing start up again, so I... it was awful. I ended up taking a nap on the couch in my office."

"So what happened?" I refilled Jane's teacup with more Earl Gray.

"Hours later, I woke up with my stomach still spinning. I could hear Tom talking behind me. He sat at my desk talking to the electrical contractor. I turned over to tell him to push for limited overtime and started coughing and gagging all over again. I wonder if they got the stain out of the carpet." Jane took another slow sip of tea. "Tom was really great. He didn't freak out that his mother was yakking all over the floor while he handled the contractor." Jane smiled wryly. "I trained him well. He says he is there to pick up the slack, but that was pretty much it. He hasn't allowed me to go to the office for more than an hour or two since."

"Do you think you'll go back after the chemo is over?"

"You bet! And the first thing I am going to do is fire that ninny, Candace. She is letting the clients walk all over her. I haven't been taking care of my daddy's company for the last twenty-five years to have the likes of her run it into the ground."

The proprietress waddled over under the weight of an immense tray of little cakes and cookies. A skinny girl, probably the teapot's daughter, followed with a tray of miniature sandwiches that fit on top of the first. Jane's eyes widened at the array of tasty morsels.

"I'm so glad you were home when I called." She looked out the window not seeming to focus on anything. "I spend the days right after each treatment lying in bed in a kind of drug-induced stupor. I've thought about you many times. When I ran into you the other day, I don't know, you seemed blue." Jane arranged the tea sandwiches into neat rows. "I think I am losing my mind some days. I don't know what to do with myself. I didn't realize how much my work filled up my life."

"I like to read," I replied. "Do you read much?"

"I don't." Jane coughed into her napkin, at first quietly, then with increasing severity. The other women in the shop stopped chatting and stared. I tried to act as if nothing was amiss. Jane was obviously more ill than she was letting on. *Perhaps her son is right to not want her to leave the house right now. What if she stops breathing?* I splashed some more tea into Jane's cup and casually stood up to hold it to Jane's lips. I pat her back and noticed that while Jane had been coughing the scarf tied jauntily around her head had slipped back to expose the edge of a wig. It was a good imitation of her blonde hair, but it did not move the way real hair would. I discreetly straightened the wig before primly sitting down. I glared at the one old woman still staring.

"Thank you," Jane gasped. "You're very sweet."

My heart did a little dance. No one had called me sweet since I was a little girl. I am not a sweet woman. I'm wicked smart, but I'm also prickly and sullen. I know that.

Jane tightened the knot of the scarf around her head. "This thing refuses to stay on. Tom bought me a pack of knit caps to keep my head covered at home. I bought this thing because I thought I would be going out to meetings. Not so much." Jane popped a cucumber sandwich into her mouth and contemplated a cracker topped with chicken salad. "You know, this whole cancer thing really shows you who your friends are. The other day I called Annemarie Stoppard to see how the gala preparations for the Art Guild were going. I felt bad that I was not able to make all the meetings and offered to make phone calls or send e-mails, but she cut me off and said, 'Oh no dear. It's all under control. You rest.' It's like she's already got me dead and buried. I have known that woman for over twenty years and she did not as much as ask how I was feeling."

"That's awful." I tried a miniature éclair with pink frosting. It melted into sweet goo in my mouth.

"How did your friends react when you told them?"

I waved off the question with a watercress sandwich. "I don't have any. Mmm, those little pink things are delicious."

"Oh come on, how could you not have friends? But you said the other day you didn't have family around here. Isn't anyone taking care of you?"

I shook my head as I popped the little sandwich in my mouth.

"Oh my God, listen to me carping about how my social contacts are snubbing me and my son is being difficult. You're all alone. I'm sorry, Lara. I didn't mean to be such a bore. You must think me so whiny."

"Not at all," I replied. "I absolutely understand where you're coming from. I'd be mad, too."

"It hasn't been all that bad. People did bring casseroles and flowers right after the news spread about my diagnosis. That was nice, but it only lasted a week or so. I haven't heard from any of those people since. Even the people who work for me, people I pay, seem to have forgotten about me."

"People don't want to know. If it doesn't affect them, they don't care."

Jane snorted in agreement while signaling the waitress to bring us some more tea. She put several scones with clotted cream on her plate then pulled her leg up under her like a young girl. "All this stuff is yummy. This is the most I've eaten in weeks," she tittered. "So what's going on with you? How are you feeling? When do you start the radiation treatments?"

"Next week." I drained my teacup and then gave in to an impulse. Maybe it was the lack of sleep or maybe the sugar rush from the tiny cakes, but I told Jane about the simulation. I told her how it felt like the simulation medium was burning my flesh off my bones and about the nightmares. Jane listened. She sat there and listened to every word. She didn't run away. She didn't poo poo me or quickly change the subject. She didn't tell me I was being silly. She listened.

When I finished, Jane reached across the table and took my hand. With tears puddling on her few remaining lashes, she whispered, "You poor thing." She wiped the tears away and laughed, "And I thought I had it bad. I hate that you are so frightened."

That night, I fell asleep and slept through until morning. Although Jane had not taken any of my fears away or solved any of my problems, she had given me a gift that I could not comprehend at the time. She had listened. In doing so, she had somehow lifted my load, or perhaps, she had simply shared it.

11
The Hive

The parking lot reserved for radiation patients swarmed with activity. A kid in a yellow polo shirt helped people out of their cars while a cluster of other young men ferried the cars to the valet section. I zoomed past the young man and nosed Ruby into the last available self-parking spots. I'd studied the information packet Rosaria had given me until its pages were as soft and creased as magnolia petals, yet I was unprepared for how crowded the restricted yellow lot would be. As I hung the special parking permit that would prevent Ellery Hospital from towing Ruby, a young woman around my age stopped in front of the car. The left side of the mud-spattered minivan beside me slid open revealing two car seats buckled into the center row. Lacrosse sticks and duffle bags were strewn across the floor of the van.

Oh no, she's a mother.

I examined the woman as she tossed her pocketbook in the closest car seat and climbed into the van. She didn't look like a cancer patient, although she did hold her head as if she had a stiff neck. If I saw her at the gym, I would have assumed she had overdone it in Pilates class.

Walking into the sunlit foyer felt like walking into a different world. Rainbows danced across the polished floor. Multicolored mobiles spun in the air currents created by the sliding doors. A crowd of people milled around a bespectacled woman perched behind a high desk in the center of the jewel box foyer. A large gold bee secured the lacy blue cardigan draped over her girlish shoulders. "Hello. Who are you?" she cooed like The Caterpillar looking down at a confused Alice in Wonderland.

I hardly know myself.

I rose on my tiptoes to look over the desktop and whisper, "I'm here to be irradiated."

The woman glanced at the large yellow book in front of her and echoed my sober tone. "Your name, dear?"

"BL2911. Lara Blaine."

The woman's face cracked open with a smile. "Oh, Miss Blaine! Rosaria told me to expect you this morning. I'm Lorraine." She signaled to the woman helping an old man with his walker to take over and climbed down from her high stool. Lorraine stepped around the desk and steered me into a sunny atrium. A handful of people sat on low couches arranged into conversation pits. Floor to ceiling windows looked out on a courtyard where workmen were replacing the spent summer annuals with decorative cabbages and pansies.

"Now, when you come in every day, check in at the desk. I'm usually here at this time of day but Diane can take care of you if I'm helping another patient. Your treatments will be with Rex in room B. Now if you bring anyone with you, they'll have to stay out here. We have coffee and soft drinks and the volunteers sometimes bring in cookies." We passed a small bookshelf filled with reference books on cancer and radiation. Lorraine noticed me looking at the books and said, "Feel free to borrow anything you'd like. They're here for you to use."

"Thank you," I replied. "Any chance I can sit near one of those sunny windows and read about radiation treatments instead of receiving them?"

"Sorry, honey. It doesn't work that way." Lorraine led me around a freestanding wall to a locker room area. Keys hung from two of the four doors. My research told me that there were two radiation treatment rooms at this facility. I assumed the other two keys were with the people now being irradiated. The cold fluorescent glow in the locker room area accentuated the creases in Lorraine's cheeks, making her appear ghoulish. "And here are your changing rooms. You can leave your pocketbook and clothes inside, but make sure to take the key. The doors lock themselves."

Lorraine consulted her clipboard and continued, "There's a pile of clean gowns on the shelf. We'll need you to take everything off from the waist down." She held her clipboard beside her face and whispered conspiratorially, "You might want to wear loose cotton clothes for the next few weeks, dear. My ladies who get the radiation to their nether regions seem to do better if they let their bodies breathe some." She took a step back toward the atrium. "Once you've changed, step around the corner and wait on the bench until Rex is ready for you. Well, I'll leave you to it." Lorraine's soft sweater brushed against the back of my hand as she scurried back to the reception desk. My fingers itched to grab it and wrap myself in its softness.

I twisted the key in the door furthest to the left and entered the changing room. A shelf along the back wall held stacks of yellow hospital gowns under a sign telling patients they could wear gowns front and back if they wanted extra coverage. Rosaria had written in my information packet that I could leave a bra or camisole on during the treatment. I didn't own a camisole. *Does Rosaria wear a camisole under her blouse? Do grown-up women really wear things like that next to their skin?*

I took off my plain white shirt and wrapped two gowns tightly around me before unbuttoning my chinos and shimmying out of my white nylon panties. I folded the flimsy fabric in my hand trying to hide the dull brown stains that no amount of bleach completely removed no matter how long I soaked them. As I tucked them between my neatly folded slacks and my shoes, I thought about the pictures I'd seen of concentration camp victims carefully stacking their clothes before they were led off to the gas chambers. *I wonder how many of them knew what was going to happen. I know what's happening to me and I'm still walking in there.*

Free will is a bitch.

Holding the gown edges together with one hand, I opened the door and padded around the corner to the bench across from the large door with a B painted on it. I pulled a paper towel from the dispenser on the wall and spread it on the bench before sitting down to await my fate. The rough paper, scratchy against my skin, felt like an accusation. The clock mounted high on the wall ticked off four long minutes as I stared at the big B. I felt very small. I looked over at the empty bench across from the door marked A. *Where is everybody?* I tried to remember if I even heard anyone walk by the changing area while I took my clothes off. *Where is the person for room A? Did something happen to them?*

I couldn't sit patiently waiting to be taken into what would likely be a torture chamber. I bounced up and paced back and forth spinning the long yellow plastic key ring on my finger. To the left of the door, a floor to ceiling curtain had a sign pinned to it that read, "Keep curtain closed; protect patient confidentiality." I couldn't resist. Behind the heavy cloth lurked a rolling rack filled with amorphous grey blobs. BL2911 had been scrawled down the side of the blob in the first occupied space. My corn flakes bubbled up my throat. There had to be fifty disembodied shells silently waiting for their people to come lie in them. The image of Winston in *1984* waiting in his little room for a cage of hungry rats to be strapped to his face flashed through my mind. I dashed back to the bench and sat on my hands.

A middle-aged woman stumbled out of the changing rooms and flopped down on the A bench. She reminded me of Mr. Badger from *The Wind in the Willows*. Her hair, a shoe polish black, had three inches of grey roots along a center part. A scowl seemed rooted in her day-old oatmeal colored skin. The edges of The Badger's single hospital gown drooped open over her elastic waist pants. A welt of a scar ran down the center of her chest. She didn't acknowledge me so I pretended not to notice her.

I straightened the paper towel I was sitting on.

"Good idea. Best not to put your bare ass on the seat," the woman said. "You shouldn't walk around here barefooted neither."

I silently glared at the painted B across from my bench and hoped she could take a hint.

"You should wear rubber thongs." The Badger still wore her brown gum soled loafers. "You're liable to pick up a fungus in there. Nothing worse than a foot fungus."

Although I thought foot fungus was the least of my worries, I made a mental note to put a pair of flip-flops in my bag the next morning.

"You in B?"

I nodded to the door. I could feel The Badger appraising me. *Where is that radiation guy?*

"Has the burning started?" The Badger croaked.

"What?" I asked. "What are you talking about?"

The Badger raised her shaggy eyebrows in derision. "The pain. It usually hits in the second week."

"I'm fine. They said the radiation would be painless."

"That's what they told you, huh?" The Badger took a long slow drink from the water bottle propped against her hip. She winced as she screwed the top back on. "Just remember, it gets better eventually."

You troll! "What makes you such an expert?"

"I know."

I rolled my eyes and pretended to examine the safety instructions posted beside the control room door. The Badger cleared her throat and gurgled, "I know all right, this is my third time through. Esophageal in '92, breast in '98 and now esophageal again. The radiation to the breast burned the skin a little but it wasn't too bad. The first time for the throat did some damage though, let me tell you."

Oh please, don't! Please stop talking.

"That's why they sent me up here. The doctors say they can give me a few special treatments that are supposed to be real focused. They say it shouldn't be too bad this time."

I remembered the woman who travelled from Florida to receive her treatments at Ellery. "What do you mean, up here? Were you treated somewhere else first?"

"I got treated in Charlotte the first two times. The hospital there is nice. I like the nurses there better. This place is like a machine."

"I know what you mean." I thought about the color-coded departments and the maze of waiting rooms. I leaned toward The Badger. "You're here to see a specialist? Are you part of a research study?"

"This Dr. Phipps is supposed to be a real hot shot. I was supposed to start last week but he made them do my blocks three times before he was happy with them. He keeps saying he wants to make sure they only hit the cancer and don't burn the stuff around it. Apparently they can focus the beams way more now than they could when I was treated in '92. Like that was the Stone Age. Dr. Phipps was probably in grade school then."

Three times?

The metal door in front of me swung open and a brawny young man in yellow scrubs emerged with an elderly man. Hairy legs stuck out below his gown. "Keep those jokes coming, Bob. And keep drinking lots of fluids." The elderly man walked toward the changing rooms chuckling to himself.

The younger man turned to me and extended his hand. "Lara Blaine? I'm Rex." I expected the man that shoots radiation into people to look like Igor in *Young Frankenstein*, not young and handsome.

"Hi," I said, pulling the gown tighter across my belly. I felt my face grow hot. *Crap, this guy is going to see the Sharpie lines all over my belly.*

Rex verified my information and patient number. "Go on inside. I'll grab your cradle."

I wandered through the heavy metal doors into a dull

grey metal room with a slim window high in the wall. Goosebumps instantly bloomed on my legs. A large stainless steel table with a machine mounted above it, much like the one in the simulation chamber, monopolized the space. Rex appeared beside me and placed the cast of my torso on the table. "Okay. Hop up here for me."

I carefully held the thin gown close to my body, as I lay prone in my cradle. Once in position, Rex laid a sheet over my upper thighs to preserve a modicum of my dignity before he lifted the gown to align the marks on my body with the register marks on the cradle and table. I flinched when he touched my thigh. My mind started to disengage from my body but pulled back when Rex gently shook my shoulder.

"Try to relax, Lara. Stay with me here. May I scoot your left hip up a bit?"

He's asking permission to touch me? I bit my lip and nodded my consent.

Rex tenderly slipped his fingertips under my hip to position me correctly. "I'm sorry my fingers are cold. They keep it comfortable for the machines, not the patients." He stepped back from the table and said, "I am going to step out now and begin the treatment. It will only take a few seconds. Try to relax, but don't move."

The immense lead door clanged shut behind Rex, leaving me alone under the machine. I held my breath and waited for a flash of light or a searing beam of heat. Despite what Rosaria said and everything I'd read, I knew this would hurt. It had to.

Before I could slip away, Rex was there again, beside me. He gently lowered my gown and pulled me up into a seated position. "You're all set. See you tomorrow."

I slid off the table and crept toward the exit. This didn't

feel right; it was as if a step had been missed. *Where was the flash of light? Where was the searing pain?* I didn't feel irradiated. I felt the same as I did when I walked in. I glanced back and saw Rex place my cradle in a large rack identical to the one behind the curtain in the hallway. There were nine other cradles already there. Nine other people had already been blasted that morning.

An old woman with a bandage on her leg sat on the bench where The Badger had been. She nodded at me as I hurried by. I pretended I didn't see her. Inside the changing room, I pulled off the gowns and shoved them through the trap door labeled "Used Gowns." *They shouldn't launder the gowns. They should incinerate them. They're contaminated.*

The next day, the radiation treatment went as smoothly. Lorraine greeted me with a smile. People came and went. I was in and out of the treatment center in less than twenty minutes. I felt fine, like nothing was different at all. I wondered if I was a frog foolishly staying in a pot of water as the flame was slowly being raised beneath me.

✶✶✶

By the fourth day of radiation, I couldn't concentrate on mineral futures. I didn't care how the tropical storms brewing off Africa would affect shipping lanes. My insides were being burned out of me a portion at a time. How could I give a damn about freighters full of ore? They could all sink off the Canary Islands for all I cared.

At lunchtime, I heard Garlic Breath and Pathetic Dog Owner in the next cubicle talking over their Big Macs. The most terrible thing in their lives was some football player being traded. I had cancer. I wanted to call Jane and ask her to meet me for tea again. I even found her number in the recent calls on my phone and dialed the number. I was afraid to push send. She had another chemotherapy treatment that week. She'd be feeling awful. I didn't want to bother her. I saved the number in my phone in case I found the courage to call another day.

I pulled my peanut butter and jelly sandwich from my backpack, took one look at it, and tossed it in the garbage can. I didn't want my usual sandwich. I wanted a watercress sandwich. I wanted a little pink fluffy petit fore with a crystallized violet on top. I slung my bag over my shoulder. My work for the day was done. Frankly, my work for the next two weeks was mostly done. I didn't really need to be in the office at all. I picked up my laptop and walked toward the elevator.

"Where do you think you're going?" Garlic Breath called after me.

"Shopping," I said over my shoulder.

I drove across town to the teashop where I met Jane. At first, it felt a bit strange to be sitting there having tea by myself, but I enjoyed it nonetheless. The little lady that ran the shop, who I learned was named Myra, taught me the difference between lapsang souchang and Ceylon super pekoe teas. The shop was empty on a Thursday afternoon so she sat down and had a cup of tea with me. I learned we had a common love of minerals. She opened the shop after retiring from teaching high school science and was obsessed with geodes.

Fortified with caffeine and sugar, I stepped into the tiny boutique a few stores down from the teashop. Lorraine had suggested that I get some loose clothes. And I'd told Garlic Breath I was going shopping. He would definitely be looking for a new outfit the next day. Frankly, any change would be noticed. I hadn't worn anything but plain blue chinos and a white shirt to work since I joined Bettel Occidental Commodities. I bought five new work outfits at Wal-Mart during the back-to-school sales. My athletic clothes got replaced every few months. I didn't care about my work clothes.

I tried to remember what Jane had worn the first time we met. She looked comfortable and self-assured even when she was feeling like five miles of scorched earth. I picked up a black polished cotton skirt off the sale rack and tried it on. It felt cool and light against my legs. The saleswoman encouraged me to try on a pair of blue wool slacks to replace my chinos. They did flatter my slim figure without showing too much and I liked the way the satin lining felt against my skin. My plain black loafers looked scuffed and clunky beside the fine gabardine wool. A pair of red leather driving moccasins, very much like Jane's, looked better and felt as soft as slippers on my feet. When I checked out, I discreetly placed seven pairs of nude cotton panties with stretch lace waistbands and a silk camisole with lace straps on the counter next to my other purchases.

✳✳✳

The next day, I was making headroom on the pomegranate report when a low rumble moved through the office like a seismic wave. I peeked around the edge of my cube, expecting to see Letitia stalking her latest victim. Instead, Vanessa Klaitner from Human Resources teetered down the passageway in turquoise wedges. Her orange hair floated around the shoulders of her hot pink sheath, like seaweed around an exotic coral. Murmuring voices followed in her wake.

"Hey," she said as she perched on the pile of file boxes outside my cube. "You know, I don't think I've ever been up here. It's efficient."

"Thank you?"

Vanessa tapped the file boxes. "Big project?"

"No bigger than usual. That pile is part of the pomegranate report for next week. Did you know that the apple in the Bible was probably really a pomegranate? You see—"

"So, how you feeling? You start—"

"Fine," I said quickly. I held a finger up to my lips and pointed at Garlic Breath's eyes peering over the wall.

Vanessa leaned over the cubicle wall and said, "Greg Blankenshipp, don't you have work you need to be doing? If you have time to listen to Ms. Blaine's personal conversations, perhaps you are not as overworked as you claim to be."

Garlic Breath disappeared with a snort.

Vanessa rolled her eyes and whispered, "Letitia tells me you took yesterday afternoon off to go shopping? I was worried something happened."

I gestured to my new skirt and shoes. "I really did go shopping."

"Cute shoes," Vanessa replied. She stood up and started back toward the elevator. She called over her shoulder so everyone could hear, "Remember, if you need anything, give me a call."

As soon as the elevator doors closed, the office erupted with conjecture. I heard Garlic Breath pick up his extension and say, "I don't know. I was hoping she'd fire her, too." I banged on the cubicle wall until Garlic Breath hung up.

12
Poached Frog

More than halfway through the course of radiation treatments, I hadn't experienced any of the fatigue or skin problems touted in the literature. My schedule accommodated the morning radiation appointments while still leaving plenty of time to workout at the Y every evening before stopping in Lucky Lee's for my dinner. This bout with cancer felt like nothing more than an icy patch in the road of life. Scary for a moment, yet easily forgotten.

In the middle of the second week of treatments, the ice broke beneath my feet and plunged me into the cold, cruel world of unintended side effects. As soon as my rear end hit the toilet seat that morning, I knew something was wrong. Dreadfully wrong. My urine had been replaced with lye. I gasped in pain and clenched to stop the burning stream.

No! It's too soon! The books said I might have "pain on urination," but later. Not like this!

I couldn't clench my muscles against the pain any longer. I

was forced to let go. Flashes of light and color turned my tiny white bathroom into a psychedelic blur. It had only lasted a second, maybe two, however the effort left me wasted. I toppled off the toilet and lay with my hip against the cool side of the tub until the room stopped spinning. I tried to twist my body into a sitting position. The bathroom was small. I jostled the vanity in the process, sending my leather bound copy of *Nicholas Nickleby* toppling to the ground. It narrowly missed falling into the toilet. "Smike!" I caught the precious volume and hugged it to my chest as I banged the back of my head again and again against the edge of the tub. *Oh my God, blood! And that didn't come out of my vagina either. My bladder is bleeding.*

As the enormity of what was happening rose up within me, I vomited into the toilet. The room reeked with the stench of fear. No amount of bleach could get rid of that smell. A memory of it would always linger in the grout and behind the fixtures.

Eventually I pulled myself together enough to dress and get to the hospital in time to receive my treatment. I was worried the radiation would burn me even more, yet I wasn't about to mention the pain. I would tough it out in silence. Alone.

✳✳✳

Even though I'd read about radiation fatigue, I was as completely unprepared for it as I was the bleeding and pain. At lunchtime I was nibbling at my peanut butter and jelly sandwich when it hit me. One minute I was a little tired. The next, my neck muscles could no longer hold up my head. I was a lone swimmer standing up to my neck in the ocean watching a tidal wave of exhaustion looming on the horizon.

Two hours later, I vaguely registered scarlet fingernails

waving in front of my face. I fully opened my eyes to see Letitia poised over me like a watchful spider. "Are we keeping you up?"

"What? No. I'm awake!"

"You were snoring," Letitia snickered. She leaned across the desk and pincered the report I had been working on before lunch. "What is with you lately? First you're here at all hours of the night like you don't sleep at all. Now your co-workers find you snoozing at your desk. I thought you were getting some help."

She dropped the report, apparently satisfied with it. "And, you didn't come in until almost ten again this morning. That woman in HR said to give you a break, but this is unacceptable. People are beginning to talk."

I avoided Letitia's eye and straightened the papers on my desk. "I go to meetings in the mornings."

Letitia stepped back and straightened her fashionably cropped suit jacket. "Well, I didn't like compiling everyone's weekly reports myself this morning."

It is your job.

"I sent you all my stuff days ago. If you ask people to email me their stuff a day or so before your meetings, I can aggregate them for you like I usually do."

"That's true." Letitia scrutinized my face. I hoped I didn't have drool on my cheek. "I might could do that… You look like hell."

"I'm tired," I snapped. It wouldn't be giving too much away to admit that. "I didn't sleep very well."

"Are you sure you're okay?" Letitia anxiously clicked her long red nails on the top of her Starbucks cup. "I noticed you spent an awful long time in the bathroom earlier."

Talk about an understatement. I had briefly fainted in the stall from the sheer pain of using the bathroom. Before this ordeal, I never would have believed that soggy Rice Crispies could go through my body like shards of glass. "I think I picked up a stomach virus. The meetings are held in a church basement. Those places are cesspools."

"Really?" Letitia sighed.

"Oh yeah, lots of people die every year from viruses they pick up in church." I expounded on flesh eating viruses until Letitia went back to her office in disgust. I knew I wasn't going to be able to keep up the charade much longer. Letitia wasn't going to tolerate my sleeping at my desk. My head felt like it was filled with cotton. I pulled my foot up under my sore bottom and hunched over the desk. If I could pretend to be studying the report on the desk, I could close my eyes again—for just a second. As I drifted off again I thought of Dante's *Inferno* and wondered exactly which circle of Hell I was currently in.

13
Standing Eight Count

The next few days were a blur. Even though cancer clearly had me on the ropes, I wasn't down for the count quite yet. The pain was no worse at this point and the radiation fatigue had temporarily dislodged the nightmares. I was punch drunk but keeping my feet under me.

On the morning of my twelfth treatment, I drove to the Yellow lot through a deluge. A line of cones blocked the entrance and the yellow-slickered valets were directing people to park along the street. I already felt like a wet rag; I didn't want to hike through the pouring rain to receive my radiation treatment. I circled the block three times before finding a spot. The narrow side street was a river of brown water. I slipped off my new red flats and tucked them in my backpack before slogging my way through the muddy puddles back to the Cancer Center. Outside the sliding doors, I recognized the minivan-driving mom talking on her cell phone under the small overhang. "I'm sorry, Dwight, you'll have to miss first period again. Give your sisters some frozen waffles and pack their lunches. They can watch TV until I get home. I'll email your teacher to explain why you're late again." She smiled at me while I rinsed my toes in a downspout. I smiled back before stepping inside. I hoped her children were all right home alone.

The reception area was a cacophonous mess. The rain hammered on the glass ceiling while a crowd of patients peppered a frazzled volunteer with questions. Lorraine was nowhere to be seen. I stepped into the crowded ladies room for some paper towels when a wave of fatigue suddenly swamped me. I needed to sit down before I fell down. People were packed cheek to jowl in the normally calm waiting room. No one spoke. They were as grey and tepid as the rain quietly dribbling down the large windows. They just sat, waiting. I drifted around the room like a fading butterfly looking for a place to land until I heard someone croak, "Hey, Blue Eyes," from the other side of the room. The Badger was waving a copy of *National Geographic* like a flag. "Over here, I saved you a seat."

My breath caught in my throat. The grumpy rodent was turning out to be a fairy godmother. I squeezed in beside The Badger on a pale yellow loveseat sprinkled with embroidered daisies.

"You look like a drowned rat. And where the hell are your shoes? You're always walking around barefooted."

I pulled my shoes out of my backpack and dried my feet off as best I could with the paper towels in my hand before slipping them back on. "Thanks for saving me a seat."

"You looked like death warmed over. I knew you couldn't stand in the hall for two hours."

"Two hours!"

"Room A broke down this morning so they were doubling up in B. Then I heard that some kid flipped out and had to be sedated. That took forever. So now we're two hours behind." The Badger scratched at her chest. I could see a discolored patch of skin there.

"Does that hurt?"

The Badger squinted at me. "What d'you think?"

I bent over and started to gather up my things. "I've got to get to work. My boss is going to be pissed if I'm gone all day. Think they would let me cut in front of some of these other people?"

"No," The Badger said with finality. "What makes you so special?"

"But I've got things to do."

"What makes your things more important than anybody else's?"

I thought about Minivan Woman's children needing to get to school.

"Hell, some of us don't have that many days left," The Badger mumbled. She cleared her throat and winced.

A jolt of compassion twisted my heart in my chest. I had researched esophageal cancer after we met. The odds of The Badger recovering from this relapse were slim. Getting to work no longer seemed quite so important. "How are you feeling? Are you in a lot of pain?"

"Might have to get a feeding tube," she replied curtly. She scratched at her chest again.

The Badger watched me shift my weight so I was not sitting on my painful parts. "Didn't talk to your doctor about the pain, did ya?"

"I'm sure he has more important things to deal with. I'm

tough. I'll be fine."

That type of response usually put people off but The Badger merely laughed. "You think you're that tough? If you think you can beat back cancer with those little fists, you're sicker than I thought." She cleared her throat again and took a long replenishing draught from a tall green sports bottle with the Ellery Hospital logo on it. She winced as she swallowed but seemed relieved afterward.

"Can I do anything?"

"There's nothing to do. The doctor gave me pain pills." The Badger took another swallow of water then said, "Just talk to me while we wait. It'll keep my mind off my throat."

"What do you want to talk about?"

"Read any good books lately?" Those were magic words. We chatted about British mysteries and suspense novels. I was surprised to find this lifelong employee of a textile mill from the mountains of North Carolina was a reader of P.D. James and Ruth Rendell. The two hours went by as swiftly as Hercule Poirot through a sitting room of lying socialites.

***

Hours later, I emerged from the changing area to find Rosaria waiting for me. She took my arm in a Vulcan grip and led me to a private alcove. "I got a call from Rex yesterday," she said sternly. "He told me you wince when you walk and that he saw black and blues on your knees." I involuntarily held my backpack in front of the fist shaped bruises where I had silently punched through the pain of using the ladies' room at work.

"Then," Rosaria continued, "when I asked Lorraine to buzz me when you were finishing up today, she told me another patient reported they were worried about you." Rosaria's starched white pants glowed under the fluorescent lights. "Now. Tell me. What is going on?"

I was touched that Rosaria cared enough to come check on me. I struggled to keep my voice steady as I replied, "It hurts. It hurts to pee and it really hurts to go... you know."

Rosaria held her pen poised over a notepad. "When did this begin?"

I was embarrassed to admit how quickly the side effects had started. "Last Monday."

Rosaria slammed her pen down on the pad. "Last Monday! *Pobrecita*! Why did you not call? I told you to tell me if you experienced any side effects."

I stared out the window and watched the rain slide down the glass. "I thought I could handle it."

Rosaria rested her tiny hand on my arm and searched my face with her warm brown eyes. "Has there been any blood?" I didn't dare respond. Rosaria rolled her eyes and mumbled, more to herself than to me, "Who knows what kind of damage has been done."

Rosaria gathered up her clipboard and grumbled, "Come to my office. I have some things to give you to help with the side effects and, hopefully, we can catch the doctor for a minute." Rosaria hustled away, muttering to herself in Spanish. I struggled to keep up with her.

I expected Rosaria's office to be cold and impersonal; however it was a warm, inviting room with large windows and a rag rug in the center. A disused desk was pushed against one wall and piled high with reference books. Along the other wall was a threadbare couch, an obvious cast-off from a waiting room. The sun broke through the clouds and shifted the shadows cast from a collection of carved angels hanging from the suspended ceiling. I imagined Rosaria sitting on the couch reviewing patient's charts with her choir of angels over her head.

Rosaria sat down on the couch and gestured for me to sit beside her. "Come. Come. Sit. I only have a few minutes." She looked at me and sighed heavily. "Dr. Obatu will want to see you. You'll just have to be patient until we can fit you in."

"But I have to get to work. I'm already really late."

"You're taking the day off," Rosaria replied. She stretched her petite form to its full height and continued firmly, "Now, have you been drinking enough fluids?"

"I don't know," I lied.

Rosaria took a tall green sports bottle out of the plastic bag at her feet. I recognized it as identical to the one The Badger carried with her to alleviate the burns in her throat. "I want you to drink four of these every day."

I gulped at the thought of passing that much scalding urine over my tender skin.

"I get it, but we need you to move fluids through your body." Rosaria shifted to look me in the eye. "Lara, this is important. What have you been eating?"

I hadn't been eating much for the last few days. I picked up my order from Lucky Lee's in order to see Helen and maintain some semblance of a schedule but had only been nibbling at the rice. I'd even been too tired to go to the gym the last few days.

"Some rice," I replied defensively. "My grandmother always said rice and bananas are good for the digestion."

Rosaria pat my knee and replied, "Your grandmother was correct. Rice is easy on the system." She stood up to retrieve a plastic bag. "Here are some liquid meal replacements to get some calories in you. You need to eat actual food, too. Isn't your family helping you?"

I set my jaw. "I can take care of myself."

"You'll need to do a better job of it then. I would feel better if you had someone to help you through all this. Now," she said, turning toward the door, "let's go find you a room." Rosaria left me in an exam room to wait for Dr. Obatu. I stripped and put on the hospital gown. It now felt natural to be half-naked whenever I was in this building. Once undressed, the fatigue started to wash over me again. I couldn't sit on the hard plastic chair and standing upright was too much of an effort. I hoisted my weary body up on the examination table and curled my feet up under my bottom. The room was warm and the fluorescent lights emitted a low buzz that made my eyelids heavy. I leaned back and quickly drifted off to sleep to the sound of muffled voices through the wall.

I was roused from my catnap by Dr. Obatu's warm laugh. "Ms. Blaine, I gather that you are experiencing some fatigue? My patients do not typically curl up on my examination table like sleeping kittens."

I sat up and tugged my gown around my legs. "Sorry. I was just so tired and—"

"Do not apologize! I am glad you were able to rest a few moments and it brought me a bit of joy on a trying day." A shadow seemed to pass across his smiling face. "But let us talk about how you are getting on. Rosaria tells me you have been having some difficulty." He sat down and opened my chart on his lap. His expression turned grave. "Oh my goodness, she writes here this has been going on for some days. When did you first experience these side effects?"

"Monday?" I mumbled.

"Well! I would have preferred that you had told us right away but that is in the past. Let us examine you and see what can be done." Dr. Obatu called Rosaria in to help with the exam. I lay back, dreading what he would say once he saw how red and swollen my body was. The doctor had to gently nudge my knees apart to examine me. As soon as he touched my skin, I gasped and arched in the stirrups. The doctor jumped back at my reaction and said, "It's okay, Miss Blaine. Although it may be uncomfortable, I need to examine you. Try to relax." He signaled to Rosaria to stand closer by and resumed the examination, moving as gently and slowly as possible. Rosaria placed her hands on my upper arm and talked to me again about how important it was to drink plenty of fluids. I could tell she was prepared to hold me down if necessary and was talking more to distract me than to impart any new information. Still, I liked the sensation of her hand on my arm.

Eventually, Dr. Obatu instructed me to sit up. He sat in the chair across the room from me and made some notes in my chart. He wiped his brow, although the room was chilly. "There is quite a bit of irritation. I had hoped we could proceed with the last several treatments with a different cradle. I no longer feel that would be a prudent choice. I suggest we stop, let the tissues heal, then re-evaluate. We can proceed with the one day-long internal radiation treatment at some point down the road." He closed the chart and stood up. "I want to see you again in two weeks. I will leave you with Rosaria now. She can give you advice on how to help you heal better." He wearily walked out of the small room into the busy hallway.

Rosaria closed the door and leaned against it for several long moments. Her eyes felt like spot lights examining every inch of my face. "You are like the girls that would wander into Antigua from the jungle—too frightened to know any better. My sister, Maria Angeles, would take a pitcher of water and some food and leave it in the back garden for them. In the morning, the food would be gone. Only after weeks of feeding them did they talk to her. My sister cried for their souls. They made me angry."

"Angry?"

"The soldiers had come into their villages, killed their families, and… well."

"Really? What happened to them?"

"I went to my father and he was able to save a few of the girls. The Church helped some. Perhaps that is why Maria Angeles is a nun and I am a nurse." Rosaria shook her head as if to shake out a memory. "I met Reg at a conference on post-traumatic gynecology. His sister runs a clinic for women in Kigali. He was supposed to go back and work with her in her clinic, but he fell in love with a girl from New York and stayed here in the States."

"Why are telling me this?"

"Because I want you to remember that you are not the only young woman who has been abused by life."

"But I—"

"*M'ija*," Rosaria sighed. "You flinch exactly like those girls who wandered, skinny and tired, out of the jungle into my father's garden. It's time to stop fighting."

Rosaria walked out of the room and left me, dumbstruck, to change. I felt a fool. Rosaria saw the way I pulled away from the doctor's touch. She saw the way I am and she didn't reject me. She didn't judge me.

I dressed and retrieved Ruby from the valet. He smiled at me and wished me a good day. He didn't give me a hard time about leaving the car there for hours or leer at me. He was nice. Dr. Obatu and Rosaria had been nice.

I drove down the interstate on autopilot. It was already

late afternoon. I realized I never called Letitia to say I wasn't coming in. The car parked itself in front of Lucky Lee's. When I opened the door and entered the deserted restaurant, Susan Lee looked up from her ledger and squealed, "Miss Lara! What are you doing here so early? Your food isn't ready." I couldn't help but be amused.

"That's okay." I leaned against the first booth. I didn't even know why I was there. I wasn't hungry. "Actually, can I get something different today? Can I have some of that chicken soup with the big noodles in it?"

"Won ton?"

"Sure, Miss Lara. You sit down and I'll go get you some." Mrs. Lee trotted off into the back of the restaurant. When she returned with a bag filled with a tall take-out container of golden goodness, she asked, "Why aren't you sitting down? You look tired." I didn't want to lie to Mrs. Lee. She had always been so sweet to me. I looked forward to seeing her and her daughter, Helen, in the evenings.

"There is something wrong, isn't there? I noticed you don't go to the gym down here anymore. Sit down. Tell me all about it. There aren't any other customers here." Mrs. Lee slid into a booth.

From the function room to the left, Mrs. Lee's mother-in-law said, "I told you she looked terrible." She padded over and squeezed my shoulder like a chicken bone. "You're too skinny."

I cracked. First Rosaria saw through my facade, and now the Lees were fussing over me. I sunk into the booth and flinched as my bottom hit the vinyl.

"What is it, colon cancer?"

"Geez, Mom! That's none of our business," Mrs. Lee chided her mother-in-law. They argued over my head in

Chinese.

"Cervical cancer. The radiation is burning me up inside. Everything hurts these days."

The older woman put her hand on my head. She seemed to be measuring my energy and then proclaimed, "You need some ginger tea and mushroom sauce."

"What?" I asked.

"You need ginger tea to sooth your system and mushroom sauce to heal you. I'll go get some!" Mrs. Lee skittered into the kitchen.

The bell rang as a family entered the restaurant and Susan jumped up to seat them in the back of the room. She quickly came back to sit next to me. "My mother-in-law and her Eastern medicine. She makes herself out to be the old Chinese sage, but she learned it all from books. I don't understand it, but when she makes me drink her teas and concoctions I always feel better. My brother is a pediatric urologist and he can't explain why they work, but they do. I'm so sorry to hear about your cancer. Is your mother helping you?"

"No, my mother and I don't get along," I replied. Susan seemed more disturbed by this news than by my diagnosis. Mrs. Lee came back with a huge container of tea, a box of rice, and another container filled with a black sauce.

"You drink a cup of this tea every hour and eat the rice with some of this sauce tonight. Tomorrow, you'll feel better. Next time, I will make a special dinner to help you not hurt so much inside. Okay?"

I stood up. "Okay. I'll come see you tomorrow. Thanks." I didn't know how to thank the Lees enough for their generosity. The sweet, spicy aromas emitting from the plastic bag filled the air inside Ruby as I drove home. I felt better already.

14
The Office Explodes

My absence the day before did not go unnoticed. Garlic Breath and Pathetic Dog Owner's heads poked up over their cubicle walls like meerkats popping out of their burrows as soon as I staggered out of the elevator. I'd planned to be safely in my cube before they arrived for the day. The radiation fatigue planned for me to sleep until 11:00.

"Rough night?" Garlic Breath jeered.

Pathetic Dog Owner stood up and gawked. "Look at the way she's walking. Is she still high?"

I edged into my cubicle and plugged in my laptop as if I couldn't hear them. Still, each word cut like talon strikes. I ached for my computer to boot-up quickly so I could lose myself in numbers and charts.

I should have stayed home. Rosaria told me to rest.

"She's really gone and done it now," Garlic Breath scoffed from behind the wall. "Letitia can't let this one go. I don't care how great that PowerPoint on pomegranates was." A quiver of conceit spread through my aching muscles. I had spent hours doing research and getting the pomegranate report perfect. "I'm going over Letitia's head this time." In the few minutes it took for the mainframe to finish syncing with my laptop, I rested my heavy head on the palm of my hand. The walk from the car had been exhausting.

Some time later, I jerked awake from my second catnap in an hour. It took me a moment to register what had woken me; the background buzz of workplace conversation had gone silent. I looked over the top of my cubicle wall and recognized a distinctive orange ponytail bobbing toward Letitia's office above the cubicle walls. Vanessa looked like a parrot in a turquoise sweater dress with a wide yellow belt that accentuated her generous curves. Letitia came out of her office to meet Vanessa. Her sleek black suit looked drab next to Vanessa's splendor. Letitia pointed in my direction and yelped, "She's taking a nap!"

Vanessa walked into Letitia's office and calmly sat down in the white leather chair in front of Letitia's sleek glass desk. Once Letitia joined her behind the closed door, Vanessa leaned back and started talking. After a few sentences, Letitia's body stiffened. She swung around and glared at me through the glass wall. The rest of the office ducked behind their cubicle walls. Vanessa wrinkled her nose and said something that made Letitia spin around to face her again. Letitia's eyes widened and her scarlet nails went to her lips as Vanessa pushed a piece of paper across the desk.

At this point, I scooted back to my desk before Letitia turned around and caught me in her gaze again. I sat there trying not to hyperventilate until Vanessa poked her head in and said, "Do you have a minute?" Her face was flushed.

There was anger just under the surface of her voice.

"Sure," I replied. I looked over Vanessa's shoulder and saw the entire department watching. Letitia stood on the other side of the glass office wall glowering at me, her thin red lips pinched into a bitter rose.

"Good," Vanessa said. "Grab your computer and purse."

I gathered my things and followed Vanessa to the elevator. I wondered if I would ever be back. Vanessa stepped in behind me and punched the button for the fifth floor. When the doors closed, she slapped me on the back of the head with the thick manila folder in her hand. "What is wrong with you? Why didn't you tell HR that Letitia has been taking credit for your work?"

I knocked the folder out of her hand and stepped back until I bumped against the wall of the elevator. "She's my boss."

"For years we've been putting up with that bully," Vanessa mumbled to herself. "Frank thinks she's so smart... Smart, my ass... and she accuses this one of... she's a user. That's what she is."

The doors opened to the hushed Human Resources department. Vanessa quickly bent to pick up the manila folder, then literally pulled me down the hall to her office. My feet were like cannonballs, heavy and wobbly on the plush carpeting. I really wasn't up to so much excitement. I leaned against the doorjamb while Vanessa unlocked her office. As soon as she got it open, I thudded into the high backed chair just inside the door.

Vanessa dropped the file folder on her desk and woke up her computer. She spoke to me over her shoulder. "I'm going to ask you this again, Ms. Lara Blaine. Why didn't you report Letitia?"

"For what?"

"For stealing your work," Vanessa snapped.

"What? She didn't steal it. She shares her bonuses with me."

"You earn your year end bonuses. They aren't gifts."

"I know that." My voice sounded slurred in my ears. I leaned my head against the back of the chair and closed my eyes. Part of me was worried that I was going to get fired, but mostly, I was too tired to care. "What I meant was that when I do a particularly good job on something, she gets a bonus. Then a couple of days later, she writes me a check for half."

When Vanessa didn't respond, I opened my eyes again and sat up. She was blinking so fast her false eyelashes were coming loose. "Excuse me?" she squawked.

"Am I in trouble?"

"How could you let Letitia take advantage of you like that?" Vanessa took out a yellow legal pad and started making notes. "By writing a check, do you mean she had AP cut you a check?"

"No, she writes me a personal check or gives me cash."

"So let me get this straight. Your job description is researcher, correct?"

"Senior Researcher," I replied. "But Letitia can't put a presentation together to save her life. She was always analyzing my numbers wrong. I do excellent research but she kept screwing up the facts in her presentations. After a while, I started just preparing the presentation slides for her. Then, a couple of years ago, she asked me to make everyone else's stuff work with mine."

"Isn't that her job as the head of the department?"

I rolled my eyes. I was too tired to spell it out for Vanessa in politically correct terms. "Yeah, but she sucks at her job." I leaned forward and reached for the folder on Vanessa's desk. "Is Letitia in trouble?"

"Not yet," Vanessa replied. She moved the folder away from me. "But if I give her enough rope I'm pretty sure she'll hang herself."

"What do you mean?"

"You see, yesterday afternoon, I was talking to her boss, Frank. He came down about something totally unrelated to you guys up on the eighth floor, but he mentioned in passing that he was worried about Letitia."

"Really?"

"He was telling me how Letitia totally blanked in this big meeting yesterday. I wasn't really paying that close of attention. That Frank, he's a real talker. Until he said something about pomegranates." I startled to attention as Vanessa popped open a can of Diet Coke from her mini fridge. "Then, Greg Blankenshipp emailed me his daily rant about you coming in yesterday. Were you feeling really sick or something?"

"Long day at the hospital."

"That's fine. You have tons of sick time." She took a sip of soda. "Where was I? Oh yeah, I remembered that you were putting together a presentation on pomegranates when we talked the other day. So, I asked him more about that meeting and he said that Letitia didn't seem to know anything about the stuff she was giving a presentation on. He said she kept texting someone." Vanessa took a gulp from the can. "Did you get any texts from Letitia yesterday?"

"Yeah, like ten, but there's no reception in the hospital."

"That's what I thought. She was texting you for the answers and you weren't here."

"So what were you arguing about in her office?"

"She thought I came by to talk about you missing so many hours lately. I wanted to know why she didn't know anything about pomegranates."

"No wonder she looked so mad."

Vanessa held her pen poised over her notepad. "Can we back-up here a sec? You and the other people up there research stuff and write reports, then Letitia puts them together and presents them to the Executive Committee, right?"

"That's what she's supposed to do," I replied. "What actually happens is this—everyone does their thing, then sends their reports to me, and I aggregate them into a PowerPoint with cheat sheet notes at the bottom of Letitia's screen. That's why she couldn't answer Frank Mariano's questions. She had to do the PowerPoint herself this week. She always forgets to add the notes section."

"And for that, she pays you part of her bonuses?

"Yup."

"How much are we talking about here?"

I rubbed my forehead with my palm. "I think she wrote me a check for $15,000 last quarter."

"Wow, no wonder she hasn't promoted you. I have to talk to my boss about this! And I'm going to ask accounting to get me a reckoning of all her bonuses, then talk to Frank again."

I had a feeling I should have said something more, but my brain hurt. I could hear Vanessa furiously typing, but I didn't have the energy to open my eyes to look at what she was doing. The back of the chair was soft and inviting. I closed my eyes and let my arms grow heavy on my lap.

The next thing I knew, Vanessa was shaking me awake. "Lara! Lara, are you okay?" It took me a moment to register where I was. I sat up and rubbed my eyes.

"I'm fine. Fine," I said. "I'm just really tired."

"Are you sure?" Vanessa bit her lip and looked genuinely concerned. "I'm sorry. You aren't in any shape to talk right now. I'm so mad at Letitia, I forgot how sick you are. We can talk about Letitia tomorrow." Vanessa helped me stand up. "Why don't I take you home so you can get some rest?"

I was so tired, I allowed Vanessa to lead me out of the office. By the time Vanessa leaned me up against the side of her pick-up truck, I could barely put one foot in front of the other. I looked up at the building and tried to make out where the eighth floor was. *I wonder if Letitia is watching us right now. She must be so pissed at me.*

Vanessa helped me climb into the truck and ran around to the driver's seat. "So, where do you live?"

"What about my car?" I whispered.

"Deal with that tomorrow. Let's just get you home. I'll cook you some dinner."

I curled up in the corner of the soft leather seat and mumbled, "I don't have any food. I get take out."

"Do I need to take the highway?"

"Go east. Get off at exit 12."

Vanessa roared onto the highway and drove thirteen miles over the speed limit. She tapped me on the arm and asked, "Did you want to stop for some take out?"

"When you get off at my exit, turn left at the bottom of the ramp. Go to Lucky Lee's in the Kroger Plaza. They know my order."

The next time I opened my eyes, I was shivering and alone inside Vanessa's truck. I rubbed the fog off the window. We were parked in front of Lucky Lee's. *When did we get here? Vanessa was just getting on the highway a second ago.* A soft rain tapped on the roof of the cab. I ran my hand across the door searching for the handle but my fingers felt like clubs. I was trapped.

A moment later, the passenger door burst open and Vanessa shoved a steaming bag of food between my feet. "Hi, Miss Lara," Helen Lee said from behind Vanessa. "Your friend bought all sorts of food even though I told her you only eat Moo Goo Gai Pan, white rice and Pineapple Surprise."

"I've got to eat, too," retorted Vanessa as she took Helen's bag and put it next to the first.

"Thanks, Helen. You okay?"

"I got a B plus on my spelling test."

"Helen! Go back inside," her mother scolded as she approached with yet another bag of food. "Can't you see that Miss Lara isn't feeling well?" Susan waited for the little girl to scamper back into the restaurant before turning to me with genuine concern in her dark eyes. "Are you all right? Who is that woman?"

My lips felt thick and sticky as I replied, "I'm fine, just really run down. I'll be better tomorrow."

"Okay then," Susan said and handed me the last bag. "My mother-in-law put something special in here just for you. I didn't put all this other food on your account. She paid."

She closed the door gently but didn't go back inside. I could see her reading Vanessa's license plate number and repeating it over and over to herself as we pulled away.

Vanessa started chattering as soon as she pulled out of the parking lot. "What an adorable place that is. It's so great to see immigrants trying to make a life here."

"Susan grew up in New Jersey. Her husband is a lawyer. Turn right at the light."

"Still, it's a cute place. The little girl said you come in every day and get the same thing."

"Turn left up here. I'm the last driveway on the right."

I used what little energy I had to jump out of the truck and push the security code into the garage door opener. I didn't want Vanessa to see the numbers over my shoulder. The garage looked lonely without Ruby. I wondered how I would get her back home.

Vanessa stormed past me as soon as I unlocked the inner door and whisked the bags of food into the kitchen. "Did you just move in?" I lay down on the couch and let her open and shut cabinets until she found plates and glasses.

She returned with fifteen take out containers arranged on a cookie sheet I didn't remember ever using. "Oh baby, this place has bad break-up written all over it. When did he leave?"

I sat up and took the plate that Vanessa wagged in my face. "I'm not that hungry. My stomach has been upset lately."

"You need to get some food in you. You need your strength." Vanessa shook some rice and chicken onto my plate. "Eat that. You'll feel better in no time."

"If I eat, will you leave and let me sleep?"

"You eat all that food and I'll leave alone." We ate in silence for a few moments until Vanessa jumped up and ran back to the kitchen. "Shit, I almost forgot. The Chinese lady sent some tea." Vanessa returned with a Solo cup full of hot tea. I held the cup to my chest and inhaled the aroma of ginger and cloves. It smelled like a hug.

Once Vanessa made a small dent in all the food she bought, she closed up the square paper containers and took them into the kitchen. She came back with another cup of the tea. She put a pillow on the arm of the couch and helped me lie down. "Comfortable? Do you want anything else to eat?"

"No, I ate more than I should have." As much as I had been avoiding food, I did feel better after eating something. My body felt heavy but better.

Vanessa pushed my feet to one side and sat on the corner of the couch with her tea balanced on her belly. "Wow, this tea is amazing," Vanessa said. Her voice sounded far away.

✳✳✳

I thought I had died. Bird song twittered softly in the distance. Nightmares didn't lurk at the edges of my consciousness. My body didn't hurt. I wasn't afraid.

This isn't too bad. Kind of wish I could remember actually dying. But maybe that's for the best. I lay still adjusting to oblivion when the loud beep of a truck backing up drowned out the bird song. *Crap, I forgot to put the trash out before I died.* My eyelids snapped open. Instead of oblivion, I was in my apartment. A musky smell permeated the room as I rolled over with a grunt. My keys sat in the center of the coffee table. I distinctly remembered hanging them on their hook when Vanessa and I came in the night before.

Dale! He's found me. Panic rushed through me until I noticed the orange sticky note with a message scrawled in purple ink.

Couldn't get in the garage.
Don't go back to the 8th floor until you talk to me 1st.
Have a good appointment. –V

I hoisted myself off the couch and went to the picture window at the front of the townhouse. Ruby was parked in the driveway. *Oh my gosh, I slept through Vanessa coming in and out of my apartment with my keys? I must have been comatose.*

I walked into the kitchen to warm up a cup of Mrs. Lee's delicious tea. *That was so nice of her to move my car for me. Vanessa didn't have to do that for me. But she did.*

15

Special Project

I dozed on the couch to reruns of *Masterpiece Mystery* when Vanessa called. I wondered when Tommy Lynley had replaced Hercule Poirot. She thanked me for sending a bouquet of lilies that morning. I'd sent the flowers because I didn't have words for how much I appreciated her help with the car, and Letitia, and in general. She said she'd had a long meeting with accounting and still needed some more time to figure out what to do with me. She told me to take yet another day off to get my strength back and meet her in HR at 10:00 the following day. I didn't argue with her. I could barely lift my head.

By Friday morning, I was less exhausted and more anxious. Vanessa had scheduled a meeting between her boss in Human Resources, Frank Mariano, and me in one of the glass conference rooms. I didn't know Frank Mariano. All I knew was that he was Letitia's boss and that she was afraid of him. I hoped he wasn't as awful as she made him out to be.

When I got off the elevator at 9:50, Vanessa was pacing in the HR foyer. "Is that what you're wearing?"

"Yeah, what's wrong with this?" I looked down at my grey trousers and white blouse. I hadn't spilled Ensure down my front or rubbed up against a dirty car while walking in. I thought I looked fine.

"Boring!" Vanessa chirped. "Thank God I saw you first." She pushed me into the ladies room, slipped off her cobalt blue blazer, and threw it at me. "Put that on."

"Why?"

"Look, Lara. I'm not going to let you go in there looking like a nun. Both our necks are on the line here.

I pulled on the blazer and held my arms out. The sleeves covered my hands. Vanessa tugged on the lapels and buttoned all five of the oversized silver buttons. "You don't have my assets to fill this out, but it sets off your blue eyes nicely. You have pretty eyes, Lara. You should wear more color." She rolled up the sleeves and folded the cuffs of my white shirt to the outside. She then took off her narrow silver belt and wrapped it around my waist.

"There, that gives you more definition." Vanessa stepped back and looked at me. "That hair," she tsked. She rolled an elastic band off her wrist and pulled my hair into a loose bun. "That will have to do," she sighed. "At least we can see your face now."

"I like my hair down," I protested. I reached up to pull out the elastic, but Vanessa slapped my hand away.

"Tough patooties. Maybe Frank won't notice those shoes."

I looked at the sensible black loafers on my feet. "I like these shoes. They're comfortable."

"That's all you can say for them." Vanessa tugged and tucked the blazer's fabric a few more times. She looked dowdy in her black knit dress without the belt and blazer. She pulled out a few tendrils of hair around my face then said, "Now go in there and act all brilliant."

When Vanessa and I entered the conference room, Vanessa's boss, a laconic man with a potbelly hanging over his belt, was talking on his cell phone. He hung up and extended his hand. "So, you must be the Lara Blaine that's been causing all the ruckus."

"I'm sorry. It's just that Letitia—"

Vanessa kicked me in the ankle and said, "It has come to our attention that Letitia has not been giving Lara enough credit for her work product. I felt we should discuss that with Letitia's supervisor before we take any action."

I sat down in one of the chairs while Vanessa's boss flipped through the file folder in front of him. He took a sip of his coffee. "It's all coming back to me now; you're the gal who wrote the pomegranate report that Vanessa was going on about."

"Yes, sir," I replied. I got the impression I should say as little as possible at this point and let Vanessa do the talking. She seemed to have a plan. A man I recognized as the balding man who drove the green sedan stepped off the elevator and walked toward me. He came in and was introduced to me as Frank Mariano. When I shook his hand, he blinked at me for a moment then exclaimed, "Red VW. You tailed me the whole way to work the other day."

"I'm sorry. I didn't mean to. I was just trying to keep heading east."

"Me, too, but I got totally lost in West Latham. I recognized your car from the parking lot, so when you kept going the same way, I felt better." He accepted a cup of coffee from Vanessa and smiled at me. "Boy, was I glad you turned out to be the same red VW. I could have gotten completely lost."

I didn't know what to say. I never considered that anyone would have recognized my car. Vanessa kicked me again and grinned at me. I smiled back at Frank and said, "Good thing we both kept going east. You're Letitia's supervisor?"

"Yes," Frank said as he turned to Vanessa. "So, why are we here? Did you figure out what's going on with the eighth floor?"

"Again, as I told John yesterday, it has come to our attention that Letitia has been taking credit for Lara's work product." Vanessa went on to give Frank all the particulars of Letitia's and my arrangement while I sat there silently trying to look brilliant.

"So, let me get this straight," Frank said when Vanessa was finished. "You did all the research, analyzed it, and prepared the presentations for the board? All Letitia had to do was show up and talk at our meetings?"

"Pretty much."

Frank took a sip of coffee. "Does everyone on the eighth floor do that?"

"Oh no," I said, perhaps a bit too loudly judging from the way Vanessa's boss started. "The others just do the research part. I put everyone's stuff all together for Letitia before your meetings."

"What do you mean, you put it all together?"

"Well," I said, looking to Vanessa for direction. She gave me a tiny nod. "Every week, we have a staff meeting, then everyone mails me their weekly reports that I aggregate into a presentation for Letitia. That is, until the last few weeks." I played with the buttons of the blazer. "I've been sick lately and missed the last few meetings."

"That's why her presentations haven't been making sense lately." Frank spoke to Vanessa's boss. "One person is out and the whole house of cards falls apart?"

"This is all very disturbing," the head of Human Resources agreed. "Especially after her numbers didn't balance last quarter."

"That wasn't Letitia's fault. Garlic Breath fudged the numbers."

Three heads whipped in my direction as they all said, "What?" in unison.

"Excuse me, Greg."

"Greg Blankenshipp?"

"Yeah, I think that's his name. He sits next to me. I heard him telling one of the other people that he had fudged the numbers on his monthly report. That's why the department's numbers didn't balance. That wasn't Letitia's doing."

"Why didn't you tell me this before?" Vanessa mumbled out of the corner of her mouth.

"You didn't ask me," I said.

Frank Mariano leaned back in his seat and steepled his fingers. "Part of me would like to wring Letitia's neck right now, but from what you told me the other day," Frank said nodding to Vanessa's boss, "Letitia hasn't actually broken any rules?"

Vanessa's boss shook himself out of his lethargy. "Since Lara here never lodged an official complaint and Letitia didn't use company money to keep her quiet, Human Resources can't take any official action. Letitia's damaged her reputation around here, but that's about it."

"Whatever," Frank said. He turned back to focus on me. I tried to arrange my features to look friendly and intelligent. "So what are we going to do with you? You obviously do excellent work, but you can't work with Letitia anymore. Vanessa mentioned you have a background in geology?"

"Yes, sir. I double majored in economics and geology in school. I've always been fascinated with minerals."

"Was the bauxite report one of yours?"

"Yes, sir."

"We have a few new markets that we're looking to get into. I'd like to set you up in a Special Projects capacity. You'd report directly to me on those markets. I can give you six months to either succeed or fail."

Vanessa kicked my chair.

"Thank you, sir. What are the areas you want me to research. I have some ideas—"

"Where will she sit?" Vanessa interrupted.

"There are empty offices on the ninth floor and on the sixth floor. She can take one of those," Vanessa's boss chimed in. "Vanessa, why don't you take Ms. Blaine to go look at those, then supervise getting all her things off the eighth floor? I'd like to discuss Letitia's future with Frank a bit more."

Vanessa and I left the room. As soon as we were out of earshot, Vanessa turned to me and said, "You know Special Projects can be the kiss of death, don't you? If you don't perform, you are out of here." She stabbed the elevator button with her long fingernail. "Well, let's go pick out an office for you and hope for the best."

We went up to the ninth floor first. The empty office there was near Frank's office and across from the large conference room where the board met. Vanessa thought I should take that office because it would give me lots of visibility and opportunities to interact with the mucky mucks. That was why I didn't want it. I didn't want to be running into executives and be forced to make small talk. Also, all the offices on the ninth floor had one glass interior wall to let light into the central area. I couldn't work in a fishbowl.

Vanessa thought the empty office on the sixth floor was atrocious; I thought it was perfect. The sixth floor was split between accounting and IT. Neither group was particularly chatty, but everyone was respectful. The room had previously been used as an auxiliary server room so it had four solid walls covered with sound proofing tiles.

"This room is on the west side of the building," Vanessa said. "It'll be dim and depressing in the morning and have blaring sun in the afternoon. You'll have to pull the shades after lunch."

"I can accept that."

"If you really want this room," Vanessa sighed, "I'm sure we can rustle up a desk for you and we can get maintenance to take this ugly foamy stuff down."

"Do I have to?"

"Why would you want drab walls like these?"

"It's not the color," I replied. I picked up a loose staple from the floor, straightened it out and poked it into the wall. "They'd be like one big giant cork board." I looked around the room and tried to imagine it without cords snaking across the floor. It was a twelve by twelve space that would be private and quiet. Perfect.

"Instead of a desk, do you think I could get two of those wide file cabinets like you have in your office?"

"Sure, there's a bunch of old file cabinets in the basement. What would you use for a desktop?"

"A big piece of glass. Easy to clean and you can write on it with china pencils." Vanessa just shook her head and called maintenance to make the arrangements.

Maintenance needed a few days to get the office together.

In the meantime, Vanessa supervised Garlic Breath distributing my file boxes to the other people on the eighth floor. She reported back that he grumbled under his breath and that Letitia pretended to be on the phone the whole time Vanessa was there. Frank Mariano sent me an email asking me to bone up on zinc futures and to expand on my last bauxite report while working from home for the rest of the week. When Dr. Obatu's office called and scheduled me for another CT scan later that week, I didn't bother telling Frank that I would be spending a day at the hospital. I didn't need three full days to do the work he'd asked of me.

16

Capped off

I t was oddly reassuring to see the worn orange chairs still squatting along the walls in the Radiology room like a line of slowly rotting pumpkins. So much was changing in my life, it was nice to know what to expect. I had settled into an armchair near the window with my bottles of Gatorade-contrast solution and an old copy of *Jurassic Park,* when a tiny plastic stegosaur hit my leg. Ten feet away, a little boy was launching an assault on a group of dinosaurs with his action figures. As he lunged Batman forward to ambush a triceratops, his baseball cap tipped off his head. A golf-ball-sized chunk of skull was missing from the right side of his head. He grabbed up his baseball cap, shoved it back on his head, and went back to playing.

The woman in the next chair picked up the dinosaur with a tired smile. "Sorry about that. Rory sure does love his action figures."

The little boy ran over and reclaimed his dinosaur. He

pointed to my book. "Do you like dinosaurs, too?"

"Dinosaurs are fun. I think it's neat how big they were."

"Some of them were like chickens," he replied with a toothy grin that transformed his grey face.

The front of his cap had the Durham Bulls logo on it. I once had a cap just like it. My grandfather took me to a Bulls game the summer I was six. PawPaw was excited to introduce me to the world of minor league baseball but worried I'd fuss during the long drive. He planned a surprise for me in the car to pass the time. Once we left the twisting mountain road and were on the interstate, he pulled a plastic box filled with cassette tapes from beneath my seat. It was an unabridged reading of *Anne of Green Gables*. He said Grammy had a much-loved copy somewhere in the attic, but he had never gotten around to reading it with my mother. The five-hour drive flew by as I saw the hills of Prince Edward Island in my mind instead of the red dirt of North Carolina. When we arrived in Durham, PawPaw was as reluctant as I was to turn off the tape.

Grammy had packed us a bag of ham and cheese sandwiches and jelly jars of lemonade, but PawPaw left them in the car. He wanted to eat hot dogs and cotton candy for lunch and stop in Gastonia on the way back for some barbecue and a bottle of Cheerwine. At the end of the day, I fell asleep in the backseat of PawPaw's old blue Volvo with a full belly and sunburned neck. Nestled in my arms was a stuffed bull wearing a cap exactly like the one now covering Rory's dented skull.

Before I had a chance to think it through, I was kneeling on the floor beside Rory. "Are you a Bulls fan?"

Rory looked up from his toys. "They gave a bunch of us kids from the hospital free tickets. It was really fun. They have a billboard of a bull that shoots out steam if a ball hits it. Do you have cancer, too?"

"Rory!" his mother scolded. The woman's face colored as she said, "You know not to ask questions like that." It improved her looks.

"That's okay," I chuckled as I poured half a Gatorade down my throat. "It's likely everyone here has cancer."

"Want to see my tattoo?" Rory asked.

I was overcome with an urge to scoop him up in my arms and hug him. I picked up a little red plastic man instead. "Who's this?" We played with his little men for several minutes until a technician came and took Rory back to the testing rooms. When he was gone, I helped his mother pick up his toys.

"Thank you for playing with him. So many people are afraid of us."

I handed Rory's red backpack to his mother. "I'm just as radioactive as he is."

"They're doing a scan today to see if the cancer has spread to his bones. He puts on a brave face, but he's really in a lot of pain. We haven't slept through the night for weeks." Her face was a collage of anguish: red rimmed eyes, gaunt cheeks, deep fissures between her brows, and a persistent flutter in her upper lip as if she was trying not to scream. "I wish I could go through this for him. I would trade my life for his in a heartbeat."

Is that what it means to be a mother? To be willing to give up your life for your child's? This woman is younger than I am. She could still have other children. She may have other children. But here she is wishing to trade places with her sick child.

I drank some more of my contrast solution.

Mama would never have sacrificed herself for me. I was her flesh and blood and she wouldn't even inconvenience herself for me. What made me so unlovable?

I reached out and touched Rory's mom's shoulder. "You are a good mom. I wish there was something I could do to help."

"Thank you," she said. "I'm afraid there's not much anyone can do. I think we're coming down to the end now." Her eyes filled with tears, but they didn't escape her lashes. I foolishly wondered if a person could run out of tears. "I just don't want him to be in pain anymore. I want this all to be over."

I felt awful leaving Rory's mother alone in the waiting room when they called my name. If I could have stayed with her until Rory came back, I would have. But I had to go. I had already drunk the contrast. The nurse was waiting for me.

✳✳✳

Forty minutes later, I waddled into the ladies room feeling a bit nauseated from the contrast solution working its way through my innards to find Jane standing in front of the sinks staring at herself in the mirror. I almost didn't recognize her. She looked awful. A grey knit cap that blended with her skin had replaced the wig and jaunty silk scarf. A too-new looking tracksuit hung off her frame. A wave of guilt washed over me. I'd meant to call Jane to ask how she was doing with the treatments. I tottered over as best I could.

"Lara! What are doing here?" Jane's eyes twinkled within their purple-tinged hollows. "You're a lucky penny the way you keep turning up."

"I had a CT scan this morning. You?"

"PET scan." I waited. Jane had more to say; I could see the words twitching around the edges of her mouth. "I think they saw something."

"What do you mean?"

"The girl. She was friendly enough when she was putting in the IV but business-like. After the test though, she was… I don't know. Too nice. Overly attentive helping me up out the machine. Then, she called me 'dear' when she gave me my paper work." Jane tugged absently at the medical tape securing the IV still sticking out of her arm. "I don't know; something about it was out of whack. I've been standing here trying to put my finger on it." I turned off the water she'd left running in the sink and handed her a towel. I didn't feel a need to fill the silence.

"When will you find out the results?"

"I see my oncologist at two."

I took Jane's arm and led her out of the ladies room. "Are you just hanging out here until then? Are you here alone?" *Listen to me. I sound like Rosaria.*

"Tom dropped me off and then went to the office. We had a huge fight on the way here."

"What's going on?" I settled Jane on a loveseat and waited for her to go on.

Jane continued to pick at the medical tape on her forearm. "I overheard him talking on the phone yesterday. He's signed an agreement with some young architect to build a green subdivision. He committed to do twenty houses!"

"Is that a bad thing? Can't you do the work?"

"We can do the build." Some color came back to Jane's cheeks as she griped about her son. "He signed on without even asking me. It *is* my company!"

"Is that legal?"

"Yes, technically. I made him a director when I started chemo so he could make day-to-day decisions, but—" Jane had reached the sticking point. She had signed over control of her company because she planned to be out for a few weeks, but now her son had taken over and made a major decision without consulting her.

"What did he say when you confronted him?"

Jane tugged her cap down on her forehead. "He can't understand why I'm even upset."

"I can. It's your company."

"Thank you, Lara. That's it. Exactly. It's mine. Everything else in my life has been for him or my mother. But the business was mine. It was my life. Now I don't know who I am." Jane played with the zipper on her warm-up jacket. "It's too much. Really, too much to bear. This cancer has taken away the one thing that made me, me.

We sat in silence for ten minutes until the contrast solution caught up with me and I had to run back into the bathroom. When I returned, Jane said, "Look sweetie, I've been thinking a lot about what you told me was going through your mind while they were making that mold of your body." Jane rubbed her eyes as if to rub away a vision. "I refuse to believe this is happening to you as some sort of retribution, Lara. I can't believe there is a God up there somewhere who would punish such a lovely young woman like that."

"I…"

"I don't care what you did to make you think you deserved this."

"But I…"

"No! I don't want to know! It doesn't matter. I refuse to believe you are anything but good. No one deserves to get cancer. I don't care what we've done. All this is totally random. It has to be. Okay, maybe I shouldn't have smoked all those years, and believe me, I tried to quit a million times. And maybe that caused my cells to mutate, but they are just cells—insidious, deadly cells—but that's it. The cells were not put there by some retributive overlord."

"You've really been thinking about what I said that much?"

"Haven't you?"

I looked across the waiting room and watched a man pacing back and forth in front of the heavy orange doors. He took a sip from the tall cup in his hand and shuddered at its foul taste. I felt a tired kinship with him and all the other souls in the room, each going through their own private hell. "Every second of every day," I admitted.

"I can't sleep at all these days," Jane said. "I've been reading some Eastern philosophy book my ex left behind. So far, I'm getting that pain is a part of life. You can't avoid it. Everyone dies so we need to just accept that. This book says that if we can let go of our desires, then we won't suffer so much. I don't really understand it all but it's an interesting way to think about what's happening to me. And honestly, I would really like to be free of this pain."

Pain and suffering I could understand. Letting go of it—I had trouble with that. "Do you want me to hang out with you until its time to go to your appointment?"

"Don't you have to get to work?"

"No," I said with a laugh. "How about we go find you a cup of tea and I'll tell you all about it?" I thought Jane could use some distraction. "I can't guarantee the cafeteria will have scones, but we might be able to find a bagel or a muffin."

"A cup of tea would be great," Jane replied weakly. I took Jane's arm to help her up and was shocked by just how much the chemotherapy was ravaging her body. We had to stop and rest every hundred feet or so on the circuitous path down to the cafeteria.

What could her son be thinking? She shouldn't be here alone. He should be taking better care of his mother.

I found Jane a table overlooking the courtyard where she could watch people walking amidst the last of the roses. A platoon of gardeners were pulling out begonias and planting pansies in the wide beds. I came back with tall paper cups of tea, a plate of muffins, and a plastic container of cubed fruit.

"You bought enough to feed a small army," Jane said with an anemic smile.

"I didn't know what you'd want, but I thought you should probably eat something."

Jane turned her face to look out the window. I got the impression I'd just been dismissed. "I think this is the courtyard I can see from the chemo room." Jane smiled wryly. "I'm terrible to those poor nurses. I always insist on getting one of the chairs near the window. It's awful enough just being there, letting them pump poison into my veins. I can't stand having everyone and their brother staring at me." Jane held the hot cup of tea against her chest. "I have to tell them every time. You'd think they'd write it down."

"Maybe some fruit would taste good."

A cold chill came over me as I remembered saying the same words to my grandmother. In the last year or so that I lived in the mountains of North Carolina, Grammy had also grown quite thin. PawPaw and I could usually persuade her to eat some fruit though, especially the raspberries and apples from her own garden. As a little girl ,my grandmother seemed like an old woman. Now that I quickly did the math in my head, she couldn't have been more than fifty years old when I lived with them—far too young to have been that frail.

"I estimate that it took three loads of gravel to do these paths. And look over there. When they put the addition on the main building, they didn't quite match the brick. The foreman should have picked up on that." Jane took a sip of her tea and winced.

"I'm sorry, Jane. I should have gotten a cup of ice."

"Details Lara, they can be the difference between success and failure." Jane half-heartedly ate a strawberry in four bites. "So, what's going on with you these days? Why did you have another CT today? Did the radiation treatments go all right?"

"Not so well. But I think that was mostly my fault."

"There you go again, blaming yourself for what has happened to your body!" Jane reached across the table and grabbed my arm. "Listen to me, none of this is your fault. It's just not. You are not responsible for getting cancer."

"But I had all these side effects. I didn't tell the doctor. I let myself get radiation burns in—inside. What if it did permanent damage?" Tea rose up in my throat. Explaining it to Jane made me realize how stupid I had been.

"Well, okay, maybe you were imprudent, but that still doesn't make it your fault. Why beat yourself up on top of having the cancer work you over? You need to be strong now, not weak."

Jane's words scalded my already raw feelings. *Could Jane be right? Am I being weak? Am I taking some sick pleasure in wallowing in self-pity? But I didn't want any of this. Did I?*

Jane nibbled on the corner of a muffin then dropped it back on the plate. "These muffins taste like cardboard. So why aren't you at work today?"

"I got my boss in trouble so I'm kind of in-between jobs

right now. I'm supposed to start working directly for this guy Frank Mariano, who is my old boss's boss. He's creating a new position for me called Special Projects in Emerging Markets. I'm not exactly sure what I'll be doing yet."

"Do you get a staff?"

"No. I get my own office with a door though."

"I can see why you'd be excited about that. I never could understand how people get any work done in those rat runs of cubicles. Then again, I've never had to." I was again struck by how easy it was to talk to Jane, as if she understood the thoughts between my sentences. "You will be getting some new clothes before you start this new position, right?"

"What do you mean?"

Jane swirled the dregs of her tea. She seemed to weigh her words before continuing. "You're around thirty right?"

"Twenty-nine."

"Aren't we all?" Jane laughed. It was nice to see her smile. It took some of the grayness away from her face. "You dress like a kid rather than a successful thirty year old. The clothes make the man—or woman—in this case. If you are going to be taken seriously, you need to have more of an air of self-confidence about you. You need some power suits. You also have the added bonus of being able to use your sexuality as a tool. Didn't your mother teach you this stuff?

I pulled my sweatshirt over my hips. "Not in the way I think you mean."

"Right, you and your mother aren't close." Jane twisted the old scratched men's watch around her slim wrist and sniffed. "Well, I guess we have that in common now, too."

"Excuse me?" I picked up one of the muffins and took a small bite.

"I had a fight with my mother. Actually, it wasn't so much

a fight as an epiphany.

"Remember that day that you and I met? Of course you remember. How could you forget? Anyway, the next morning I drove to Greensboro to see my mother. Stupid me, I thought I should tell her. The whole way up, I rehearsed what I was going to say. She's getting old. I didn't want to give her a heart attack. I don't know what I was thinking, really.

"Anyway, I got all the way there and she wasn't even in her room. I had to wait around in that glass and chrome mausoleum, drinking watered down coffee for an hour. Of course, what I really wanted was a cigarette. It's crazy. I've bleached the stains out of my teeth and got collagen injections to erase the wrinkles around my mouth but, even with the cancer, I still can't break free of the need."

I picked at my muffin and let her go on. I was pretty sure Jane wasn't aware that I was even there anymore.

"Eventually, Mother showed up, pink cocktail in hand. Typical Mother, she didn't even say 'Hello,' or 'Janie, great to see you.' She said, 'What are you doing here? It's not Sunday.'

"You know," Jane continued, staring out the window at the mound of discarded begonias. "I have gone to see her every Sunday since she moved there in '85 and she never, not once, has said thank you. Heaven forbid I want to go away for a vacation or anything. My ex-husband hated that.

"I abandoned my plan and blurted out, 'I have cancer.'

"Mother just sat down in one of the lobby chairs and sighed, 'How long? Six months? A year?' She crossed her arms and scowled at me as if I had admitted to committing a crime. I couldn't believe she was angry at me for cancer. 'Didn't you ask for some kind of estimate?' she demanded.

"'My God, Mother!' I said. 'I haven't even had the surgery yet.' That was when they were still holding the surgery carrot out in front of me.

"'Bah, they never tell you the truth,' Mother scoffed. 'They make you get that chemo crap. All your hair falls out. You're sick all the time. Might as well take rat poison.' She had the gall to pick up her compact and apply a fresh coat of lipstick. For a second there, I thought she was going to say something kind to me. 'So when are they going to cut your breast off? You'll be all crooked after.'

"'It's not breast cancer. It's lung cancer. You know this cough I've had—'

"'Lung cancer?' she said. 'Why even bother with chemo? Lung cancer's a killer. I told you, you should have smoked lights like me. And you're always around all those diesel fumes. If you'd have had a job more suited to a woman, this wouldn't have happened.'

"'Mother, this didn't happen because I took over Daddy's business. Dr. Pemachokatha said—'

"'An Indian! You're seeing an Indian doctor?' Mother rifled through her pocketbook for her address book. 'Look, Mimi Greenberg's son is a doctor. I'm sure she can ask him to pull some strings for you and get you an American doctor.'

"'Sanjay Pemachokatha is as much of an American as I am. He sounds like he's from Texas.'

"'Well, you do whatever you want. You always do. Just don't expect me to nurse you like I did your father. It is extremely selfish of you to get sick. That is not the way it is supposed to work. Who'll take care of me now?'"

Jane shook her head as she relived their conversation. "You know, Lara. Maybe it's best that you don't see your mother anymore. I wasted my whole life trying to make up for the fact that my father loved me more than he did her. For what? I told her I have cancer and she essentially gave me the back of her hand."

"Have you seen her since?" I asked.

"Nope, we haven't even talked on the phone." Jane shook her head, making the cap fall over her ear. "No, I'm not going to apologize for walking out on her that day."

"She's still angry with you?"

"Oh yeah," Jane replied. She took a sip of her tea and set the cup down between us. "She called Tom while I was driving back and gave him an earful. He thinks we should simply stop paying her bills and see how long it takes for her to come crawling back." I wasn't sure if Tom's attitude made me think more or less of him.

"So when do you start this new job?"

"I'm not sure. Next week sometime?"

"We should go shopping. I love shopping! I used to wish I had a daughter to dress up in pretty little dresses and go shopping with. We should go this weekend."

"Wouldn't that be a lot of walking for you? Maybe I should go by myself. The sales lady at the boutique near the—"

"Sales lady? Don't listen to them! They just want to earn their commission."

"They get commission?"

"Lara, where have you been?" Jane rolled her eyes. "No, I will take you shopping." I could see how excited Jane was getting at the prospect of getting out and having some fun. I wanted to be a part of that. "We'll make a day of it. We can eat lunch in the café in Nordstrom's. We'll be ladies-that-lunch."

Jane didn't ask me to come with her to get the results of her PET scan, but I wasn't about to leave her alone. What if she collapsed or got lost getting to the office? Who would run for help? When it came time for Jane to go, I simply gathered up our things and led the way. Even with my help, it took us nearly an hour to work our way to the green waiting room from the cafeteria. Jane's breathing had not fully recovered before Stephanie, Dr. Pemachokatha's nurse, pushed a wheelchair through the heavy green doors.

"Good afternoon Mrs. Babcock-Roberts," she said quietly. This nurse was nothing like the nurses that worked with Dr. Lander. I wondered if nice doctors tended to have nice nurses working with them and brutal people like Dr. Lander attracted curt cohorts. "Would your daughter like to see Dr. P with you?"

"She's not my daughter. She's my friend," Jane exhaled loudly in a half laugh. "Do you think she could?"

"I think it might be a good idea to have someone with you today." The nurse pursed her lips as if to keep herself from saying more and nodded once to me over Jane's head. "To take notes," she added lamely. Perhaps I was succumbing to Jane's sense of trepidation, but the nurse seemed too solicitous as she left us in one of the many identical examination rooms. The chill had not faded from the plastic chairs when the doctor bustled in carrying a mammoth envelope.

I was surprised that Jane's doctor was so young. He couldn't have been more than 35. With his jeans and running shoes under his lab coat, he looked like he should have been coaching a peewee soccer team instead of ministering to the sick and the dying.

"Mrs. Babcock-Roberts—"

"Please, it's Jane. And this is my friend, Lara." He shook my hand enthusiastically and flashed me a ready smile. He washed his hands again and paused a moment while drying them as if gathering some inner reserve of courage before turning again to Jane. "Jane, I have the scans from this morning here, and, well, they are not what we hoped for."

"That bad?" Jane asked. I moved to slip out of the room but Jane grabbed my hand and squeezed it hard.

"Well," Dr. Pemachokatha hesitated. *It must be so hard to be an oncologist. This poor guy has to give people bad news all day.* "It is not what I would call good." He pushed Jane's scans into a light box mounted in the wall. "These two scans are from before the chemo and these are from this morning." Jane stepped over and studied the multicolored blobs representing her internal organs. The blue blob on the right was far larger than the corresponding blue blob on the left. She ran her fingers over the shiny film leaving long smudges.

"Is this the main tumor here?" she asked. "Shouldn't it be smaller after the chemo?"

Dr. Pemachokatha wiped his forehead with his palm. "Well yes, that was the desired outcome."

Jane turned away from the films and sat back down. "It's all right Sanjay. I know you're doing your best." He blushed and Jane said bitterly, "You reminded me so much of my son just then. You both do that thing with your forehead when you don't want to say something difficult." Dr. Pemachokatha went on to explain that the chemotherapy had been ineffective at reducing the tumors in Jane's lungs but had stopped the cancer from spreading.

Jane stared at the floor for a moment. She seemed to be reviewing the last three months in her mind—losing her hair, losing her strength, losing her independence, losing her mind—and questioning what it was all for. "So what's next?"

"I recommend we try a different approach. I suggest you rest for a few weeks to regain some of your strength and then we'll proceed with a course of radiation."

The doctor went on to outline what focused radiation could do for Jane's type of tumor and how she could restart the chemo down the road. I could see Jane slipped further into a shocked daze with each passing moment. I remembered being there myself. I grabbed a notepad emblazoned with a drug company's logo and scribbled down most of what the doctor was saying. He was encouraging and seemed to have a plan for how he could help her in light of the many different eventualities. Jane would need this information later. Getting it down was the one thing I could do for her right then. I thought about how concerned Rosaria had been that I didn't bring anybody with me to my appointments. I now understood why. Jane didn't hear half of what Dr. Pemachokatha had just told us. I took a deep breath. I was grateful I could.

Dr. Pemachokatha stopped talking long enough to notice that Jane was not following his words. He picked up her pale hand and checked her pulse before turning to me. "I'm afraid she's had quite a shock. I'm glad you were here. Did you get the gist of what I was saying?" I nodded and held up my notes. "Good. I've got other patients waiting right now but could you make her another appointment for a day or two from now? I would like for us to sit down again when she is in a better frame of mind and go over her options again." The doctor shook Jane's hand again to which she nodded numbly. Then he was gone.

What would have happened if I hadn't been here? Would the nurse have eventually come back and found her and called her son to come get her?

17
Sand Flies

ane didn't say anything as I led her back through the hospital maze to the beast of a parking garage. She slumped in Ruby's passenger seat and watched the trees go by as I drove through Northwoods and found the house with only a few grunted directions from Jane. I lingered to look around the grounds before walking up to the geometrically carved doors with Jane's heavy ring of keys. Jane's fingerprints were all over the house from the sleek roofline to the splashes of chokeberries in the landscaping. I made out the seedpods of poppies amongst the foliage and could picture the big red blossoms nodding beside the walkway. That was what a front walk should look like.

Once inside the house, I found Jane's cell phone in her bag and left a message for Jane's son at their office to inform him that I had taken her home. "I'll wait for your son to get here then go on home."

"No, please stay for dinner."

"I couldn't intrude like that. You've just received some awful news. I'm sure Tom will want to talk about it without me being here."

"Exactly." Jane left me in the foyer. "Please don't leave me alone with him."

"Okay, but just until Tom gets home." I thought it best that Jane lie down. It seemed like the thing to do in this type of situation. Jane was sick, really sick, far sicker than I was. I followed Jane to a sunken living room at the back of the house and propped her up on the couch. I found some oversized pillows covered in pewter silk to put under her head and pulled a cashmere throw off the back of a side chair to drape over her.

Jane immediately closed her eyes. "Thank you; make yourself at home for a bit," she whispered dreamily. "I need some time to rest and gather my resolve."

The entire room was dove grey from the soft carpeting to the low-slung grey linen sofas. A wall of softly pleated drapery was closed against the fading sunlight. As Jane nodded off, my fingers itched to pull back the curtains and see what was outside, until I recalled that first morning in the radiation treatment hallway when I pulled back the curtain and found the impressions of other people's areas of anguish. The urge passed.

I was thirsty, but I was afraid to move. I didn't want to disturb Jane's rest and I didn't dare leave her side. Not right now. Not today. I was rattled by my diagnosis and the radiation was worse than even I could imagine, but I never really believed I wouldn't survive. I fantasized about the cancer devouring me from the inside out, yet I always knew, at least on some level, that I was only torturing myself. Both Dr. Lander and Dr. Obatu had been so confident that I would be fine. *Had Jane's doctor been less certain? Had he lied to her?* I didn't think so.

The room slowly darkened as the sun expired behind the drapes. I dozed off thinking about Susan and Mrs. Lee. I hoped they wouldn't worry too much when I didn't come in for my dinner.

Sometime later, the garage door rumbled open at the other end of the house. I tiptoed into the kitchen and flicked on the lights. I didn't want Tom to come in and find a strange woman standing over his sick mother in the dark. I perched uneasily on the counter.

Tom came in casually flipping through the mail. "Mom? Whose car is that in the driveway?" There was mud caked on his work boots and he wore a polo shirt with the company logo embroidered on the chest. He did not look like a company president; he looked like the president's kid.

"Shush!" I scolded. "She's sleeping." He looked up from the envelopes and magazines in his hand and looked at me as if I were a plate of milk and cookies left out for his afternoon snack.

"Who are you?"

"Lara Blaine."

"Is that your Beetle?" Tom tossed the mail on the high counter and retrieved a beer from the fridge.

"Yes," I replied in a whisper. "I ran into your mother at the hospital today. I brought her home. You shouldn't have left her at the hospital all alone like that."

"She insisted on going alone today and… Wait a minute, you're the girl I met at the hospital." Tom chuckled into his beer bottle. "You're the Lara she snuck out to meet for tea?"

"Yeah, what's so funny about that?"

"Nothing, I had pictured Mom sipping tea with some

little grey haired lady complaining about their wigs, not, well, *you*." I felt him appraising me. "You have cancer? You look good, maybe a little skinny but…"

I bounced down from the counter and advanced on him. "You shouldn't have abandoned her at the hospital today. What if I hadn't run into her?"

"I'm sure she was glad to see you." He started taking ingredients out of the refrigerator for dinner. "Are you staying for dinner?"

"You're supposed to take care of her." I had an urge to rip the bunch of celery out of his hand and smash it over his head. That would have wiped the smirk off his face. "She shouldn't have been alone today, of all days."

"What are you talking about? It was only blood work. And I didn't abandon her. She got pissed at me and stormed out of the car."

I had been thinking of Tom as a callous brute who had blithely dumped his sick mother and gone off to work. The young man chopping vegetables didn't appear as heartless as Jane made him out to be. "You didn't know she was having a PET scan this morning?"

Tom choked on his beer. "A PET scan? Hell no! I never would have let her go for a PET scan by herself." He dropped his knife and shouted into the living room, "Mom!" like an indignant seven-year-old.

"Shut up!" I shoved him away from the counter. "She's resting. She's had a rough day."

Tom turned as if registering my presence in his house anew. He blanched so that the sprinkling of freckles across his nose stood out. "Shit! Why are you here? What happened?"

"I think she's in shock. Essentially, the doctor said—"

"I'll tell him later, Lara." Jane's voice was anemic but

categorical. She had quietly come over to the counter from her place on the couch. "I didn't want to deal with you pacing around like a caged tiger all day." She laid her hand on my shoulder. It was too light to be comforting. "I was glad that Lara turned up though. She took very good care of me."

"Mom, you should have told me," Tom scolded. "I would have cancelled the meeting with Elliot." A coughing jag kept Jane from responding. She hung onto the counter with one hand and covered her mouth with the other. I still saw the blood spattering her fingers.

"Mom!" Tom gasped. He grabbed a dishtowel and bound over to his mother. While Tom was concentrating on Jane, I picked up my keys and slipped out through the garage. Jane was in her son's hands now.

I was halfway to the car when Tom ran out. "Wait! Where the hell do you think you're going? You can't just leave. What happened at the hospital?" The wind had changed while I had been inside. The low clouds had slid away leaving the evening air biting. I leaned on the car door rubbing the goose bumps from my arms.

"You need to talk to your mother about her appointment." I turned to get into my car.

"You better come back in," Tom said plaintively. "She wants you to stay." Part of me wanted to go back in the house with Tom and stay for dinner, as Jane asked. This place was magical. I had dreamed of eating family dinners at a wide table with matching china and cloth napkins like the ones I saw in the kitchen. But not like this. Tom would understandably be crushed by the news of Jane's cancer not shrinking. I couldn't intrude. "Look Tom, I can't stay."

"I take it you know what the doctor said? Please tell me. Mom doesn't seem to be giving me all the info these days, does she?"

I understood how Jane could be keeping her illness primarily to herself but her son seemed to care about her, even if he was a bully. I pulled the notes I took in Dr. Pemachokatha's office from my bag and handed them to him. "I wrote down everything I could. Her doctor wants her to come back in a few days to talk about her options." Tom's lips quivered. He seemed so young although he couldn't have been more than a few years younger than me. I felt sorry for him having to take on this burden. "Look, essentially, the chemo didn't work and the tumor is bigger than ever." Tom took a step back as if I'd shoved him. "Perhaps you should go with her this time and talk to the doctor yourself. He can answer your questions better than I can." I got in and started Ruby's engine. Before I closed the door, I stammered, "I'm sorry, Tom."

✱✱✱

A new nightmare crept into my head that night. I was tied facedown in burning sand. Blaring sun blinded me as soon as I lifted my head from the sand. The more I struggled, the tighter the knots around my wrists and ankles became. The sand itself seemed to be humming in the heat. A massive bird landed nearby and extended its long wings to cast a shadow over my face. After several moments, my eyes adjusted enough to see more than burning sand and shadow. I strained to see the bird, but I could only make out the edges of its scarlet body against the sun. It hopped around me as the sun moved and perched on a giant rock. Beyond the rock, I sensed movement. A line of people were trudging through the sand, some quickly, some at a snail's pace. I could see them but they didn't see me. They were all looking forward toward the end of the trail. I opened my mouth to call out but no sound came out. The more I tried to scream the more the burning air shriveled my lungs. Tears of exertion dripped across the bridge of my nose. Within seconds, sand flies came to lick them up. The bird flapped its wings making the flies float away momentarily, but they came right back. I couldn't tell if the bird was protecting me or saving me for a snack. I turned my face to the sand.

When I opened my eyes again, the wind had buried my right arm in the sand and the sun was high in the sky. I couldn't tell if I had been unconscious a few minutes or a few days. I turned my head to look over my blistered shoulder. All around me were brilliant red feathers. In the shadow of the rock, a skeletal person quietly wept. As soon as I moved, the ropes around my wrists broke away. I heard the hunched form gasp and drop to its knees as I freed my legs. Jane crawled out of the shade toward me.

"Lara? Thank God! I thought you were dead. You stopped moving ages ago." I didn't have the strength to stand but managed to awkwardly crawl over to Jane. Jane slipped off the white silk robe she wore over satin pajamas and draped it over my shoulders. It was a cool salve on my sunburned skin. "I thought that bird was some kind of vulture the way it was hopping around you on the sand. It kept pecking at the ropes and eating the bugs crawling on your skin. I tried to shoo it off but it was a tough old bird."

I wanted to ask how long she had been there, but I still couldn't speak. I clutched at my throat to try to get Jane to understand.

Jane magically pulled cool bottles of water and a pair of sandals from the air. She pressed the water and shoes into my hands. "Take these. You should get going. Quickly, follow the others to the scanner."

I stepped around the rock and saw that the line of people stretched as far as the horizon and ended at a row of chairs in front of a set of gleaming doors. As I watched, the doors opened, a person in the front row disappeared through the doors, then everyone moved over one chair like cogs in a machine. I felt compelled to join the line despite my burning skin and scorched throat. I held my hand out to help Jane up but she wouldn't leave her place in the shade.

"I can't go any further. I kept thinking I was almost there but I never seemed to get any closer. You take the water and go on." With a superhuman strength that I could only possess in a dream, I picked Jane up. I felt suddenly powerful and Jane was easy to carry. Closer to the chairs, we met little Rory sitting on the side of the path. I stopped and Jane asked, "Where's your mother, sweetie?"

He pointed to a rock several yards away. "Behind that rock. She has to stop and cry sometimes. We'll catch up."

I wanted to take him with us but I couldn't carry Jane, Rory and his mother. I had to leave him behind. Before we moved on, Rory handed me his backpack and asked, "Could you take my men with you? They're getting too hard to carry, with my mom on my back." I took the red backpack and looped it over Jane's arm.

It was difficult to see the path. I started to run. I passed thousands of other people on the trail but never got any closer to the chairs. Jane begged me to put her down and run ahead. Before I could respond, I awoke in my bed with the alarm blaring in my ear.

I rolled over and swatted the clock to the floor. The sheets were drenched. Sweat plastered my long hair to my neck. The details of the nightmare washed away with a cool shower, but as I buttoned up my plain white blouse, I had an overwhelming urge to call Jane. If I couldn't do anything to help Rory and his mother, I could certainly make sure Jane was okay.

Part Two

18

Teamwork

The Christmas lights flickered on outside my office window before the December gloom fully crept in. Inflatable snowmen and plastic reindeer dotted the front yards of the neat mill houses that abutted Bettel Occidental Commodities' parking lot. The house at the end of the street was the one exception. In the morning, an old man and his wife had fit a collection of long and short pipes into holes in the ground until the yard looked like a battered comb. At lunchtime, they sat on the front steps while their grandson pounded tent stakes all over the lawn then, at some point in the afternoon, stretched strings of lights between the tent stakes and pipes. What looked like a tangle of pipes and wires during the day transformed into a twinkling forest of Christmas trees in the dark.

I stood at my office window with a mug of spearmint tea and let out a contented sigh. It had turned out to be a good day. Frank Mariano had stopped by to say he was pleased with my preliminary report on zinc futures. He seemed impressed by how well I was doing overall. In the new year, Frank planned to have me supervise two interns from the local business school. He hinted that if the interns worked out, he planned to reassign a few of Letitia's people to me. I was tempted to tell Frank that I didn't want to be responsible to, or for, anyone, but I understood he was offering me the interns because he had faith in me. I needed to live up to that faith. Instead, I'd smiled the way Vanessa taught me and thanked him for the help.

Pradeep from IT popped his head in my door. "Are you looking at that house with the pipe trees?"

"Yeah, the old guy had the kid working all afternoon."

"I was watching him earlier. I can't get my kids to do anything, never mind banging stakes in the ground. I'm sorry for disturbing you. I thought you accidentally left your lights on."

"Are you going home? What time is it?"

"Almost 6:30. I've got to get home to help my kid with a project." I thought that sounded like fun. I loved school projects as a kid. "How's the new office working out?"

"So far, so good."

"Well," he said with a shy smile, "it's good to have you on the floor. See you in the morning."

I waved goodnight to Pradeep. The IT people had all made me feel welcome. I liked how they all chipped in to keep their little break room clean and well stocked with tea.

I went over to my desk and disconnected my laptop from the network. It was the first day in weeks that I was still feeling good at the end of the day. The radiation fatigue was finally lifting. I had been itching to get back to the gym, and since I felt pretty good, decided to give it a try.

✷✷✷

I walked into the Y lobby and heard someone shout my name. Liam was standing on a ladder updating the bulletin boards inside the large trophy case. "Long time, no see. You been traveling for work lately?"

"I've been kind of sick. It's taking me a really long time to bounce back," I said, hiking my gym bag up on my shoulder. "I thought I'd try to ease my way back in tonight."

"Cool," Liam said. "There's a guy using the Schlein bike right now but he shouldn't be long. He's just starting to get in shape for this race." He climbed down the ladder and pulled a flyer off the bulletin board. "Hey, you would be perfect for this Women's Cancer Run!"

My head started to tingle and my tongue became a dry sponge. I dropped my bag to steady myself on the wall. Liam jumped down from the trophy case and ran over to me and put his arm around me. "Oh my gosh, are you okay? Here, sit down a sec." He pulled the stool out from behind the reception desk and made me sit down. "Are you okay?"

"How?" My voice sounded shaky. "How could you tell?"

Liam's head jerked back in confusion. Then, he blushed to the roots of his floppy red hair. "Shit! I am so sorry. I didn't know. I mean, how could I?"

"But you said I—" I cleared my throat. "You said I would be perfect for a Women's Cancer Run."

Liam moved in front of me to block a group of middle-aged men coming off the basketball courts from eavesdropping on our conversation. "Yeah, because you're in fabulous shape. And a girl. That's all I meant. I had no idea you—"

"Have cancer?"

"Well, yeah."

Liam's obvious discomfort helped me calm down a bit. It was funny how embarrassed he was. "You can say the word, you know. Cancer. It won't hurt you. Cancer. Cancer. Cancer, cancer, cancer!"

"I know." Liam's shoulders relaxed. He stepped away and picked up my gym bag. "My Aunt Dee had ovarian cancer when I was a little kid. My cousin and I organize the race every year. The swimming part is murder for some people, but it's always a good day." Liam handed me my bag. "So, how are you feeling?"

"Okay. Not a hundred percent yet. But better."

Liam jumped up on the counter and swung his gangly legs over the edge. "You really would be a good addition to the team, you know. We could use some younger women. Can you swim?"

I picked up one of the brochures from where they had fallen to the floor. "I had to pass a swim safety class in college. I can do a decent crawl."

"They call it freestyle now," Liam said. "The leader of the team is the swim coach here. I'm sure she'd give you a hand."

I stood up and picked up my bag. "Do you really think I could compete in a triathlon?"

"If you can run or swim half as well as you attack that bike in there, I'm sure you'd do fine."

"Excuse me? Was that a compliment?"

Liam blushed again and straightened his shirt. "You'll need to get a road bike. The Schlein TdF99 is great, but it's not anything like training on real roads." Liam fished through the top drawer of the desk and handed me a business card. "Evan at Cosmic Cycles has the best selection. They even have special seats to protect your—"

"Lady parts?" It was kind of fun to watch Liam squirm.

I put the flyer and card in my bag and started toward the locker room. "I'm not saying I'll sign up, Liam. But I promise I'll think about it."

I did think about it. I thought about raising money to dispel the stigma of cancer while I changed into my workout clothes. I thought about helping other women with gynecological cancers while I peddled the stationary bike at a leisurely pace. I thought about actively doing something to help other women. It felt good.

Before I could talk myself out if it, I called Vanessa as I drove to Lucky Lee's. "Lara!" Vanessa shouted through the phone. Voices and music blared in the background. I suspected she was in a bar.

"I'm thinking of signing up to do a charity run with some people at my gym!" I shouted back. "You want to do it with me?"

"You're asking me to run in a race?"

"Well, yeah."

Vanessa removed the phone from her ear and laughed. I heard her telling someone that her friend wants her to run a marathon. When she brought the phone back to her mouth, she said, "On one condition. We get matching running outfits."

✷✷✷

The next evening, Vanessa and I battled the Christmas crowds in the sporting goods store. Vanessa tried on some form fitting running tights with Day-Glo orange stripes down the sides and a matching bright orange lycra top. She looked like an oriole with hair. I suggested we also get plain black warm-up jackets to wear over the lycra and tone down the orange. When we got to the swimsuit department, Vanessa held up a skimpy pink and yellow suit with Hawaiian flowers all over it. "This one's cute," she cooed.

"No way." I put the flimsy suit back on the rack. "I'm nervous enough about putting on a bathing suit without you making me look like a lei exploded in my face."

Vanessa flipped through the rack of suits. "But these are all so boring," Vanessa pouted.

"We'll be doing laps, not laying on a beach. I think we're supposed to think about durability and compression, not aesthetics."

Vanessa held up a yellow suit with a purple stripe. "I want to look good in my suit."

"You do know how to swim, don't you?"

Vanessa considered a tie-dyed racing bikini then put it back. "Do you think we'll have to get our hair wet?"

"Oh my God," I groaned. "This is going to be a disaster. What are we doing?"

Vanessa picked up another suit, black with hot pink trim. "Don't worry, Lara. I was just pulling your leg. I won't embarrass you. I swam in high school. I'm not very fast but I can get down the pool. Did your high school have a swim team?"

"We didn't have a town pool. We had a lake." I turned around to face another rack and recalled watching the popular kids walk past the library with their beach towels and coolers on their way to Lake Winnewipple. They spent hours sunning themselves on the floating platforms moored several hundred yards out in the water. I used to hope their toes would be bitten off by snapping turtles.

"What do you think," Vanessa asked, "should I go for shiny black?"

I shook the memory of Hawthorne out of my head like rank water. "Yes, but in a larger size. Your boobs would pop right out of that suit."

✷✷✷

Vanessa and I changed into our matching outfits in the Y locker room before joining the growing crowd of spandex clad women milling in the lobby. "Why did I ever agree to do this with you, Lara? I can't run," Vanessa whined. "I'm going to make a fool of myself."

"No you won't," I replied. "Look at these women. They're all old and flabby. Someone's bound to be slower than you."

"Gee, Lara. Way to make a girl feel good about herself." Vanessa walked up to a lumpy grandma-type and introduced herself. Within five minutes, she knew everyone's name and something about each of them. I stuck to her side like a barnacle and smiled insincerely until Liam clapped his hands to get everyone's attention. Beside him stood a trim woman with close cropped grey hair and keen blue eyes.

"Okay ladies, let's get started. I'm Elkie Templeton. Welcome to our team. We are jointly sponsored by the Y and the Cancer Center at Ellery Hospital. This is my sixth year leading the team and my twelfth year of survivorship." The women reflexively clapped for her still being alive. "For those of you who are new to the team, which many of you are, we start our practices on time and end on time. Tonight, we will be going for a short conditioning run and then we will give out the training schedule leading up to the race in late March. We won't be collecting the registration forms until after the first of the year, so you still have time to back out." Several women giggled nervously. "After we collect the registrations, we expect you to train together over the next fourteen weeks to compete in the race. We'll start in the pool next week and add the bikes in January." The women nodded dumbly as they herded themselves out to the parking lot.

"All right," Elkie said once everyone was outside. "We'll

do an easy run down to the phone company parking lot and back. If you have any questions, flag me down. Bridget, could you lead us out?" A woman in teal running tights took off. The others followed. "Now take it easy tonight. We are still getting our legs under us."

I took off to catch up with the leader. Vanessa lagged behind and was gasping for air within five hundred yards. She stopped and hung her head between her knees. I doubled back and ran in circles around her. "Come on, Vanessa. They're going around the bend. We've got to catch up."

Elkie and another woman ran up beside us and stopped. She patted Vanessa on the back and handed her a water bottle from the pouch at the back of her running top. "Catch your breath for a minute," she said. "There's no need to sprint. When you're ready, Celeste here will keep you company. You two go as far as you feel comfortable, then walk back."

Elkie stood up and glared at me. *Crap. Now the coach is pissed that I stopped. It's not my fault Vanessa is slow.* "And you. What's your name?"

"Lara." I jogged in place beside Vanessa.

Elkie appraised me as if I were a filly in a paddock. "You'll run with me tonight." She took off down the pavement like a startled deer. Once I recognized the challenge, I left Vanessa behind. When I caught up, Elkie said, "Oh, there you are? What took you so long?" I couldn't respond. My lungs burned. Elkie was setting an ambitious pace. "I applaud you for joining the team to support your friend's recovery but we don't normally suggest you run the patient ragged the first night out."

"She's not sick." I panted.

"Really? I could have sworn that was a wig. Are you doing this as a memorial?"

"No, I finished radiation a few weeks ago."

Elkie swerved to watch me run beside her for a moment. "*You* are the survivor?"

I nodded, momentarily unable to speak. I didn't accept the label of cancer survivor. It felt like a hand-me-down coat.

Elkie upped the pace. Her legs were a tangle of sinew as she pulled ahead of me. My shins burned and my thighs screamed for me to stop, but I wasn't about to be bested by a woman in her sixties. We rounded the electric company lot, flying past the women who were walking. When we were in sight of the Y again, Elkie kicked it up yet another notch. My lungs burned but I managed to keep up. Elkie was grinning wildly and yelling, "Come on! Come on!" the last few yards. She touched the door two paces ahead of me. We both collapsed on the grassy area in front of the door, gasping for breath. When she recovered, Elkie said, "I think you'll be a fine addition to the team."

Vanessa and I went back the next night and every other night that week. Vanessa continued to run with Celeste, a fifty-seven year old uterine cancer survivor, and I tried to keep up with Elkie. Training on pavement was different than running on a treadmill. The surfaces were uneven and there were obstacles like cars and gutters to avoid. Elkie lectured me on learning to set a pace and envisioning a whole race, as opposed to just running headlong until I couldn't go any further.

The camaraderie was amazing. I was surprised when one of the women asked the group's opinion about whether or not she should continue in her unsatisfying, but stable, teaching position or open the jewelry boutique she dreamed of. She repeatedly said her diagnosis and treatment for uterine cancer was motivating her to stop thinking about what she might do someday in the future and do what made her happy today. I admired how she was able to embrace the immediacy of life. I had read the survival statistics for uterine cancer; they were bleak.

By the end of the week, I had settled into a new routine. I enjoyed training with the team then reviewing the day with Vanessa over dinner at Lucky Lee's far more than I had ever enjoyed going to the gym by myself. The radiation fatigue kept me from performing at full-strength, yet it felt good to work my muscles again. I fell into bed physically tired and mentally relaxed. Vanessa, on the other hand, was still questioning the wisdom of joining the team. She had a nice figure, curvy in all the appropriate places, but she was not in very good shape. That first week of short training runs left her sore and frustrated.

When the team started training for the swimming portion of the race, Vanessa hit her stride. She looked like an alien with her massive hair tucked into a pink silicone cap, but she swam with the fluid grace of a dolphin. I appreciated her good cheer that first morning in the pool when I didn't want people looking at me in a swimsuit. "Get over yourself, Lara. It's 5:00 a.m. No one cares what you look like." She literally pushed me out the locker room door onto the pool deck. Even though I was half-naked, no one looked at my body. Everyone was focused on his or her own swimming. By the third morning, I was able to walk by the male lifeguard without feeling self-conscious.

Running was relatively easy where training in the pool was a challenge. Luckily, Elkie was a patient taskmaster. I mastered the freestyle and could swim four lengths of the pool by the end of the first week. Some of the other techniques came more slowly and required more help.

Celeste took time away from her own workout to help me learn how to do a flip turn and Maureen, a forty-five year old mother of four and a ten-year breast cancer survivor, talked me through my unreasonable fear of diving off the blocks.

At the end of the third week, the roster was settled. Elkie gathered the group together to officially name that year's team. The tradition was to use the name of the woman with the most recent diagnosis in the team name. They had been Estrella's Stars and Elkie's Bounders in past years. "This year," Elkie said with a crooked smile, "we will be Lara's Ladies." I protested but was outvoted. I had the most recent diagnosis and, as Elkie put it, I was going to "kick some University Hospital ass."

19
Heart Aflutter

When I worked on the eighth floor, I looked forward to the week between Christmas and the New Year. The office was quiet; I could get things done without anyone bothering me. Now that I knew and liked the people on the sixth floor, I looked forward to the Accounting and IT people coming back after the holiday break. I missed hearing Melissa in Accounting singing to herself as she stood at the photocopier and the way Randy in IT invariably spilled his coffee walking around the corner. I almost missed listening to Pathetic Dog Owner and Garlic Breath talking about sports on the other side of the cubicle wall. Almost.

On December 27, I took a break from updating the bauxite report to stretch my sore shoulders. I had overdone it in the pool that morning. Vanessa hadn't been there to make me take breaks. She was in Texas visiting her sister. It had been easier to swim in a lane by myself but not nearly as fun as clamoring for space with the other women. I'd rushed through the set, showered, and came to work. As I rubbed my sore shoulders, I regretted not warming down.

I propped my foot on the windowsill like a ballerina at the barre and stretched my aching hamstrings. I wasn't worried about someone seeing me with my feet in the air. The sixth floor was deserted. The only other person working that day was Pradeep Thacker. His wife had taken their kids to visit her parents in Louisiana over Christmas break. He stayed home with the dog.

The old man in the next street was taking advantage of the warm afternoon to disassemble the Christmas light display in his front yard. I wished he would leave it up a few more days. This had been the first Christmas since my grandparents died that I enjoyed the holiday. For the past few years, I had gone to Lucky Lee's for their special buffet and movie ticket deal. Mrs. Lee said it was a treat for their Jewish patrons. I doubted the people hunched over their plates of sweet and sour pork and shrimp fried rice had anything in common other than being alone. This year, I ate Christmas dinner at Jane's house. Tom had roasted a huge turkey. Jane said she hated to have him eat the whole thing by himself and had invited me to join them. I bought a Buche de Noel from the French bakery near the Y for dessert.

I picked a banana out of the fruit bowl I now kept on my file cabinet. Elkie had lectured me about eating a more varied diet. Product of Costa Rica was printed across a stylized sun on the peel. It made me think of the picture hanging in Jane's front hall. Jane had snapped a photo of a young Tom screaming his head off while hurtling through the rain forest canopy. When I asked Jane if Tom was excited or frightened when she took the photo, she replied, "He loved that trip."

"I was scared out of my mind," Tom had called from the

kitchen. "It was great!"

That summed up my life over the last few weeks. It felt like I was hurtling through the treetops on a thin metal wire. It was invigorating, but I was afraid I'd smash into a tree at any second. I tossed the banana peel into the trashcan and pulled my cell phone out of my new black leather tote. I dialed Jane's number.

She picked up quickly; a good sign that Jane was awake and willing to talk to the outside world. "Lara, sweetie! How's my favorite emerging markets analyst?"

"You're in a good mood." I pushed a strand of hair out of my eyes. It seemed to always be in the way lately.

"I am. I just fired the visiting nurse."

"Nurse?" *When did Tom hire a nurse? What does that mean?*

"Tom and Dr. P think I need a babysitter while Tom is at work."

"Well, do you?"

"Maybe. I don't really care. I don't want some little ninny telling me what to do in my own house."

Poor Tom. He must feel it's necessary to have a nurse there all the time. Jane's not going to make this easy for him.

"Hey, why don't you come over and keep me company tonight? Tom has a client dinner with that idiot, Candace. I made a nice turkey rice soup with the leftovers from Christmas dinner."

"Has Candace been selling people cement counter tops again?" I straightened the icons on my computer desktop into rows.

"No," Jane said with a sigh. I couldn't tell through the phone if it was from exasperation or difficulty breathing. "She is encouraging him to pursue this green housing project."

Heaven forbid someone encourage Tom. Tom had told me about the planned community he was looking to invest in while we did the dishes after our Christmas dinner. The houses would all be LEED certified. He was taking his grandfather's company by the horns and pulling it kicking and screaming into the 21st century. If Tom was getting encouragement from Candace, more power to her. "How awful," I replied sarcastically.

"Don't be snippy with me, young lady," Jane said. I smiled to myself. I loved it when Jane got riled up and called me young lady. It meant she was feeling relatively well. "Are you coming over for soup, or not?"

"I'll be there around 6:00. There's a bike shop not far from you I want to check out. I'll come over after I talk to them."

✱✱✱

Cosmic Cycles was a prefab metal building filled with a panoply of bicycles. There were rows of bikes spread across the concrete floor, bikes hanging from the ceiling, and child-sized bikes along the walls. Even though I'd ridden a few different types of stationary bikes at the gym, I didn't know anything about the wider world of cycling. My cursory on-line research did not prepare me for the sheer number of choices in front of me. A slender young man looked up from his workbench at the back of the store. "Do you need some help?"

"No," I replied reflexively and wandered around the store touching each machine. *This one is aluminum. Do I need something made out of aluminum? Do I need something called an aero-bar?* I could feel the young man watching me wind my way through the maze of bikes. "I guess I do need some help," I finally said. "I need a racing bike."

He turned off some kind of welding tool and sauntered

my way. "What kind of bike do you have now?"

"I don't," I admitted. "I've taken spinning classes for years but I don't have an actual bicycle."

"Well, this is a good all around road bike." He put his hand on the silver bike I stood next to. "Will you be doing any off-road biking?"

"I don't know. I'm buying it to do a charity race." I backed away. I was in over my head in this conversation and didn't like being at such a disadvantage, especially with a man. "Maybe I should wait and ask the coach which bike I should get."

He stepped closer, closing the gap. "Which race are you doing? Maybe I can tell you what kind of terrain you'll be on."

Good, good. Use the available data to come up with a prediction. Get information. "It's the Rose Buckman Race for Women's Health." My mouth went dry. "I'm on the team sponsored by the Y."

"Good for you! That's a great race to start out with. Elkie's great. She's still leading the team, right?" I stepped back again nearly knocking over a row of bright yellow bicycles. I didn't like the way he was looking at me, like I was a cupcake.

"I have cancer!" I blurted out. I thought that would make him back away. He stepped closer. He brushed against my hip as he pulled one of the bikes over to show me its special features, as if saying I had cancer was as normal as saying it was Wednesday. "Pick it up. Feel how light it is?" He grabbed my elbow to help me mount. I pulled away, tipping another bike. The salesman caught it before it tipped over the whole row like a line of dominos.

My cheeks burned as I frantically looked around for something to focus on. "I don't think I want to test drive any bikes today. The guy at the Y said I need a special seat for, um, women with, um,—"

"Liam?"

"Yeah. Why?"

"I knew it! You're the girl that uses the Schlein machine. Liam told me about you."

"He talked to you about me?"

"Yeah, he said to keep an eye out for a cute girl…"

Cute?

"… with a slammin' body. He says you're a beast on that machine."

I turned away to hide my burning cheeks. *I can't believe Liam talked about me. That little twerp.* "So this is the bike I should get?"

"It's a good all around racing bike and it's not so expensive you'd feel you have to do a race every week."

"What about a special seat?"

"I can fit it with a different saddle. Can you come back in a few days?"

I put down a deposit on the yellow bike and got out of there as quickly as possible. *What was that? He knows I have cancer, a gynecological cancer no less, and he's flirting with me? That isn't right. He was supposed to shun me. Wasn't he?*

∗∗∗

The sun was low in the sky as I drove between the tall stone pillars marking Jane's driveway and up the gravel drive. The remains of Tom's tree house in the pin oak beside the driveway cast long shadows over the sprawling ranch. A plump wreath of holly and fir branches graced the heavily carved front doors. I knocked and let myself in to save Jane from having to come to the door.

Jane thrust a cocktail in my hand seconds after I hung my

coat next to hers in the hall closet. "Try it. It's a Negroni."

"It's bright red." I took a sip and put the glass down on the foyer table. The drink was pungently bitter.

"I've been experimenting." Jane picked up my glass and carried it to the kitchen. "They called the poison they pumped into my veins a chemo cocktail. I've been trying to find a real cocktail that same color for months."

"Should you be drinking these days?"

"Absoposilutely," Jane replied. She drained her glass before lifting the lid from a cast iron pot on the stove. The room filled with the scent of simmering turkey stock. "I hope you don't mind if we eat in the kitchen."

My response stuck in my throat. Jane had no idea how flattered I was that she considered me eligible to sit at the high counter and eat off their plain white kitchen dishes. I climbed onto one of the heavy oak stools. Jane had laid out brightly striped placemats and glasses of sweet tea. I took a sip of tea to clear my throat.

"So Tom hired a visiting nurse?"

Jane scooped some turkey broth into a soup bowl and added a scoop of brown rice. "That woman was driving me up the wall. She actually stood outside the door when I was in the bathroom and asked if I needed any help. I can still wipe my own ass, thank you very much."

"But how are doing, really?"

"Shitty," Jane admitted. "I've got that woman stalking me in my own home. I hurt all over. I feel like there's a hole in my chest. I am having trouble swallowing, and if I as much as walk to the bathroom, I need to take a nap." She scratched at her scalp. "I'm so tired and you'd think I would be able to sleep. But no. I just lie there and stare at the ceiling."

Jane handed the steaming bowl of turkey rice soup and

heel of French bread across the counter to me. She then joined me with a small bowl of clear broth for herself. I remembered how the burning was at its worst just after the treatments ended and worried. "How are the radiation treatments going?"

"Fine, I guess. I only have two more treatments, thank God."

"Do you have any burns?"

"Not on my skin."

"How about on the inside? Can they help you with the swallowing thing?"

"That nice young guy who lines me up in the machine told me to keep eating and drinking. I just don't have any appetite."

A pang of regret twisted in my stomach. "They know what they are talking about. Please try to drink more."

"He told me to drink green tea with honey to soothe my throat. It seems to be helping a bit." Jane took a sip of my cocktail. "Not as much as these though."

I dipped some bread in my soup and made a mental note to talk to Mrs. Lee about what kind of green tea would be best. I would also call Tom. I wondered if he knew Jane was drinking so much.

"But I don't want to talk about that. I am having a nice dinner with my friend Lara—who looks adorable today." Jane touched the collar of my blouse. "I like this blouse."

"Thank you. It's new."

"I could never pull off peach."

"But you always look so elegant."

A wry smile spread across Jane's face as she adjusted the grey scarf tied artfully around her wispy locks. "Elegant can be another word for boring. I was always afraid to look too feminine. You know, construction, the whole 'a woman in a man's world' thing." Jane took another sip from my cocktail. "Hey, why don't we go shopping on Saturday? I bet we could pick you up some great outfits on after Christmas clearance."

"Do you feel up to walking around that much?"

"Dr. P has me on Prednisone right now, so I feel great—at least for the short term."

Short term? What does that mean?

"Why don't I pick you up around ten?"

"Are you sure? I don't want to tire you out."

Jane pushed a strand of hair behind my ear. "You should pull your hair back from your face like that more often." I reached up to pull the clip out of the loose bun I'd hastily gathered while concentrating on a report earlier. "No, leave it. You look pretty. You've got that just-got-out-of-bed tousled look."

I remembered the way the Cosmic Cycles guy had looked at me. "Oh my God, Jane. It was so embarrassing. This guy in the bike shop was showing me this yellow bike, and he wanted me to try it out. Well, I couldn't do it because the seat would hit me, well, there, and I'm still sore."

"Oh come on, he couldn't have known you were sensitive."

"But he did! I had just told him that I had cancer. And get this, the guy at the Y had told him I was cute. Can you believe that? Cute!"

"Oh, I don't know," Jane said, taking a sip of broth. "Maybe he doesn't care that you have cancer. You're a pretty girl who likes to ride a bike. Maybe that's enough."

I blushed. I liked that Jane thought I was pretty. "I guess. It still felt creepy."

"So, you're swearing off men in general because you've had cancer?"

"That's the plan."

"Good luck with that." Jane put her spoon down and took another sip of my cocktail.

"Are you making fun of me?"

Jane waved off the question. "So you and your friend are both on the team?"

"Yes, there are eleven of us training for the race in March."

"It's not one of those pink ribbon brigade events, is it?"

"Teal, I think. It's to raise money for gynecological cancer research."

"Good, because I am sick and tired of those breast cancer people. Breast cancer is like the pretty cheerleader of the cancer world, all pink and popular. Lung Cancer is the greaser off in the shadows smoking a butt with his buddy, Mouth Cancer. People are very sympathetic about my having cancer until they find out it's lung cancer. They actually have the nerve to ask if I smoked." Jane stared into space for a few moments. I ate my soup.

Jane carefully swallowed several shallow spoonfuls of broth. Her hand shook as she lifted the spoon to her mouth, making the charms on the silver bracelet clack against each other. I remembered how awful it had been to eat a bowl of cereal or a piece of fruit while still going through radiation. It should not be terrifying to eat soup. I put my spoon down.

"Nice bracelet."

"Thank you," Jane smiled. "I hadn't worn it in ages. It doesn't go very well with a business suit." She pinched a silver stepped pyramid between her forefinger and thumb. "I picked them up in Cancun when we were on a cruise. I think that was the year Tom went parasailing and we toured Chichén Itzá. Have you ever been there?"

"The only traveling I've ever done was the bus trip from

New Hampshire to here."

"Oh Lara, you don't know what you are missing. I loved to travel. I love to see how other people live, try the different cuisines." Jane's color heightened and she finished her entire bowl of broth while she showed me each of the charms on the crowded bracelet. She had a tiny giraffe from the safari she and Tom took to celebrate him finishing his MBA. A blue enamel webbed foot prompted her to tell me about their trip to the Galapagos Islands. The last charm on the bracelet was an intricate silver Eiffel Tower.

Jane blinked back tears as she rolled the tiny building between her fingers. "This was the first charm I bought. My father took me to Paris the summer between high school and college. It was the only time we ever travelled without Mother." A sad smile graced Jane's lean face. "We ate so much rich food on that trip, my father had to buy a new pair of trousers. You've got to go, Lara. Don't wait."

20

Small Packages

*C*ould I wear the peach blouse with a pair of jeans to go shopping? It's clean, but I don't want her to think I only have one nice shirt. What does one wear for a day of shopping? Sweats and a T-shirt would be the most practical. It's supposed to be cold out today. Maybe a sweater? I pushed my few decent outfits around the closet when the doorbell rang. At first, I thought the hollow ding was the text message tone on the new smartphone Frank Mariano gave me. He said he wanted to be able to reach me whenever he needed to talk to me. I wasn't sure I wanted to be available day and night.

The bell rang several more times, in quick succession, before I connected the sound to the front door.

Geez Jane, break the doorbell why don't you?

I shook the towel off my wet hair, pulled a bathrobe on, and ran down the stairs to ask Jane to wait in the car for a few minutes. I didn't want Jane to see my empty apartment. A cobweb stuck to my thigh as I wrenched open the stiff dead bolt. When I swung the door open, instead of Jane impatiently tapping her toe in the frigid air, the monster from my nightmares glared at me through the screen door.

"About time!" Dale bellowed. I screamed, slammed the heavy steel door, and threw the bolt home. "Open the door, girl."

Suddenly, I was sixteen again, hiding in my closet. "Go away!" I yelled.

Dale rattled the lock on the screen door handle. It provided flimsy protection, but I appreciated each thread on the screws holding it in place.

"Larissa, honey." That name, oozing from between his lips, made me cringe. "We need to talk."

I crouched behind the door and screamed, "Leave me alone!"

He kicked the doorframe and pounded on the screen. "Open the door, Larissa."

"Go away!"

I had been preparing for this day for eleven years. I had a plan. Everything I needed for a quick getaway was packed in Ruby's trunk. I should have run to the car, crashed through the garage door, and disappeared in a cloud of fiberglass and blue smoke. Preparations forgotten, I cowered in the corner like an animal.

Dale's heavy boots thumped in time with the blood pounding in my ears as he paced past the door. I squeezed my knees to my chest and tried to think. *I need to go. Is there still a hole in the fence out back? It's a Saturday. Is the little girl there? I can't risk Dale seeing that little girl.*

I need to run. It's taken him this long to find me; I could hide again. I'll do a better job this time. Go overseas. Change my name more. I stood up and stepped away from the door.

But, what about Jane? And Vanessa? I don't want to leave them behind.

The pacing stopped. Dale's red nose pressed up against the picture window. He shielded his eyes with one spotted hand to peer into the dark condo. I realized that, from where I was standing, I could see him but he couldn't see me. Over the last eleven years, Dale had become the beast in my nightmares. Time had been hard on the very real man peering in the window. He was hunched and worn. His hair was reduced to wisps hanging over his ears and collar. His once hawk-like eyes were now milky with cataracts. A tattered flannel shirt hung off his once broad shoulders. He was no more than a used up old man holding a wrinkled paper grocery bag.

"What do you want?" I yelled through the door.

Dale craned his neck in my direction. The old predatory smirk spread across his face. I could feel his eyes on me even if he couldn't actually see me standing behind the door in a flimsy flannel robe. I would have preferred a set of armor.

"You know why I'm here. You owe me," he spat. "You and me've got a score to settle." He banged on the door again. "Come on girl, I drove a long way to see you."

"How did you find me? Did the hospital tell you where I was?"

"That bunch of vultures? They don't tell me nothing. They just want to get every damn penny out of me."

I quietly slid over to the window frame.

"Open the door, girl," he cooed. "We need to talk about your mama." He leaned into the glass and licked his lips like a fox eying a hen house. I slapped the glass in front of his face.

"What the hell!" he yelped.

"What do you want?" I wished my hand had gone right

through the glass and cut his face to ribbons. Dale recovered his balance and returned to the window to leer in at me. I was very aware of my bare legs sticking out below the robe.

"I need to talk to you about your mama," he keened. "She's dead, Larissa."

I reeled back from the window. "What? When?" The words caught in my throat. *Mama can't be dead. She's like a cockroach. She could survive nuclear winter.*

"She passed away three weeks ago." Dale wiped at his eye as if he were actually weeping.

Mama is dead?

I stood in front of the glass. "She died?"

"I scattered her ashes up on your grandparent's property yesterday."

"Why are you really here?" I knew not to believe anything Dale said. There had to be money involved. Dale would never drive all the way from New Hampshire to North Carolina just to scatter Mama's ashes. He'd ship them UPS or dump them in the woods beyond the back pasture. "What do you want?"

"Larissa. Honey." Dale's voice was like sulfured molasses. Broken blood vessels covered his nose from years of hard drinking and he was missing some of his teeth. "Won't you let your old step-daddy in for a cup of coffee? Talk about old times?" I could think of nothing I would like less than to talk about "old times" with Dale. I tightened the belt around my waist and tried to breathe under the suffocating weight of memory.

"Why. Are. You. Here?"

Dale glared at me for a moment then looked down at the paper bag in his hand. A greasy smile spread across his stubble-strewn face. "I've got a present for you. Now why don't you open up and I'll tell you all about your mother's sad final days? You and me are the only family she had left. Even if you did run off."

"Fuck you!"

Dale dropped the amiable mask and snarled, "Shut your mouth and let me in!"

"I am never letting you in. This is my place. Mine!"

"Then come out here." He slapped the paper grocery sack in his hand. "All you've got to do is sign a few papers and I'll be on my way. I'll never bother you again. Promise."

I was considering whether or not my reflexes were fast enough to unlock the screen and safely grab the bag out of his hand, when I heard a voice growl. "Don't do it, Lara! You stay right there."

The color drained from Dale's face as he looked cautiously over his shoulder. Jane stood in the driveway beside her shiny little sports car. It may as well have been a coach and four. Dale stepped away from the door and retreated to the edge of the small front porch. He was trembling. "Just having a friendly conversation with my stepdaughter." He turned back to the window and hissed, "Why did you call the lawyers?" I had no idea what he was talking about but liked that he looked scared.

"Lara?" Jane called. "Is this man bothering you?" She paced slowly up the overgrown walkway. If I didn't know she walked so slowly because she was ill, I would have found Jane in her full length black coat and dark glasses intimidating, too.

"Yes! Yes, he is."

Jane calmly pulled her cell phone from her pocket. "I am calling the police. I suggest you leave. Now."

Dale scowled at me through the window. "You need to

sign these papers, girl."

Jane started dialing numbers. "Then leave the papers and go." She turned away and spoke quietly into the phone. When she turned back, she made a show of being surprised that Dale was still there. "It should only take the police a few minutes to get here, so be quick about it." Jane stepped a few paces away as if he were already gone. She kicked at the weeds in the neglected flowerbeds. The only flowers growing there were some overgrown chrysanthemums planted by the builder.

Dale seemed to vacillate between leaving and staying to get what he came for. He kept one eye on Jane and dropped the wrinkled paper bag on the stoop. "You sign these papers and mail them in, or I'll come back to make you sign them. You hear me, girl?" He winked at me through the window. "You know, you can change your name and act as high fallutin' as you like, but I know who you are. You're still nothing more than a little tramp from the trailer park."

My stomach dropped as Jane spun around. I was sure she would never speak to me again after she heard what Dale had just said. I certainly didn't expect Jane to poke Dale between the shoulder blades and seethe, "I think you have said just about all you are going to say today. If you have any more information for Ms. Blaine, I suggest you contact her by post."

Jane stared at Dale until he shuffled back to his truck and drove away like the coward he was. She walked up the steps and picked up the bag before I opened the door. "You all right?" she asked. I didn't know if I was. I felt numb. All I could think was that I needed to call the landlord to get the cracks in the front walkway fixed.

My hands shook as I bolted the door behind us. "What

am I going to tell the police when they get here?"

"I didn't actually call them, Lara. I called Tom and told him to stand by the phone if I needed him to come over. I know guys like that. They're all bark and no bite."

"Thank you," I whispered. "That was my mother's husband." I was trying to act calm but my heart felt like a little bird flying against the bars of its cage. "She's dead. My mother is dead," I said again, letting the words sink in.

It felt good.

Jane turned back toward the door. "I'm sorry. Do you need to be alone? I can go."

"Could you stick around for a bit?" I felt lightheaded. Everything seemed to be out of focus, as if I were looking through a dirty camera lens. Jane put the grocery bag down inside the doorway and enveloped me in her spindly arms. That hug was wonderful. I had not been properly hugged in so long it was overwhelming.

"I just can't believe my mother is dead."

Perhaps it was the hug, or the adrenaline associated with seeing Dale, or the news that Mama was dead, or Jane standing up to Dale, or a combination of them all; I started to weep into Jane's chest. Sob after sob after sob shook my body. Eventually, the sobbing quieted down and Jane said, "Why don't we get out of the doorway and have a cup of tea? I need to sit down."

"I have Earl Grey. I bought some the other day," I said proudly.

Jane glanced around the dusty empty rooms with raised eyebrows on our way to the kitchen but was too polite to ask where all the furniture had gone. She situated me on the couch and pulled the old blanket around my shoulders.

Reality seemed elastic. I could see Jane banging around

in my little kitchen looking for something to boil water in and some cups, yet I was also still seeing Dale's face leering through the window.

How did he find me? He couldn't have driven all that way just to tell me Mama was dead?

Mama is dead?

For three weeks?

Jane returned and pressed a steaming cup in my hand. She looked around for a place to sit and settled on sitting on the arm of the couch.

"I didn't realize you recently moved."

"I didn't."

"Oh?" Jane balanced her teacup on the makeshift coffee table.

"I can't believe my mother died weeks ago and I didn't know it."

"Was it sudden? Had she been ill?"

"I don't know. I haven't talked to her for eleven years." I sipped some of the tea. "Well, for all intents and purposes, fifteen years. Since she married Dale."

"A charming man, I could see."

"He thought you were my lawyer."

Jane choked on her tea. It had been remarkably satisfying to see Dale so intimidated by Jane, especially since she was so frail these days. He could have taken her down in one fell swoop if he had tried. Then again, he looked pretty weak, too.

"Speaking of lawyers, what are the papers he wanted you to sign?"

"I don't know. You showed up before I got a chance to find out."

Jane got up and retrieved the bag from the front room. She

gently put it down in front of me. "Let's take a look. Maybe it will explain what made him turn up at your door today." Jane pulled out a battered FedEx envelope addressed to me, a manila folder of crumpled documents, and a painted cigar box.

"Mama's box," I murmured. The box sat on the top shelf of her closet hidden under a grey wool blanket in every cockroach-infested apartment and ramshackle trailer we ever lived in. She had been willing to sell our few possessions to put cheap clothes on her back and liquor in her belly, but she hoarded that box like it was filled with gold. When I was little, I imagined it contained a fairy that could whisk me away to a magical world if I would only free her from her confinement. I imagined us living happily ever after in a fairy world where no one was sad or hungry. After we moved to the farm, the box disappeared.

I had been forbidden to touch this box for so long I was afraid to touch it now. I ran a finger over the top of the painted surface. There were pale green leaves painted around the edges and the name "Elise" painted in lavender across the curved lid. Elise was my grandmother's name. From the crude nature of the lettering, she must have painted it as a child.

Jane picked up the folder and envelope and started to flip through the papers inside them. "Well? Are you going to open it?" she asked. I lifted the hinged top. Inside was a piece of paper ripped from a spiral notebook and crudely folded in quarters. Underneath the paper was a lavender envelope that I recognized as being from my grandmother's stationary. Under the envelope was a small white leather box. I unfolded the notebook paper, recognized Mama's childlike handwriting and immediately tossed it back on the coffee table.

I delicately pulled the lavender envelope out and held it to my nose. It smelled like my grandparent's house: cigarette smoke and Murphy's Oil Soap. Tears welled up in my eyes. I placed it on the table and lifted the small white leather box out. Inside was a simple gold band with leaves etched around it. I recognized it as my grandmother's wedding ring. I remembered how the smooth band felt against my young fingers when I held Grammy's hand as we walked into town or to church. I pushed the small ring on my right ring finger. It fit.

At the bottom of the box was an ornate silver cross. My grandmother had worn it at all times on a long silver chain. I'd asked Grammy about the cross one morning. Even as a little girl, I knew that it was out of place in my grandmother's restrained wardrobe. She had travelled to Mexico as a young woman on a mission trip. Grammy and her friends had met people who were living in the simplest of houses and had only tortillas and beans to eat yet had a faith that sustained them. She had bought the ornate silver cross in a village market and had worn it as a reminder of her time in Mexico. I pulled the chain over my head. The cold metal against my skin was like my grandmother's cool kisses on a fevered brow.

I turned to Jane sitting in front of piles of paper. "What are those?"

Jane gestured to the first pile. "This seems to be a copy of the deed to some property in the town of Alders, North Carolina; these are old stock certificates for a bunch of different companies, mostly asbestos mines; and this is a life insurance policy in the name of Larissa Scott."

"That's me. I changed my name when I was in college."

"It looks like Elise Anne and Robert Blaine Elliot left all their property to you upon Robert's death. Was Robert your father?"

"My grandfather." The words caught in my throat. "I don't know who my father is. It was always just Mama and me. Then it was Dale and Mama and me. But I don't understand. They left their house to me? I was only seven when my grandfather died. Why didn't they leave it to my mother?"

"I think you need to talk to a lawyer about all that. I wonder why your mother never gave you these papers. They belong to you."

"I'm surprised she didn't try to sell the stocks. She sold everything else I ever had."

Jane sipped her tea. "What's in the purple envelope?" I turned the envelope over and carefully pulled it open. The rough-cut pages were covered with my grandfather's compact handwriting—

Little Lara (I refuse to call you Larissa),

I'm getting ready to join my Elise in the hereafter. I fear your mother will continue to refuse to bring you to see me. I have asked her time and time again, but she seems to resent how much we love you. I want you to know that the six years you lived with Elise and me were some of the happiest years we had together. Even though the leukemia was making her feel poorly, you brought sunshine into her last days. After your mother took you away, Elise truly began to wither. But I knew I couldn't care for you alone with her in failing health. Perhaps I should have tried harder to find a way. Now I, too, am failing. The doctors say it's my lungs, but I think it's as much my heart. I miss your grandmother too much. I am looking forward to seeing her waiting for me at the pearly gates.

I have put the property here in trust for you until you are old enough to make your own decisions, and I am leaving you my shares in the mine. They may be quite valuable some day. Perhaps you can use the money to go to college. Your grandmother wanted you to go to Amherst because you reminded her of Emily Dickenson with that serious little frown, but you go wherever you please. I know you will use your sharp mind to do something wonderful. I have read and re-read *David Copperfield* and *Anne of Green Gables* in the last year because they remind me of you and the hours we spent reading together. I treasure those memories. You are always in my prayers.

Your loving PawPaw

I read the note several times through with silent tears streaming down my face. My heart was breaking all over again. All these years, I thought my grandparents didn't want me. My mother had said they couldn't wait to get rid of me.

That was a lie.

That changed everything.

I remembered my grandmother as being weak, but I never realized how ill she had been. My mother had kept that from me, too. Looking back from the perspective of an adult, I could see that my grandmother was easily tired and had trouble doing the household chores, but the Grammy in my memories was a woman reveling in her flower garden and cooking delicious meals while listening to my stories of school.

Jane wiped my cheeks with her soft linen handkerchief,

bringing me back to the present. I turned to Jane with a watery smile and said, "My grandparents wanted to keep me, but my grandmother had cancer. They *had* to let my mother take me away. They wanted to keep me."

"You never knew?" Jane got up and returned with a glass of water. "You've had an awful shock. Drink some water and let it sink in a bit." She gestured to the documents strewn across the coffee table. "Do you have a lawyer?"

"No, I've never needed one."

"I'll call Celeste Brigham and set up an appointment for you. She specializes in real estate law, but I bet she, or one of her associates, could help with these stock certificates."

The enormity of what was in front of me began to hit me. I'd had property and a stock portfolio. I had a family that loved me, even if they were dead. I didn't have to be poor and alone all those years. I picked up the note from my mother and balled it up.

"I'm glad she's dead. I wish she'd died when I was born. Then my grandparents would have found a way to keep me and I never would have met Dale." I tossed the ball of paper across the room. "I wish he would die, too. And I want it to be slow and painful."

I started to explain about Dale and Mama but before I could say much of anything, Jane stopped me. "No, no. I don't want to know the whole sordid story. I'm sure it was awful for you. But it's over now. In the past."

I was taken aback. It wasn't that simple.

"Look he can't hurt you anymore. Today is a new day. You can't go back and change it. You have to move forward. Why don't you go upstairs and get dressed?"

I went upstairs and took another shower. Merely seeing Dale made me feel dirty. I needed to scrub his eyes off me.

I felt a little better once I was clean, but also exhausted. The morning had been an emotional roller coaster with the sickening stomach-dropping sensation of Dale knowing where I lived and the heart-in-your-throat thrill of learning Grammy and PawPaw had wanted to keep me. I pulled on some clothes and climbed into my bed intent on closing my eyes for just a moment. I could hear Jane talking on her cell phone.

21

Kindred Spirits

ours later, when I opened my bedroom door, Jane was gone and Vanessa was sitting downstairs sipping a Big Gulp. As soon as I started down the steps, Vanessa clicked off the television and ran up to me.

"Hey there, Sleeping Beauty. You'll really have to give me the 411 on this place sometime. Why don't you have any furniture?"

"What the hell are you doing here? Where's Jane?"

"Hello to you, too." Vanessa took my arm and tried to help me down the stairs as if I were an invalid. "She had to go. Is she your aunt or something? I take it you two were supposed to go shopping, but... something came up?"

"What did she tell you?"

"Not enough." It was obviously killing Vanessa to not know what was going on. "She called me an hour or so ago and said you'd had a shock and she didn't think you should be alone. Apparently I was the only person programmed into your cell phone. I'm flattered, but that is pretty pathetic."

I pushed her off. "I just got that phone yesterday. And the only reason you are programmed into it is because you put the number in there yourself."

"Do you need to lie down? Can I get you something to drink?"

I got a Coke out of the fridge and pressed it to my forehead. "I'm fine."

Vanessa followed me into the kitchen. "So it's not the cancer coming back?" She opened one cabinet and then another. "You're okay?"

"My mother's husband showed up and... and..."

Vanessa stopped snooping around the kitchen and looked at me hard. I wanted her to stop.

"And?"

Where to begin? "I guess my Mama died a few weeks ago and her husband wanted me to sign some papers and..." My voice quavered and my hands began to shake again as Dale's lecherous face appeared in front of my eyes. "And... and I really hate that guy. I can't tell you how much I Really. Hate. Him." It was like expelling toxic gas just to say the words.

Vanessa took the soda from my hand and thoughtfully placed it on the counter. She cautiously stepped closer and put her arms around me. Vanessa hugged me for several awkwardly long minutes before she whispered in my ear, "It's okay, honey. I think I understand. We won't let him hurt you again."

"What? I didn't say anything about—"

"Lara, honey, you don't have to say it. I saw the go bag in your car when I drove it over here that time. I recognized the way you're always looking over your shoulder. I know the sound of fear in your voice whenever you answer the phone."

"You knew?"

"We're like alcoholics, we can spot each other at twenty paces."

"You?"

"My stepbrother." Vanessa rummaged through the lower cabinets. "It sounds like your family should hang out with my family. I'm sorry your mother passed away."

"I'm not."

Vanessa shooed me aside and looked in the fridge. "That Jane lady was right to call me. Do you think he'll come back? Do you want to get a restraining order?"

"I don't think so. Jane scared him off pretty good."

"That's the spirit! Screw him!"

"No thank you."

Vanessa swatted me on the arm. "Do you actually live here? There is no food."

"There's breakfast stuff. And you know I eat at Lucky Lee's every night."

"Still. What do you say we get a pizza?" She stepped into the bathroom and put on some lipstick. "We can stop on the way back and get a bottle of tequila and some limes," she called from the bathroom. "We'll make some margaritas. Swap stories." For once, I was thankful that Vanessa was so nosey.

Hours later, Vanessa passed out on the couch. I curled up in my bed and stared at the ceiling. Thoughts were coming at me too fast to register one before I was confronted by another. *Mama is dead.*

She died of cancer.

I have cancer. My grandparents both died of cancer.

Grammy and PawPaw wanted me. They left me everything they had.

Mama is dead.

*Mama knew PawPaw left me his stocks and never told me.
Mama let Dale rape me. Mama knew about the money and
still let Dale hurt me. Mama lied about not having any money
and needing to stay with Dale.*

Mama is dead.

✷✷✷

The next morning I woke up face down in the center
of my bed. My mouth tasted like I had been chewing on
cotton balls. I rolled over. The morning sun reflected off my
grandmother's silver necklace still around my neck and cast
rainbows on the ceiling. Knowing my grandparents loved me
buoyed me, but I couldn't stay afloat long. The possibility of
Dale coming back weighed me down.

I snuck down the stairs, careful to not wake Vanessa, to
retrieve the pile of papers and Mama's crumpled note from
the floor. I went into the living room and laid them out on
the floor in front of the windows. I needed to understand
what they meant. I smoothed out the piece of notebook
paper. I could hear Mama's cigarette ravaged voice in my
head as I read:

> Larissa,
>
> I hoped I would see you in person but now I don't
> think that's going to happen. I've got the cancer
> just like Mama and Daddy. It's in my stomach and
> the doctors don't think I have too much time left. I
> called you, but you didn't talk to me, so I made Dale
> promise to give you this when the time comes.
>
> I'm sorry, baby. I made a lot of mistakes in life but
> the biggest was letting Dale ever touch you. I was
> real young when I had you and I guess I thought you

needed to learn the ways of the world early so you didn't end up like me. I should of known you were better than that. You were always so smart reading those big books. Dale says you're too smart for your own good, but he don't know the half of it. I was real proud when I found all those empty Mason jars. I don't know how much you got, but I hope it was enough. Remember, I fixed it so he didn't know. That's all I'll say.

All the things in this box are yours. Daddy gave it to me before he died and I was keeping it until you were grown. When you left that day, I never thought you wouldn't never come back.

I hope you have a good life.

Mama

I refolded the note and put it down beside the box. Her words meant nothing. I felt nothing but emptiness.

Then I remembered that Mama was actually dead now. A sense of relief spread through my chest. Maybe the world isn't as cruel a place as I had thought? Mama had taken pleasure in telling me that I had no one else in the world and that my grandparents had thrown me out as so much human garbage. That was not true. They did want me. They had turned their backs on their daughter, or perhaps simply grew tired of her antics, but they wanted me. They loved me.

Mama was such a pathetic liar. I am not all alone in the world. Jane thinks I'm a valuable person or she wouldn't have defended me against Dale. She could have just driven away yesterday, and she didn't. She even left a message while Vanessa and I were out to see how I was doing. She didn't have to do that.

Slow footsteps advanced behind me. They stopped every

few steps, then resumed. My first thought was that Dale was back. *Oh no, he's killed Vanessa and is going to kill me now.* The footsteps stopped then started again.

"I made tea," Vanessa said. "Careful walking to the kitchen. I spilled a couple of times."

Vanessa set a steaming cup on the floor beside me and plopped down. "What do you say? Brunch at O'Reilly's? You look like you could use a mimosa and some French toast."

***

Two hours and three mimosas later, Vanessa pointed a waffle-laden fork at me. "You know what you need? A good man to help you forget all that shit that happened to you back in New Hampshire."

"I don't see that happening, Vanessa. I'm damaged goods." I took a bite of strawberry blintz and savored the creamy fruit laced filling. I wished Jane were with us to enjoy the food. "Anyway, Jane says I need to stand on my own two feet. That I need to claim my power, whatever that means." I filled my fork again. "Then again, she did give me a hard time about the flirty guy in the bike shop."

"Guy? Bike shop? What guy in the bike shop?"

"We start training for the bike portion of the race next week. Remember?"

Vanessa rolled her eyes and took a huge bite of fried chicken.

"Liam gave me the name of a bike shop near Jane's house in Northwoods. So when I told her how this Evan guy was totally coming on to me, she was like, 'Maybe he likes you.'"

Vanessa chewed for a moment. "I don't get it. You expected him to run you out of his shop with a ratchet wrench?"

I laughed at the idea of Evan chasing me through the maze of bicycles with a wrench. "I guess not."

"So what kind of bike did you get?"

"Yellow."

"Do they come in orange?"

"This guy, Evan, said it was the right kind of bike for what we'd be doing. He's even fitting it with a special seat for me."

Vanessa licked her lips. "You mean you haven't picked it up yet? Why don't we go over there and get it?"

"I don't know. It's all the way over in Northwoods."

"How were you going to get it home? In the back of your bug? We have my truck."

"I don't think—"

"I need to buy a bike too, don't I? You could help me pick one out."

I realized there was no way I was going to get out of taking Vanessa to meet Evan. "Fine. We'll go."

Cosmic Cycles was thankfully empty when Vanessa and I arrived. Evan was again working in his workshop at the back. I recognized *Wait, Wait Don't Tell Me* playing on the boom box. "Hey," he called and walked toward us.

"You didn't say he was gorgeous," Vanessa whispered. Evan was tall and lean with a shaved head, not what I would call gorgeous. Striking maybe.

"Is my bike ready yet?"

"Sure is. And who is this pretty lady?"

Oh my god, what a horn dog. "Vanessa needs a bike. She's doing the Women's Cancer Race, too."

"Can I get an orange bike?" Vanessa said, batting her heavy lashes.

"You can if you want to," Evan said with a broad smile. I couldn't take it. I walked over to a rack of padded bike shorts and loudly clacked the hangers around the rack to drown out the sound of Vanessa making a fool of herself. Twenty minutes later, we left with two bicycles, matching black and teal bike shorts, and Evan's phone number.

"How can you flirt with men like that after what your stepbrother did to you?"

Vanessa didn't respond right away. I sensed she was biting back one of her sassy remarks. "You really should get some counseling, honey. I've seen a slew of therapists. Some good, some not so good. One lady told me the best revenge is living well. I know that's true. I can't let what Derrick did to me hold me back." She roared up an on-ramp. "I can hook you up with a support group if you want."

"Oh my god, Vanessa. I couldn't talk about Dale to total strangers."

"They wouldn't be strangers anymore once you talked to them."

22
Breaking The Chain

onday morning, I pushed through a gaggle of girls to get into the Y's locker room. Half-naked teenagers were shedding their flannel pajama pants like winter plumage before shoving their long hair into silicone swim caps.

Seriously? The one morning I was actually looking forward to the pool being deserted so I can do some real thinking, I have to listen to a bunch of chickie-poos complain about their American history homework?

I stowed my things in a locker, then climbed over the pile of backpacks blocking the door to the pool deck. Elkie stood beside the pool talking with the head lifeguard. "What's the deal, Elkie?" I asked after looping my towel over the skimmer hanging on the wall. "Why are all these kids here before dawn?"

"The city pool is closed for repairs. We'll have to share the pool with the high school swim teams for the next week or so. I was just trying to negotiate us a couple of lanes. Dwight can only give us one today."

"It's amazing that high school kids would voluntarily get up this early to practice."

"When lane space is scarce, you take what you can get. Where's Vanessa?"

"I think she's sleeping in this morning. We had kind of a hard weekend."

"You need to take it easy on that woman," Elkie said with a wry smile. "At least we'll be down one person this morning. I'll try to figure out if there is a better time for us to train before tomorrow morning." As it turned out, Lara's Ladies only consisted of Elkie, Celeste, and me that morning. We were easily able to share the one lane without swimming into each other. Still, the increased noise and splashing coming from the other lanes made it difficult to find my rhythm. I had to stop twice and restart my stroke count. At one point, I hung on to the wall and pretended to be drinking from my water bottle in order to watch the girls in the next lane chat. They seemed so comfortable with each other. High school would have been different if I had felt the support of a team.

I pushed off the pool wall to do another thousand yards. The water muffled the high school kids' voices into a soothing ambience. I drifted further into a meditative state with each repetitive motion. The revelations of the paper bag floated through my mind as if they were scenes in a book. Each time I read through its pages, the truth became easier to absorb.

Mama was gone; I was still alive.

Dale had found me; I was still alive.

He knows where I am. I can stop running.

I flipped over and switched to backstroke for a few lengths. I looked up at the spinning fans in the roof releasing noxious fumes from the room. PawPaw's letter had released poisonous lies from my memory.

My grandparents wanted me. Mama did not.

I tried to feel something akin to compassion for my mother. I wanted to see her as a girl that didn't know any better, but that wasn't the truth. She had parents that were good, loving people. She had a home. It might have been difficult, but she could have gone back to Alders.

And where was she during those years I was with Grammy and PawPaw? Rehab? Jail? Why bother coming back at all? If she didn't want me, she could have put me up for adoption or given me to the state. For Christ's sake, an orphanage would have been better than the farm.

I tried to empty my mind and concentrate on counting my strokes until my heart stopped pounding in my ears. *Mama is dead. Really, really dead.*

I am alive.

I flipped toward the concrete pool bottom and kicked off the wall. I felt powerful sliding through the water in a streamline position. It felt strange to think that I could ever be free of my memories of Mama and Dale. It would be painful to loosen the heavy chain of hate around my heart; my heart muscles had grown around the iron links.

✳✳✳

Swept up in a wave of youthful exuberance, I followed the girls into the locker room at 6:30. Like an ornithologist observing a flock of birds, I watched them while I slowly brushed my teeth. Their slender limbs bent at odd angles as their pink bodies quivered in the cold locker room air. They showered in their bathing suits, hiding their nearly perfect young bodies under wet lycra as they lobbed shampoo and bars back and forth. A hush fell over the room when Elkie entered the shower room naked. Her well-muscled body was beautiful, although time and disease had left their marks on it. Her right breast sagged next to the neat pink scar marking where her left breast had once been. An older scar, now faded to a slick white line, snaked across her belly. Elkie proudly wore her scars like badges of honor.

Are they grossed out by Elkie's scars? Do they think she should hide them under a towel? What are these girls hiding under their suits?

When I was their age I would have been hiding the black and blue handprints on my arms and hips. I would have been hiding my shame.

What am I hiding from now?

I spit out the toothpaste in my mouth and stepped into the closest shower. I turned my back to the girls and stripped off my suit. Nothing happened. No fireworks. No earthquake. The girls didn't laugh at me. I didn't offend their sensibilities because I didn't carry my scars on the outside of my body. They ignored me and accepted me as being part of the same species. I let the warm water relax both my muscles and my nerves. Standing naked among strangers was a big step and I wasn't going to rush through it.

The girls continued to flap around until I heard someone yell that the bus was there. Suddenly, the girls were gone. Only Elkie and I were left in the locker room. "What a madhouse!" Elkie said, shaking her hair out. "They put their bags everywhere and they used up all the hot water. Celeste was smart to do a few more yards and let them clear out before she showers." Elkie dried off and stepped into a pair of jeans. A faded sweatshirt completed her outfit. From the back she could have been one of the teenagers. She hooked a pair of heavy suede gloves to her belt loop and stepped into yellow work boots for her volunteer work at the local raptor rehab center. "I'm off to nurse an owl that was hit by a car. Will we see you tonight?"

"Yeah," I replied as I wound a towel around my torso and grabbed a second out of my bag. My skin tingled as I dried off. I had opened myself up to scrutiny and had been accepted. When I left the pool that day, I felt cleansed of another small portion of the shame still weighing down my heart.

✳✳✳

On my way to the office, I called Jane. She'd left four messages on my cell phone in the last two days. The most recent message was about contacting a lawyer about the deeds in the paper bag.

Tom answered the phone. I could hear him cooking something in the background. "Is she eating again?" I asked.

"The Prednisone seems to have kicked in. She's eating everything in sight." Jane mumbled something in the background about paying him back for his teenaged years. Tom chuckled under his breath. "I'm making omelets. You want to come over?"

"Thanks, but I'm already on my way to work. She called earlier. Can I talk to her?"

Tom handed the phone to his mother. Jane's voice sounded stronger when she said, "Did you get my message? I keep thinking about those properties. I was doing some research on the web last night. Was one of those mines the Alders Asbestos mine?"

"I don't know. Probably. My grandfather managed several of the mines in Alders."

Jane sucked in her breath. "Lara, that land is worth a fortune. You have got to talk to a lawyer about that."

"That's nice, but the money is not what's important to me at this point. Look, I'll call the lawyer that drew up the will today, okay?"

"Are you in the car?"

"I just left the Y. I'm pulling into the Bettel parking lot now."

"How's the training going?"

"It's going well. I think I'll be ready for the race in March."

"I think it's great that you're doing this. I never did things like that. I jogged every day for years but always by myself. In retrospect, it would have been nice to have people to run with. I was never very good with the whole friends thing."

"Something else we have in common." I pulled into a parking space near the entrance and sat in the cold car to finish our conversation.

"Yeah but you're young. You still have time to do something about that. You don't want to end up like me, old and decrepit. Can you believe, not one of the people from the Rotary Club or the museum board have even as much as called to see how I'm doing? I've known those people for decades and—*poof*—totally forgotten. Stick with this triathlon thing. It's good to have people who understand what you've been through."

"We don't talk about it very much."

"Still, they know." I could hear Jane cover the mouthpiece and cough. The coughing seemed shallower these days. "So, what do you say we actually go on that shopping trip? I'm still feeling pretty good." I smiled at myself in the rearview mirror as I tucked a loose strand of hair into the loose bun on the top of my head. Jane had yet to directly say anything about meeting Dale on Saturday. I suspected she was too polite to say what she thought about him. She preferred to talk around the subject like this.

"Sure. It's a date. We'll go this weekend." Just then, Letitia minced her way between the cars and yanked the lobby doors open. She was carrying a tall cup of coffee with a gas station logo on the side.

"Jane, can we talk about this later? Letitia just walked by. She must be in a wicked bad mood if she stopped at the Kwiky Mart for coffee instead of going to Starbucks. I want to save my new interns before Letitia starts stacking up bodies on the eighth floor." I hung up and texted Stacy and Brad, the two interns Frank Mariano had assigned to me: "Letitia in bad mood. Don't work at the empty desks on the 8th floor. Work in my office today."

23

Periwinkle Pops

Saturday morning, Tom opened the door before I could ring the bell. "I think you two are insane for even attempting to go to the mall today. You should take the nurse with you."

I stepped into the foyer and pulled off my coat. "Good morning to you, too. Is there coffee?" I walked into the kitchen and helped myself to a cup of coffee. I could hear Jane humming in her bedroom.

Tom followed me in and held out a plate of scones dotted with dried cranberries and currants. He baked when he was upset. Judging from the volume of scones and muffins on the counter, he was beside himself.

I bit into a scone and talked through the crumbs. "No nurth. Sheth no fun."

"She's not supposed to be fun." He put the plate down and ran his fingers through his hair. "All right, Mom can go to the mall. But you have to follow some ground rules."

No wonder Jane wants so desperately to get out of the house. Poor Tom is having a nervous breakdown. I took another scone and said, "I'm listening."

"Number one—now that she's finished with the Prednisone, she's feeling weak again. She has to use a wheelchair."

"That's fine, I can rent one from Customer Service. I already checked it out and—"

"No," Tom interrupted. His face was flushed. I recognized the signs of panic; I had felt them all too many times myself. "She is not going to use some gross public wheelchair. Her immune system is too weak. She shouldn't be out in public at all." Tom took a sip from a coffee cup on the counter. "The hospital leased us a chair when she was doing chemo. Not that she's used it. She is so friggin' stubborn."

The trait's hereditary, buddy.

"I've put it in the trunk of her car. You'll take that car. Who knows what kind of germs are in your car." I felt offended on Ruby's behalf.

"Number two—you are not to let her go touching anything. I put disinfecting wipes in her purse. Use them. Wipe everything down before she touches it—the seats in the restaurant, the table, the silverware, everything. Number three—she has to eat a good lunch. She needs to eat at least 800 calories. If she doesn't eat enough at lunch, she needs to drink the can of Ensure I put in her bag. Number four—if she gets tired, she has to come right home." I looked up to see Jane in the doorway shaking her head. I agreed to all of Tom's demands so we could make our escape. As I helped Jane into the car, Tom stood in the garage and said, "I'm relying on you, Lara. Don't let her do too much."

"I've got this, Tom," I said as the Jaguar roared to life.

Once at the mall, I did as I had promised and carefully pulled up to the curb, set up the wheelchair, and helped Jane out of the car. I left Jane sitting comfortably in the winter sunshine while I looked for a parking space. *It's odd that Tom thought nothing of giving me the keys to this beautiful car. He doesn't really know me. I could just drive away right now.* I parked the car far from potential hazards and jogged back to Jane. There were tears on her cheek when I got there. "You okay?"

"Oh, don't mind me," Jane said, brushing her cheek with the back of her leather glove. "I'm just being silly. A little boy waved to me and his mother told him not to bother the old lady. Is that who I am now? A sick old lady?"

"Perhaps today was a mistake." I tucked the cashmere blanket in around the legs of Jane's velour tracksuit and turned the chair towards the parking lot. "I'll take you home."

"No." Jane grabbed the wheelchair's tire, nearly spilling herself onto the pavement. "I've been looking forward to this for days." She sat up straighter in the wheelchair. "I'm okay Lara, really, it just gets to me sometimes. I forget. And then it surprises me all over again, kind of like standing up and realizing you're drunk."

I carefully pushed the wheelchair into Nordstrom's and let Jane direct me wherever she wanted. She was in control today. Jane made me try on outfits I would never have looked at on the rack, much less considered wearing. The idea of spending more than thirty dollars on an article of clothing seemed preposterous. As I zipped up a periwinkle dress with layers of chiffon floating around my knees, I glanced at the price tag. $230! For a dress.

I stepped out of the dressing room. "This dress is so expensive!"

"But it's gorgeous on you," Jane beamed. "If you'd wear your hair up, your eyes would pop."

"But it's over $200."

"Then I'll buy it for you." Jane pulled at the sleeves and adjusted the waistline.

"That's not the point. I can afford it. I just don't see why anyone would pay so much."

"Turn around and look in the mirror. Does that girl look like a million bucks, or what? Could she wow any man in the room? You bet. That is why the dress costs that much." I twirled around in the three-way mirror. The dress did flatter my slim legs and muscular shoulders.

"But I thought I needed suits. Why are we even trying on dresses?"

"'Cause it's fun. And this new job has cocktail party requirements, right? One does not wear a suit to a cocktail party, and believe me, I have done as much business over a martini at a party as a cup of coffee in the conference room."

I closed the door of the dressing room and stripped the lovely dress off. "I'll think about the dress. Maybe I'll get just the one. For parties. Because it's necessary for business."

I could hear a triumphant smile in Jane's voice as she said, "That's my girl. You're coming around. You do drink, don't you?"

"Vanessa orders us piña coladas when we go out." I wrestled a suit off the hanger.

"No, no, no, little girls drink those. If you want to be taken seriously, you need to drink serious drinks. I have cultivated a taste for scotch, but you might want to start off slower. Gin and tonics would be okay, as would red wine, but no girlie drinks. Nothing with obscure liqueurs or fruit. And definitely nothing that comes in a fancy glass. You don't want them to think you are anything less than formidable. That suit looks terrible on you."

I looked in the three-way mirror at the long straight black skirt and elongated blazer. I looked like a stewardess.

"Take that off. Try on the taupe one."

The morning progressed in the same vein with me stripping and dressing while Jane gave me advice between fashion critiques. Jane knew what she was talking about. The outfits I bought made me feel fabulous. Jane picked out pieces around a navy palette so I could mix and match the suits, slacks, skirts and blouses into outfits for whatever an occasion required.

Just after noon, I emerged from yet another dressing room and found Jane slumped in the wheelchair. I rushed over and shook her shoulders. Jane perked up a bit but was still not quite right. "I think we should get some lunch soon," she slurred.

Tom is going to kill me. Thinking of Tom made me remember the can of Ensure in Jane's bag. I riffled around in the huge red leather pouch slung over the back of the wheelchair until I found the small can of chemical fortification. I desperately held the can up to Jane's mouth. "Drink this." She screwed up her face and turned away like an obstinate toddler. Worry bubbled in my stomach. *What if she collapses? I refuse to be responsible for her having a setback.* I forced Jane's hands down in her lap and pushed the can against her lips again. "I'll take you home right now if you don't drink this."

"You're as bad as Tom," Jane scolded after taking a sip. I made Jane keep drinking until she sat up a bit straighter and the crisis seemed to have passed.

"I'm going to change back into my own clothes now. I

want to see that can empty by the time I get out."

"Are you sure you're not a mother?"

"Absolutely." I flashed Jane a sly smile and teased, "Now if you're a good girl, I'll get you a cookie for dessert."

Jane stuck her tongue out at me.

24
Moving On

"'m Walking on Sunshine" jangled overhead while I strolled through the drug store. It was time to feel good. My meeting with Frank and the rest of the board had gone better than I could have hoped. He said my analysis of the effect of China beginning to mine tungsten on the global mineral markets had nuance. In front of a room full of people, he said I was a valuable member of the team. Letitia never made me feel part of a team. Now I had a team. I credited my two interns on the last slide as contributors and emailed them a modified copy of the presentation to use in job interviews.

I contemplated shampoo and wondered if the executive board would have taken me as seriously if I hadn't been wearing my snazzy new suit. Jane insisted I get the skirt shortened to make me look taller and bullied me into wearing a lilac silk blouse beneath the understated fitted jacket. I wanted to think that they appreciated my work on its own merits but suspected Jane was right—the clothes do make the woman. I still wasn't comfortable wearing skirts that showed my knees, but I did feel powerful in purple pointy-toed pumps.

I tossed a bottle of bargain shampoo in my cart and caught my reflection in a display of hand mirrors. *Is that my hair? I look like crap.* Chlorine had stripped my long hair until it resembled an overused mop hanging down my back. Broken strands stuck out at odd angles and it had taken on the color of wet cement. I needed help.

I'd parked in front of a new salon a few doors down from the pharmacy. I gambled that I could walk in and get a new hairdo that evening. The space had once been a paint-your-own-pottery place. It had been completely transformed. The walls were electric blue and the floor was a checkerboard of black and white linoleum tiles. The front window was dominated by a line of black pleather chairs perched over tubs of bubbling water. As soon as I opened the door, a woman who matched the shop accosted me. She wore black from head to toe, which was for the best. Any color would have taken away from the impact of her blue spiked hair. "Hello!" she squealed. "Do you have an appointment?"

I resisted the impulse to make some excuse and get out of there quickly; I needed a change. "No. I was hoping to get a haircut tonight."

The blue hair did not move as the woman checked a large appointment book perched atop a glossy black podium. There were no names written in it. The woman flashed me a grin. Her eyeteeth were crooked. "I think we can squeeze you in."

There was no one else in the shop. *Who are "we"?*

She pranced around the podium and led me toward a chair. "What are we doing today?"

"I need a haircut."

"We're running a winter special. A cut and style, a pedicure, and a facial, all for $199. What do you say?"

"I don't know."

"You save $75. It's like getting the facial for free!" Maybe it was residual adrenaline from my meeting with Frank or maybe I was dazzled by the blue hair. "What the hell, it's only hair. Give me the works."

Did I really just say that? I can't believe I'm doing this.

"Great, I'll even do you myself. I'm Cherie, by the way. This is my shop. Let's start with the facial." She reclined the chair.

"Can we do this sitting up, Sherry?"

"Don't worry, it won't hurt. And it's Cherie, as in *ma cherie.*"

Cherie was right. It didn't hurt. It took a few minutes, but once I closed my eyes and surrendered to the rhythm of Cherie's fingers moving in time with the bells and gongs of the eastern inspired background music, it was wonderful. Cherie, of the ridiculous name and clownish hair, had magical fingers.

When she was done, Cherie wrapped a cotton candy blue cape around my shoulders and started washing my hair. "Where are all the other stylists tonight?" I asked.

"It's just me. You know what they say, 'build it and they will come.'"

"So it's just you all the time?"

"Yeah, well, it's always been my dream to have my own salon. Here I am—living the dream." She didn't sound very sure of herself. As Cherie ran her long fingers through my hair, I tallied up the costs of running a salon—rent, insurance, supplies. Finally getting what you always wished for was a daunting proposition. I had wanted to be free of Mama and Dale and, now that I was, I wasn't entirely sure what to do with myself. I took a deep breath and tried to enjoy the feeling of Cherie massaging my scalp. *How could I have wasted so much time worrying about Dale and Mama? They were never even looking for me. They were lying, cheating, awful people, but after I left, they just went on with their miserable lives. They couldn't have cared less about me.*

Cherie wrested the chair upright. I looked in the mirror. The towel wrapped around my head matched Cherie's hair. Now we both looked demented.

"What are we doing here?" Cherie asked.

"I have no idea." My heart skipped. Like swimming a mile the first time, trusting was hard work but it felt good. "Do whatever you think would be best."

"Really?" Cherie smoothed the smock over my shoulders. "Wow, what a treat!" She was like the cat that caught a canary but didn't quite know how to eat it.

"All I ask is that it's easy to maintain. I swim several times a week and have to get dressed for work at the pool."

"Do you want to keep this color?"

"I don't know. I guess not. I'm open to… Well, not blue…" I thought of the pictures I'd seen of Jane at my age. "How about a goldie blondish color?"

"Goldie blondish it is." Cherie spun me around so I couldn't see what she was doing. I knew I was getting far more than a $199 special should have covered. First Cherie hacked off what felt like years of growth and then parked me in a massage chair with my feet soaking in bubbling water while she stood behind me and folded silver and bronze foils all over my head. I watched my reflection in the front window. I looked like a Halloween costume gone bad with the foils all over my head and a bright blue smock wrapped around my shoulders. While my hair "cooked," Cherie pulled up a stool, drew my left foot out of the water, and inspected my toes.

"Haven't you ever had a pedicure?"

"I don't like people touching me."

"That would make it difficult. What color do you want?" I shrugged. Cherie held up two small bottles. "Bubblegum or Twinkle toes?"

"Twinkle toes," I laughed. I watched Cherie deftly wield small instruments of torture on my toes. It was fascinating. "I never knew you were supposed to cut the skin around your toenails."

"I can see that."

I expected Cherie to quickly clip my toenails and paint some polish on them but was pleasantly surprised when she started rubbing my feet and massaging my calves. The tension from running on hard pavement and wearing awkward flippers in the pool quickly melted away. The chair was kneading my back muscles, the music was whining affably and my feet were being rubbed. Someone was touching my body, and it was glorious.

With my feet encased in foam slippers, Cherie led me back to a shiny black throne to finish my hair. She rinsed and lathered and clipped and re-clipped until I thought I would end up bald. When Cherie finally holstered her hair dryer and spun me around with a flourish, my long mousey hair was gone. In its place was a halo of soft waves. I hardly recognized myself.

"Go ahead, play with it." Cherie pushed the hair back and forth across my scalp. "It's all different chunky layers so there's no right or wrong way to do it. All you have to do is wash it and you are good to go. No blow dryer, no curler, nothing."

I played with the pieces around my face, tucking them behind my ears and then pulling them forward. I looked altered, but in a sense, I looked more like me. I smiled at myself in the mirror and then at Cherie beaming behind me.

"What do you call this color?" It was somewhere between café au lait and bamboo with gold streaks running through it.

"Goldie Blonde," Cherie giggled. "I used four different colors. But don't worry, I wrote everything down so we could replicate it next time. Or we could adjust it a little this way or that."

"You, Miss *Cherie*, are an artist. This was exactly what I wanted." Cherie looked like she could float she was so pleased.

I didn't know how to thank her enough. I felt new and improved. On the way out, I took a handful of business cards and stuffed them in my coat pocket. People were bound to notice my haircut and I would be sure to tell everyone about Auberge Cherie. Stupid name, but a great place.

✳✳✳

A week before the big race, I pulled a muscle in my left shoulder. I fully intended to keep training regardless of the pain, but Elkie, when she saw me favoring my right arm, suggested I skip training in the pool for a day or two. She said I should be tapering anyway. The concept of letting up on my training regimen in order to be more powerful on race day seemed silly to me. "You should go get a massage and have them work on that shoulder."

"You've got to be kidding," I said. "A massage? How about applying ice or hot packs?"

"It'll help. But you don't need to be afraid, dear," Elkie assured me. "You can ask for a female masseuse." I wondered if Vanessa had said something to Elkie about my "issues." The idea of letting someone touch my shoulders and back made my hands feel clammy, but I trusted Elkie. I took the number and made the appointment right then and there before I had a chance to talk myself out of it. Impulsivity had led me to Cherie and my great new hair cut. Perhaps a massage would help me, too.

The lobby of the day spa Elkie sent me to was completely white with sleek white furniture, plush white carpeting, and plain white walls. A lone pink peony blossom floated in a giant glass bowl on the reception desk. The receptionist, also all in white, spoke slowly and deliberately as she led me down a dim hallway to a tiny room. She murmured about how the platforms were heated for my comfort and I could choose to have aromatherapy as she opened a door. I froze in the doorway. The only thing in the small room was a table.

Holy crap! Why do I keep ending up naked on a table?

My heart jackhammered against my ribcage. I had the urge to run but I stood my ground. *Elkie said it would be okay. Trust Elkie.* The receptionist said something about starting face down and left me in the close dark chamber. I took a deep breath and repeated, "I'm okay, I'm okay, I'm okay" until the initial panic passed.

I closed my eyes, and for the first time in years, I prayed. *Okay, God. I take it you are trying to show me something here. The parallels between this place and my nightmare are not lost on me. I'm just going to go with it and trust that I will be okay. Elkie said it would be okay. But I'm telling you right now, God. Don't screw with me.*

I took off my clothes and climbed onto the table.

Fortunately, I realized I was supposed to get under the light cover rather than lay on top of it. I adjusted my face in the padded headrest and waited. For what, I didn't know. I was letting go, letting things happen. I needed to trust. After several minutes of listening to tropical bird songs and waterfalls splashing, the masseuse came in. She was an average enough looking woman with a kind voice. She didn't look like she would hurt me.

"I'm Brianna, we'll be together for the next hour. What kind of massage do you like?"

"I don't know. I'm new to this."

"Why don't we start with a gentle all over relaxation technique then? Are there any areas you want me to concentrate on this evening?"

"Yes, I pulled something in my left shoulder swimming. Maybe you could help me with that?"

"Certainly. We can work the kinks out of that joint." I stuck my arm out. Brianna rubbed the shoulder and said, "Just relax." A pulse of anxiety shot down my spine, but as Brianna rubbed her hands over my back and shoulders in long gentle strokes, the tension began to melt away. "If I am pushing too hard, just say something, okay?" Once I let go of my fear, the massage was a fabulous experience, completely different from any other. I focused on each muscle Brianna kneaded and repeated inwardly, *what does this mean?* I was determined to get the message God was trying to send me. I imagined Brianna pushing out the years of pain and sorrow with each pass over my back. Brianna moved to my feet and pulled on each of my toes. I imagined her tugging out splinters of resentment and regret from my soul. The holes filled with the soft music from the room. I felt waves of emotion bubble up from my core and burst in the lavender scented air.

Suddenly, I was aware of my body again. Brianna was rubbing my lower back. She pressed a spot along my spine that shot a bolt of searing pain down my legs and out my toes. I flinched and she backed off. "Does that hurt? I feel a lot of tightness through here. Do you carry your emotions in your pelvis?"

"You could say that," I replied. "I have cancer." *Oh my God, I just told another total stranger. It wasn't hard at all.*

"I see," Brianna stepped back. I was afraid she was going to stop the massage.

"But I am doing much better now. You don't have to stop. You go ahead and wail on those muscles if you need to. I can take it."

Brianna lightly touched the center of my back with her fingertips. "Let's try a different technique to see if we can release some of that built up tension, hmm? Are you familiar with hot stone treatments?"

I lifted my head to look over my shoulder. Brianna had a smooth black stone in her palm. She appeared to be praying over it. "Hot stones? Like lava?"

At first all I could feel was a burning sensation but, slowly, the warmth from the stone radiated out through my pelvis. "Oh, that feels nice."

"Good," Brianna replied. "Let's push that tension right out of your body."

✶✶✶

It had taken being diagnosed with cancer and withstanding the pain of treatment for me to stop seeing my body as an instrument of evil. It was work, but I was determined to integrate my mind and body into one entity. I still visited with the Lee's every Tuesday and chatted with

Susan over a large bowl of her delicious hot and sour soup, but I had also bought a twenty piece set of enameled cast-iron pots and pans and planned to put them to good use in my tiny kitchen.

As spring approached, my self-confidence blossomed along with the fruit trees and daffodils. Swimming daily gave me a sense of calm I never got from working out at the gym. The muffled sounds under water and repetitive motions transformed my morning workouts into a daily meditation practice. I enjoyed training with the team a couple times a week in order to keep in touch with the other women. The team was fun to be with, but they ran at half my pace.

My most consistent running partner was now Barkis, a pit-bull mix. We found each other outside the local food co-op one Saturday morning in early February. The local animal shelter had set up an adoption booth. To one side, several dogs with jaunty red bandanas were tied to a bicycle rack. They all sat politely and smiled at the passing shoppers, except for one brindled brown dog with a black patch across one cheek. He squatted, shaking, under the table. The dog growled when a little boy leaned over to look at him. The boy's mother hustled him away squawking about the shelter exposing the public to such a dangerous animal. I could see in those big brown eyes that the dog wouldn't have attacked the little boy; he was afraid of him. I quickly threw my groceries in the car and went back to look at the dog more closely. When I knelt down next to the table, the volunteer pinning flyers to a bulletin board warned, "Careful with that one. He's part pit-bull. He's liable to do anything."

"Really? He's not that big." I slowly extended my hand under the table. The dog came over and sniffed it.

"You're brave. He could have bitten your hand clean off.

He's been at the shelter for months now. Nobody wants him."
The dog nosed my leg then looked at the volunteer as if he
understood the derision in the woman's voice. I ran my hand
over his back. As soon as I touched his soft fur I knew I had
to take him home.

"What do you know about him?" The dog sat at my side
and looked up patiently.

"He's two years old and had all his shots. Like I said, he's
been with us for a long time. We think he was abused as a
puppy. He's part pit-bull. He won't get any bigger than that."

"This is the dog for me." I didn't know the first thing about
caring for a dog but was determined to give this creature
another chance in life.

"Are you sure? That lab over there is a good dog. Let me
bring him over."

"No, I want this one," I said. I paid the fee, collected the
free bag of food, and loaded the dog into Ruby's back seat.
He quietly trembled behind me during the ride back to my
apartment. I couldn't tell if he was excited or terrified. We
spent the rest of the day getting to know each other. The dog
was hesitant and alternated between letting me pet him and
sitting close by but just out of reach.

The next morning I woke up to find the dog staring at
me from the foot of my bed. "Well dog, you want to go for
a run?" He gave a joyful bark in the affirmative. "Barkis is
willing!" I said with a laugh. I searched around the garage for
a piece of rope to use as a leash and tied it to the dog's collar.
"We'll need to go to the store later and get you some more
food and a real leash. Maybe I can pick up a book on how to
be a dog owner."

Barkis enjoyed the run as much as I did. I had found
my new running partner. Later that day we bought a pile

of manuals, an assortment of dog toys, and a large gold identification tag engraved with *Barkis Blaine.*

25
Silver Strider

R ace day had come and Lara's Ladies were ready. The eleven of us lined up in front of the sign-in desk to collect our purple and teal T-shirts with Ellery Hospital Cancer Center proudly printed across the front. Positive energy buzzed in the crowd of colorful T-shirts and bright smiles and allowed us to overlook the cold March drizzle as we pinned race numbers to each other's backs. I wouldn't be cold during the run though; Vanessa had seen to that. She'd dragged me to the sporting goods store again and squawked at me until I bought an insulated warm-up jacket and special socks. I also splurged on a new technical swimsuit to wear under my T-shirt. I had overheard the high school girls talking about how they wore their race suits a size smaller than their practice suits. I bought a black knee skin suit with bright blue silicone straps that was three sizes smaller than my original suit. It made me feel like a bullet ripping through the water and could double as both running

and biking gear. Vanessa bought pink padded bicycle pants and special gloves with rhinestones embedded in the leather. We might not have been the fastest competitors, but we were definitely the best dressed.

Liam gave the group one last pep talk and sent the other Ladies off to the start zone. Since there were eleven of us, and none of the other Ladies could keep up with me, Liam had recruited a running partner for me. He waved a slightly balding boyish-faced man out of the crowd and introduced him as Sebastian Lincoln. I said a polite hello and stepped away to stretch. I had been training for this race for months. I wasn't going to let some dude Liam dug up slow me down.

When the crowd began to move in the direction of the starting line, Liam and Sebastian found me at the edge of the parking lot. "You ready, Lara?" I nodded even though my stomach was in knots. "Remember what Elkie said and try to have fun. You don't need to win."

"Yes I do."

Liam snorted and turned to Sebastian. "It looks like we're going to start soon. I'll hang on to your warm-ups for you." Sebastian leaned over and unzipped the sides of his pants. They fell away to expose a curved alloy prosthesis where his left leg should have been.

"Holy shit!" I exclaimed. "Where the hell's your leg?"

Sebastian looked down and feigned shock. "Golly gee! Where could it be? I know I had two legs when I left the house this morning!" he said in falsetto. He started jumping in place to warm up. "Liam, you said she was prickly, but you didn't say she's an ass."

Liam shook his head as he took the pants from Sebastian. "Good luck out there, you two. I'm not sure which one of you needs it most." He turned and disappeared into the crowd.

"I'm sorry," I whispered. "What happened?"

"Cancer, just like you. You can just see my missing parts better," Sebastian said with a smirk.

I am going to kill Liam. He has got to stop talking about me behind my back. I don't care how sweet he is. The crowd began to move, walking at first then building to a slow jog.

"Can you really run on that thing? It looks like something out of a science fiction movie."

"Faster than you can."

"I doubt that."

"I'll bet you dinner I can. The winner picks the restaurant." The crowd sped to a run, allowing me to not respond. This man intrigued me. He was damaged.

"When'd you lose your leg?"

"I didn't misplace it. They cut it off. Five years ago. Bone cancer. I was 26. When were you diagnosed?"

"August. Did Liam tell you about my cancer?"

"No. Liam's cool about stuff like that." We started jogging faster. "The team's name is Lara's Ladies and you are said Lara. Ergo, you must have cancer. I take it you're feeling okay. You run well. You look good. Better than good." I felt my checks get hot. I somehow didn't mind that this Sebastian was flirting with me.

"I'm doing really well. I still get tired. Better though."

"Liam said you had a great pair of legs when he asked me to do this with you. Were you always a runner?"

Sebastian didn't even sound out of breath yet. I picked up the pace a notch, testing how fast Sebastian could go.

"I was a gym rat... before." I ruefully thought about my days of endless cycling to nowhere in sterile rooms with a booming bass beat drowning out all conversation. "This is my first race outside." It was getting harder to talk. "Like the

swimming best."

"Me, too. At least now that I've got my one-legged kick down."

I was impressed by Sebastian's gait. We had left most of the pack behind by the two-kilometer flag. The curved foot of his prosthetic was efficient. I struggled to keep up with his pace. "Different footie thing for the bike?"

"Yeah. Bike shop hooked me up. Custom prosthetic."

"Cosmic Cycles?"

"Damn thing cost more than my first car."

"Train with a team?"

"Nah. My greyhound, Mitzi, every morning. Forces me out of bed. Doesn't care if I only have one leg."

I thought about Barkis. He couldn't care less if I had an intact cervix or not. "Me, too. Pit-bull mix. Looks mean. Big baby."

We ran on in companionable silence for two more kilometers, passing the runners who had taken off too fast and could not maintain their pace. We crested a hill at the front of the pack. At the side of the road was a young couple with a sable greyhound quivering on the end of her leash. As soon as she saw Sebastian come over the top, she tried to launch into the road.

"Mike!" Sebastian yelled. "Mitzi!" The young man tugged on the leash keeping the dog from knocking me down. The greyhound barked and whined until we turned the next corner.

"Your dog?"

"My brother gets bored. Starts talking."

"Why bring her?"

"Hate leaving her at home. School all week. Take her everywhere on the weekends. My students say I'm obsessed."

"Teacher?"

"English. Bunch of miscreants. Can't tell Hemingway from Hawthorne."

"Both American. Different centuries. Lavish description. Hardly any."

"Thank you!" Sebastian said. "What do you do?"

My thighs were burning. I wanted to stop running, but I didn't want to stop talking. "Research. Commodities firm. Minerals."

"Like banking?"

"Investments."

"Do people scream and run away when they see you coming?"

"Not everyone," I giggled. I was having fun. "Just lazy people. Or those bad at math."

"Like it?"

"Yeah. Changed jobs. Same company. Change can be good. Thinking about moving closer. Don't know."

"Why not?"

"Maybe I should wait."

"For what?"

When we rounded the last corner, I could see Vanessa jumping up and down like a toddler at the finish line. She and her partner were in a later start group. "Look," Sebastian said. "Toy poodle."

I laughed and almost broke stride. "My friend. Vanessa."

"I'm sorry. Sure she's a lovely woman."

"She is. And brightly colored."

We sprinted to the finish line. Sebastian let me cross the line first and made a show of pretending to have been bested. I turned to say I knew he let me win, but in the hustle and bustle of finding my bike and getting back on the road, I lost him. I didn't see him on the road. He may have been ahead of me or far behind. As I found my cadence, I smiled thinking about the intriguing man with the silver leg. I wondered if he was serious about having dinner with me. I hoped he was.

The bicycle portion of the race went well. The saddle that Liam had installed supported my pelvis so I could concentrate on staying in the pack of mostly men and hit the pool with only a handful of other competitors. I lost some ground during the mile swim but ended up finishing the triathlon as the third woman and in twenty-fourth place overall. At the closing ceremony, Liam picked me up and twirled me around until Elkie came over and made him put me down. "I'm so proud of you," she said. "It's a rare woman who can do a race like this so soon after radiation."

"I encouraged her to do it," Vanessa whined from behind Liam.

"Yes you did, dear," Elkie said dismissively. I felt a surge of satisfaction at being the favored child. I stood in the bleachers ostensibly to watch the winning teams receive ribbons, but I was looking for Sebastian's balding head and silver leg. He was listed as coming in thirty-third. My stomach rumbled loudly as I heard a voice directly behind me say, "So what kind of food would you like?"

I whipped around with a grin. "I don't know, but I could eat a horse."

"That's what I like. A girl with an appetite."

"Who are you?" Vanessa asked, stepping protectively between Sebastian and me.

"Vanessa, this is Sebastian." I gently nudged Vanessa to the side. "He's the guy Liam paired me with for the run. He bet me dinner that I couldn't beat him."

"Dinner?" Vanessa raised an eyebrow and gave us a

knowing look. She stepped away toward the rest of the team. "I think I'll ask Celeste if she'll give me a ride to the pizza place. Catch up with us later. Or don't."

Crap, she thinks I'm ditching her to go on a date? "Bye," I called after her. "I'll call you later."

Oh my God! I am ditching her to go on a date!

After the ceremony, Sebastian and I joined the stream of people flowing to the parking lot. He no longer hopped along like he did with his running leg. His gait was fine. I wouldn't have guessed he had an artificial leg. "How about barbecue? I know a place where we can split a quarter of a pig plus hush puppies, onion rings, and slaw. And they have these great Cheerwine floats."

"Cheerwine? I haven't had that since I was little." I remembered how my grandfather had loved the sticky red soda. A bottle of Cheerwine would be the perfect way to top off a good day.

26
A Length Of Rope

Frank Mariano stepped into my office and burst out laughing. "This place looks like the secret room they always find in a serial killer's attic on TV. What are you doing in here, Lara?"

I turned from where I stood on top of my filing cabinets and tried to see the room from his perspective. It did look odd. My office walls were a storyboard of my upcoming presentation to the steering committee. Possible presentation slides flowed across the walls and leaked behind the door. Each section was plastered with charts and graphs and sticky notes.

"My notes for Friday's meeting."

"Do you need some help getting down from there?"

"No, I'm fine," I said as I jumped down from the filing cabinet. I slipped my spectator pumps back on and tugged the edge of my blue and white striped sweater over the hips of my navy linen trousers. "Can I do something for you?"

Frank inspected one of my charts on the wall. "These look good. You won't need this level of detail though. We don't have that much time." He turned to leave.

I stepped toward the door. "Is there anything I should know before the meeting?"

"Basically, you'll have thirty minutes to talk. Use them wisely. Oh yeah, you should coordinate your slides with Letitia's."

"Excuse me?"

"Well yeah, I only get an hour on the agenda so you and Letitia have to both fit in that hour."

I clamped my fingers around the edge of my desktop and arranged my face into a smile. "I understand. No problem."

Frank stepped into the hallway. "Well, I'm off to see the IT guys. My laptop is acting up again."

I waited until Frank was talking to the people in IT before quietly closing my office door. "Shit!" I grabbed a stack of sticky notes and lined them up end-to-end along the front edge of my desk, then stacked them back together in a flower pattern. Coordinating my presentation with Letitia's sounded awful. Letitia and I hadn't talked since I changed positions. Vanessa suggested I keep my distance for a while, especially while my interns were using the empty desks on the eighth floor. Letitia and I had exchanged a few terse emails over the last few months but we had both avoided meeting face to face. At one point, I was about to get on the elevator in the lobby and Letitia pushed the button to close the doors before I got there.

I climbed back up on top of the file cabinets and worked to hone my section of our presentation. I pared down my discussion of copper trends to the nub, until Vanessa knocked on my door two hours later. "What you doing up there?" She dropped a Chipotle bag on my desk. "Are you tripping? Come on, share."

"Sorry. No drugs." I jumped down and closed the door behind her. "And please don't give me any crap today. Frank came by earlier and dropped a bombshell. I have to coordinate my slides for Friday's meeting with Letitia. I'm totally freaking out about my presentation now."

"You'll do great," Vanessa said. She pulled a series of smaller bags from the larger bag. "I got you soft tacos instead of hard ones. I hope that's okay."

"You get extra guacamole?"

"Yes, money bags," she sighed. "I got your extra guacamole. You owe me twelve dollars. So why are you freaking out?"

I laid a napkin down for her to use as a placemat. "I have to go talk to Letitia about her presentation. What the hell am I going to say to her?"

"As little as possible," Vanessa replied. "You show her your slides. She shows you hers. You talk about any conflicts. Then you walk away." She continued with half a taco in her mouth. "The less you two talk, the better. Remember, you let her think you had a drug problem, so if she asks you anything, say you are in ongoing treatment and leave it at that."

"So I should just keep my mouth shut about the bonuses?"

"Believe me, she has heard quite enough about the whole bonus thing." Over the last few months, Vanessa had implied that Letitia was being punished for passing off my work as her own but couldn't tell me any details. Vanessa finished her taco and took a sip of her sweet tea with a smug smile on her face. "Actually, I bet she is none too happy to be presenting with you, either. Rick in Accounting told me that her department has been in free fall this quarter. I don't think Frank fully understood how much you were carrying Letitia for the last few years. You play your cards right, you may be sitting in her office next year."

"I don't want her job. I'd be happy with one or two permanent people to help me out. I don't want a whole department." I nibbled on a tortilla chip and thought about the possibility of working closely with people. "How do you get people like the guy in Accounting to tell you things like that? No one ever tells me anything."

"Years and years of practice, honey," Vanessa giggled. "No really, I studied organizational psychology in school. I have a degree in messing with people's heads on a large scale."

"Are there any books on how to supervise people?"

"Thousands of mediocre books and a few really good ones. Management books are a growth industry. You should track them as a commodity."

After Vanessa left, I looked up books on the mechanics of interpersonal relationships. If I could research how to do it, maybe I could supervise people after all.

✳✳✳

At 5:20, my phone buzzed on my desk. It buzzed all day but it was unusual to receive an email after five; Bettel Occidental Brokerage was a strictly nine to five kind of place. I stretched my shoulders and climbed down from my desk chair to see who was emailing me. It was time to stop anyway, numbers and statistics had become jumbled in my brain. And I was famished.

The phone rang in my hand before I could access my messages. It was Jane. "Lara dear, how are you?" Jane's breathing was labored.

"Busy, but good." I gathered up my laptop and pocketbook. "How are you?"

"Would you like to come here for dinner tonight? I'd

really like to see you. It's only pot roast but Tom does a pretty good job." I could tell that Tom was standing right there and that Jane was teasing him with her words.

"I was planning to take Barkis for a run—"

"I understand if you don't want to come." Jane sounded like a petulant teenager.

"I don't know, Jane. You sound tired."

"No, I'm not. Come and eat. You've got to eat. The two of them can't eat a whole pot roast." I heard Tom scold "Mom!" in the background.

The two of them? I locked my office door and started toward the elevator. "Does the nurse stay for dinner?"

"We're having a guest. Candace is coming."

I snickered to myself as I stepped into the elevator. I understood why Jane was calling now; she wanted me to run interference between her and the hated Candace.

Jane briefly coughed. "I'd really like to see you."

"Okay," I replied. "I'll be there in an hour or so." I zipped home, took Barkis for a quick walk, and called the Lee's to tell them not to expect me that evening.

The wind made pale petals rain from the ornamental cherry trees lining the wide winding avenues of Jane's neighborhood. I wished I lived in such a place. The gridded streets in my apartment complex that I once found comfortably predictable now felt sterile. I rang the gingko leaf doorbell and immediately heard heavy footfalls approach. Tom swung the massive door open with a smile. "Lara! Come in, come in. Mom's really excited to see you."

"Am I late?"

"Not at all. Candace and I just got home a few minutes ago."

Candace and I got home? This is going to be interesting.

He took my coat and stopped me from going into the bright kitchen. "Look, you've got to help me out here," Tom whispered. "I had no idea that she was having a tough day when I invited Candace over for dinner. The nurse told me that they saw her doctor this morning and her white blood count is way too low. She's feeling really down so I hope you can cheer her up." He stepped into the kitchen and left me overlooking the modern sunken living room. The few times I had been there before, the wall of sleek linen drapes had been closed. This evening, they were open. My eyes were drawn out the back wall of windows down a gently sloping lawn to a pond. A lone goose floated in the cold water. "Wow!" I exclaimed.

"It's quite a view, isn't it?" Jane was propped up on a soft grey pillow on the low sofa. The intricately woven shawl draped over her legs made her blend into the furniture. Across from her was a plump red head with a toothy grin plastered on her face. Her eyes pleaded with me to say something nice.

I thrust my hand out to her. "You must be Candace from Babcock Construction." She took it gratefully.

"Yeah," Jane croaked. "This is Tom's accomplice in sinking my father's company."

"Oh come on, Jane," I replied. "I'm sure Tom's doing a great job." I looked over my shoulder and caught Tom smiling at me. *You better appreciate this, buddy.*

Jane sat up and tucked her feet under her. "Come, sit over here next to me, Lara dear. You look thin and lovely today." I did a tiny spin and pulled up my pant leg so Jane could see my spectator pumps. "You should wear hose with those shoes."

"No one wears hose anymore, Ms. Babcock-Roberts,"

Candace chuckled. *Oh my God, Candace. Shut up!* Tom loudly cleared his throat, signaling Candace to come help him in the kitchen.

"The yard looks beautiful."

"The view is gorgeous in the spring. Tom and I planted the red tulips and white narcissus all around the pond about ten years ago. They've spread more than we could have dreamed. It really is a sight, isn't it?" Jane's fingers quivered over her lips as she stared out the window for a moment. I wondered how many more times she would see the flowers bloom.

Jane inhaled through her fingers as if pulling on a cigarette. "Tell me, what is going on in the big world. My oncologist has put me under house arrest. He says my blood counts are too low and I can't risk getting exposed to any germs."

I squirmed away from her on the soft couch and wondered if I had carried any germs into this house. "How are you feeling?"

"Crappy. I could barely lift my head from the pillow this morning and my throat feels like it's lined with sandpaper."

"The fatigue should slowly start going away. It takes a long time."

"My brother was supposed to come visit later this week, but if my counts don't go back up I may have to ask them to cancel. I just hate the idea of my family being considered infectious agents." Jane wiped some perspiration from her forehead. "And on top of that, Sanjay gave me this nasty shot that's making me feel achy all over. As if I didn't feel lousy enough."

"Maybe Candace and I should go and let you rest."

"No! Stay. Talk to me. I'm just feeling sorry for myself. So, now that the race is over, will you still see Lara's Ladies?"

"Probably not too much. We're all going to get together in a few weeks for dinner."

"Have you been seeing more of that young man?"

"Yes," I replied, ignoring the smirk on Jane's face. Sebastian and I had grown close in the weeks after the triathlon, yet I needed our relationship to move slowly. I liked Sebastian. I didn't want to sabotage any relationship I might have with him by acting like a scared squirrel. "We might get together this weekend for a run."

"Good. I don't like the idea of you being alone." Jane took a slow breath before talking again. "How's work?"

"I've got a big presentation Friday. Unfortunately, I have to coordinate it with my old boss."

"That's going to be awkward. What's your game plan?"

I leaned back and stared out the window. "Vanessa says I should play it cool and not say anything about anything."

"I agree. Keep the upper hand. Take the high road." Jane pulled the throw tighter around her. "What are you going to wear when you meet?"

"I don't know yet. Maybe the robin's egg blue blazer?"

"I've got—" Jane's face froze as she started to cough. Tom came running from the kitchen with a rag. He held it to her mouth and thumped her back until the spasm passed. Tom was quick but I still saw the bloody mucus he wiped from Jane's lips. Jane fell back on the pillow spent and whispered, "Thanks sweetie, I'm okay." She smiled at her son looming over her. "You can go back to playing with Candace in the kitchen."

Tom glanced over at me. "I hope you like pot roast." He couldn't hide his concern behind his even smile.

"I don't know," I replied, watching him try to casually fold the rag in his hands. "I don't think I've ever tried it."

"Didn't your mom make it?" He brushed his mother's shoulder. "It can be made in the crock pot so it was one of my mom's favorite recipes."

"You make it sound like I starved you," Jane said with a smile. "It was all I could do to keep your gapping maw filled. I swear you had a hollow leg."

Tom turned to me. "Were you raised on gourmet food, Lara?"

I recalled the years of cast-off food from the diners my mother worked in. At one point, before she married Dale, Mama and I had lived on peanut butter and crackers for weeks. The only decent food I ate as a child were the school lunches and those, only because I forged my mother's signature on the forms for the free-and-reduced lunch program. "Mama reheated well."

Jane winked at me.

"Well, I hope you have a good appetite," Tom said as he headed back into the kitchen. "There's plenty of food. Can I bring you ladies a cocktail?"

"Thanks, Tom," I said. I wanted to ask about the bloody rag. The treatments didn't seem to have halted the cancer. Jane seemed weaker each time I saw her. I selfishly thought it unfair for Jane to die after I had become so attached to her.

I blurted out the first thing that came into my head to break the silence. "That shawl is neat. Did you pick that up in your globetrotting?"

"Guatemala," Jane replied. A bittersweet smile crossed her face. "Tom's father and I went to see Tikal before we split up. I picked this up in the market in Chichicastenango. Each of the patterns is supposed to mean something. The little girl I bought it from was a force to be reckoned with. Smart as a whip. I ended up paying way too much for it because

I just couldn't haggle with a child. You really should travel, Lara. There is nothing like it to give you some perspective." A companionable silence settled between us as Tom and Candace murmured together in the kitchen and Jane was lost in her memories. I thought about Rosaria and wondered if she had ever been that little girl selling shawls in the market.

Tom appeared behind me with a tray of cocktails. "Gin and tonic?" He offered me a tall glass. I took a tentative sip of the drink. Its bitter bubbliness was refreshing. "Dinner should be ready in about ten minutes."

"Thanks, sweetie," Jane said. "When you get a second, could you bring me that red bag I put aside for Lara?"

Tom bit his lip and quickly nodded. He disappeared into the master bedroom for a moment then returned with a large tooled-leather tote. He dropped the bag full of scarves and other accessories at my feet. "What's all this?" I asked.

"I've been cleaning out closets and I want you to have these."

"I can't take your things."

Tom cleared his throat awkwardly and returned to the kitchen. I saw him wipe a tear from the corner of his eye with the heel of his hand before he returned to making a salad. Candace put her arm around his shoulder.

Jane rolled her eyes and turned to me. "I want these things to be used and appreciated. Tom will end up giving everything to Good Will." I didn't like the way Jane was talking. She wasn't even pretending she would ever use these things again. I picked up a long scarf in tones of grey and moss green. The silky fabric slipped through my fingers like water.

"There is a beautiful grey dress that goes with that scarf. Unfortunately, it wouldn't fit you even if you got it hemmed.

You're so little. Tom will have to take it to the consignment shop on Broad Street. You should wear this with that peach blouse and some grey slacks. Anyway, dig in there and find the silver cuff. You should wear that with that pale blue blazer."

***

The next morning, I spun the silver cuff around my wrist as I rode the elevator to the eighth floor. After doing some research on the Internet, I decided to go on the offensive and speak to Letitia in her office. I didn't want her seeing the extent of my background notes or polluting my workspace. I wiggled my toes inside my purple pointy-toed pumps and wondered what Garlic Breath and Pathetic Dog Owner would think of my outfit. I'd selected a pearl silk shirt and navy pencil skirt, an homage to my old navy chinos, to go with the robin's egg blue fitted blazer. I hoped the outfit made me look feminine yet strong. When the door slid open, I fluffed my hair and strode out with an air of self-confidence that I did not fully feel. I expected to see a shocked look on Pathetic Dog Owner's face but his cube was empty and his monitor was covered by a yellowed plastic dustcover. A kid sat at Bald Guy's desk. The few faces that did peek over the line of cubes were all strangers to me.

Letitia and Garlic Breath were talking in her office as I strode in that direction. Neither one looked happy to see me. Letitia rapidly said something to Garlic Breath before I opened the door. He quickly gathered up the papers strewn across the desk and shoved them in a file folder. Letitia smoothed her ponytail, straightened the pens on her desk, and stood up as I pushed open the heavy glass door.

"Good morning, Letitia," I said brightly. "Greg, could you excuse us for a moment? I need to discuss something with Letitia." Garlic Breath's mouth hung open vacuously for a moment, then he looked away and lumbered out of the room. He stared at me through the glass wall all the way back to his cube.

"Wow Blaine, I hardly recognized you! Special Projects obviously agrees with you." Letitia squeezed the paper cup of black coffee in her hand. There were two more cups with a gas station logo in the trashcan under the desk. *Hmm, no more Starbucks. Can't she afford a $4 cup of coffee anymore?*

I pushed aside a stack of folders and opened my laptop in the center of the desk. "Frank said we need to coordinate our presentations for Friday."

"I, um, haven't finished mine yet." Letitia crossed her arms over the front of her sleek black suit. "We still have a few days."

I sensed a dozen eyes on us through the glass walls. They couldn't hear what we were saying, yet they were all experts at reading body language. My research into interpersonal relationships told me how to act. I leaned on Letitia's desk with my fingers splayed out. "I've emailed you a list of my slides. I will need yours by the end of the day," I said with a big smile that showed my teeth.

"Sure," Letitia said a little too quickly. "I can get those to you today."

It was too soon to leave so I tucked a curl behind my ear exposing a set of silver drop earrings, another gift from Jane, and casually sat on the corner of Letitia's desk. "So, how's everything going around here?"

Letitia fell into her chair and crossed her legs. The heel of her right pump was worn down to the metal shank. "It's been insane. I've lost four people in the last two months to rank incompetence, and now Peter is out on disability."

"Peter?"

"Didn't you hear? Kidney cancer. It's been terrible. He went to see the doctor because he thought he had the flu and well, they found it. Greg's taken it really hard. First he had to step up the workload after you moved downstairs and now his best friend is sick. He's even been going over and walking Peter's dogs every morning."

When Letitia mentioned the dogs, the pieces fell into place. Pathetic Dog Owner had kidney cancer. *I never knew Pathetic Dog Owner's name was Peter. His email is Ppappert, so I guess Peter would be right.*

Pathetic Dog Owner has cancer? I closed my eyes and took a few deep breaths before rubbing my eyes.

"I'm sorry, I assumed you knew."

"It's just such a shock," I sighed as I stood up and picked up my laptop.

"I know," Letitia scoffed. She twisted her ponytail around her forefinger. "I can't believe I have to keep his job open while he's out. That Vanessa Klaitner won't let me fire him. Some federal statute or something."

A bitter taste in my mouth made me swallow hard. *I knew it! She totally would have fired me if I told her I had cancer.*

I stepped toward the door. The websites said to stay at least five minutes, but I needed to leave before I slapped Letitia silly.

"It's not like I have any less work without him," Letitia continued, more to herself than to me.

As I stepped out of the office, I recognized one of my old file boxes inside the cubicle of a petite woman with blue wire framed glasses. I stopped beside her cubicle. "Hi, I'm Lara Blaine." Through the glass office wall, I could see Letitia stumble around her desk and teeter after me.

"Nice to meet you, Ms. Blaine. You're a bit of a legend around here."

I felt my cheeks turning red. "I see you were assigned the pomegranate report. That used to be mine. So if you need any help, please come see me. I'm on the sixth floor."

"Granger will be fine," Letitia seethed from behind me.

Garlic Breath's head popped up over the cubicles. I stepped around Letitia to speak to him. "I was sorry to hear about Peter's illness. I remember what good friends you are."

"I… ummm… well," Garlic Breath stammered.

"Well you tell Peter I'm thinking about him. Okay, Greg?"

"Ummm…" Garlic Breath looked to Letitia for guidance. She was saying something, probably mean, to Ms. Granger. "Okay."

"I hope he's back soon. I know you're down a few people up here," I said in a loud, clear voice. A sea of eyes watched me walk to the elevator. "I'd hate to see this department suffer. I know how much you all rely on getting your quarterly bonuses." The word bonus rattled through the cubicles like a breeze through dried leaves.

Letitia stiffened. "I can't believe you brought that up!"

"Really?" I whispered as I punched the elevator button. "'Cause you seem to be able to believe all sorts of nasty things about people."

Letitia's eyes bugged out of her head. "What do you mean?"

"I'm not on drugs, Letitia. I have cancer." I stepped into the open elevator and turned around before saying, "Your slides better be good because mine are awesome." As the doors slid shut, Letitia bit the crimson lipstick off her lower lip. I had only seen her do that when talking to Frank on the phone.

That's right, Letitia. Be afraid. Be very afraid.

27
Tiny Bubbles

After our first meal of barbecue and Cheerwine, Sebastian and I spoke every night. We each sat on our respective couches, with our dogs by our sides, and watched TV together. He liked to shoot holes in the logic of police procedurals and I complained about how homicide detectives could never chase down criminals in high heels and tight slacks. In dribs and drabs, Sebastian told me how his fiancé left him the same week he was diagnosed with cancer and how his students had kept him going through the last few years. I related enough strategic details of my life to explain my shock at seeing Dale a few months before. Sebastian pronounced my life story Dickensian.

Our conversations helped. Telling my story, even without some of the more lurid details, drained it of color. My memories were beginning to fade into the past. Still, for three weeks I didn't let Sebastian closer to me than a telephone connection. Finally, after much coaching from Vanessa, I agreed to meet Sebastian at the botanical gardens for a run. The gardens seemed like a good choice for our date. If we ran out of things to talk about, I could comment on how lovely the roses were or how many different varieties of dogwood the gardens had. They had eighty-two. I looked it up. It was just a running date, yet I was as excited as a sixteen-year-old getting ready for the prom, or so I imagined. I gave Barkis a bath that morning and strapped his jaunty new dog pack to his back. I wanted Mitzi to like him.

It turned out my anxiety was unfounded. It was as easy to talk to Sebastian in person as it was on the phone. We chatted about current events and the books we were reading. We had similar taste in novels, short on sentiment and long on plot. At the end of the two-mile loop, we tied the dogs' leads to a picnic table in the cafe area. I put my foot up on the table to stretch my hamstring. Sebastian took off his prosthetic and readjusted the sock over his stump. I thought it was a good sign that he felt comfortable enough with me to do that.

"How did that big presentation go yesterday? Did that woman ever send you her stuff for the meeting?"

"No. I sent her, and our boss, a list of the topics I planned to cover but she never replied to my email." I switched legs and leaned into the stretch. "You know, actually, the meeting went way better than I could have dreamed. Letitia showed up late, her PowerPoint looked like she threw it together the night before, and she just kind of rambled. At one point, our boss cut her off and asked me a question about what she was presenting."

"Could you answer it?"

"Sure, it hasn't been that long since I worked for Letitia. I still know that stuff." I did a few lunges and remembered Letitia's petulant frown when one of the directors thanked me for clarifying a point. "The best part, though, was after the meeting. My boss pulled me aside and told me that this guy Greg, who I used to work with, asked him if he could work with me instead of Letitia."

"I didn't think you had anyone but those interns working with you."

"I don't right now," I said with a devilish grin.

"So what did your boss say?"

"He didn't say anything definite, but he hinted that if I keep doing good work and Letitia keeps screwing up, he might reassign some of her markets to me. My goal is to have a whole team in place by the time this other guy, Peter, gets back from disability."

"He's the guy with kidney cancer?"

"Yeah, I used to call him Pathetic Dog Owner in my head."

"Speaking of dogs and your competitive streak, are you planning to do any other races this year?"

"I hadn't planned to," I said. "Are there many others to do?"

"Oh yeah, there seems to always be a couple pink ribbon runs." I thought about Jane's disdain for the pink ribbon brigade and smiled to myself. "There's a triathlon to feed the homeless, a walk for AIDS research, there's one for the ASPCA. We should do that and take the dogs with us."

"That might be fun." The idea of raising money for orphaned animals appealed to me. I touched my toes and continued to stretch out my muscles. I could feel Sebastian watching me and held the stretch.

"And then there's always the big brain tumor run."

I stood up and spun around. "There's a race to help people with brain cancer? When is that? Could I still sign-up?"

Sebastian strapped his prosthetic back on and looked at

me, head akimbo. My heart skipped a beat. "Why that race in particular?"

"I met a little boy. He had a huge dent in the side of his head, but he was so…" I sat down and extended my legs out to rest on the bench next to Sebastian. I recalled how free Rory had been when we played with his little men, "… innocent. And his mother. She was such a mess."

"So, it's personal." Sebastian played with the stitching on my running shoes, almost touching my feet. "I think if everyone knew a cancer patient, we wouldn't need to go begging for research funds."

"I always thought cancer only affected old people, but the people I've met were just… well… people."

"At least you met people, got to know them. I was so angry for so long I could barely speak at all. It wasn't until after the leg was gone and I was well into PT that I realized how many of us there are wandering around out here." Sebastian stared at the fading azaleas without seeing them.

I wondered who he was thinking about. Did they make it?

When he came back to the present, Sebastian whispered, "I'd been afraid of stuff all my life, but I never knew to be afraid of getting cancer in my twenties. If I hadn't fallen off that ladder and broken my tibia, it may have been too late."

"They found the cancer when you broke your leg? Wow, that's rough."

Sebastian untied and retied my shoelace twice before he replied, "Yeah, it was. How did they find yours?"

"I collapsed at the gym. I had symptoms, but I'd been ignoring them."

Sebastian started to say something just as my phone rang in my pocket. Tom Roberts came up on the caller ID. Anxiety gripped my heart. *Oh no, she's dead.* "Excuse me, I need to take this." I jumped up and stepped behind a tree. "I'll just be a sec," I said as I answered the phone.

"Lara?"

"Jane?" My heart raced in my chest. "Are you okay? Why are calling from Tom's phone?"

"He changed the name on the account. Now his name comes up whenever I make calls." Resentment dripped through the phone line. "He's out with that Candace looking at lots. Anyway, I did some more digging on the Internet about those mines in Alders. Did you make an appointment with that lawyer?"

"I'm driving up to see him on Tuesday. Do you want to come with me?"

"I'd love to, but I'm still under house arrest. Do you want to come here for lunch today?"

"I'm sorry, I'm out." I took a deep breath. "I'm out with a friend."

"Sebastian?" Jane teased. She was obviously enjoying making me squirm.

"Yes," I replied coolly. I felt my cheeks getting hot.

"Don't let me keep you. Call me later and tell me all about it."

I tucked the phone back into my jacket pocket, returned to the picnic table, and took a sip of cold water from my water bottle. I wanted to splash it on my face.

"Sorry about that."

"Vanessa?" Sebastian asked. He poured water into a collapsible bowl for Mitzi.

"Actually, that was my friend, Jane, on the phone. One of those people I met during treatment. We used to go out for lunch every once in a while but she can't really go out much anymore." I sat down and pulled my knees up under my chin. "The traditional treatments didn't work. Her doctor—he's a great guy—found this new drug that's in its final trials. She won't even try it. They self-insure and she says it would bankrupt her family's business. You should hear her rant on about how she and her father worked too hard to get the company to where it is today to let freakin' lung cancer take it away from them."

"How long does she have?" Sebastian asked.

"I'm not really sure."

"It was nice of you to befriend her, especially with your mom passing away and all. That's a lot for you to handle in a year."

I knew Sebastian was trying to be nice by showing concern. Normal people love their parents and would need comforting after they died. I was not normal people. I was twisted and strange inside. I had to accept that and move on. "Actually, that was one of the reasons she called. Jane keeps bugging me to meet with the lawyer that handled my grandparents' estate."

Sebastian laid his hand on my shoulder and turned toward me. I hadn't noticed the golden flecks in his hazel eyes before. "You should go. See the lawyer. Finish this thing."

I hugged my knees tighter to my chest. The idea of going back to Alders was terrifying. What if it didn't live up to my memories?

Sebastian gave my shoulder a little squeeze. "Do you want me to go with you?" His hand felt wonderful on my shoulder. I wanted him to touch me but I didn't want the memory of Dale to be in the room with us when that happened.

I jumped up and shook out my legs. "Look, the snack bar is opening. You want an ice cream?"

Sebastian nodded like he understood that I needed to stop

talking about Alders and Mama and everything else that had happened to me. He began to pull himself up to a standing position. "Chocolate or vanilla?"

"I'll go." I pulled my wallet out of Barkis's pack. "I want to see if they have jimmies."

"Jimmies?" He rolled his eyes. "What part of New England are you from, anyway? Do you call water fountains 'bubblers,' too?"

"The great state of New Hampshire. And yes, they are bubblers. They bubble." I sauntered over to the snack bar distinctly aware of Sebastian watching me walk away and exactly how well my running shorts showed off my rear end.

28

Alders

ane was right. Sebastian was right. I couldn't put off
meeting with my grandfather's lawyer any longer. I needed
to climb that mountain. I didn't know what I would find;
it could have been a dragon or Shangri La. I had to climb
to the top to find out. Even though both Jane and Sebastian
volunteered to keep me company on the four-hour drive up
to Alders, in the end, I decided to take Sebastian's advice
and take Barkis. When I returned to the town where I had
been happiest, I needed a companion that both loved me and
didn't talk.

Spring dawdled in the mountains. The azaleas in my
apartment complex already had their gaudy Easter dresses
on. The azalea and mountain laurel along narrow route 934
were still dreaming of spring. The only life along the whiplash
turns blasted out of the mountainsides was the ephemeral
redbud dancing between the pines and the occasional
dogwood reaching its lobed fingers over the road. I followed

the few hundred feet of pavement I could see at a time until the road hugged the mountain around a blind curve and opened out over a narrow valley. Alders was tucked in the valley like a sapphire in a pile of mica. Below me I could see the rusting machinery of the abandoned asbestos works. Someone was using the employee parking lot to store broken down school buses and a handful of smashed mail trucks.

As if I had been there the day before, I still recognized the plain granite pillar that marked the turn off for Alders. Barkis let out a bark and dove under the dashboard as I wrenched the wheel to the left and seemingly drove into space. The road down was scarred with broken tree trunks and the rusting hulks of trucks that had tumbled down the mountainside. Savvy truckers knew to take the long route around to come up through Black Mountain. PawPaw always took the treacherously thrilling road down from the ridge. Ruby's short wheelbase and excellent suspension made bumping down the rutted road feel like a roller coaster rather than a death spiral.

A white-pillared bank, a Rite-Aid, and three churches marked the center of Alders. If the residents wanted to shop in a big box store or see a movie, they had to drive almost an hour over the mountain roads to Asheville. I found the lawyer's office tucked between a bead shop and Hispanic market in the neat block of brick shops that were as old as the town. I pulled into a spot directly in front of the wide front window. The name William Longley, III, Esq. was painted in gilt and black letters across the bubbled glass. The paint on the final "I" was still sharp.

I collected my laptop and purse from the backseat but didn't go inside right away. Barkis needed to take a potty break on the tiny grassy area beside the parking lot and I needed a moment to gather my courage. An enormous fichus tree dominated the many paned windows along the front of the offices. It was easily twice the age of the young man sitting at a massive mahogany desk. Dark shelves, sagging with moldering law books, lined the office walls, and moth-eaten oriental rugs covered the worn yellow pine floors. The young man and his sleek twenty-first century laptop seemed out of place in the nineteenth century furnishings. Once Barkis was relieved and packed back in the car, I pushed open the glass-paneled door. A bell tinkled happily over my head. The room smelled of stale cigarettes and late nights.

The young man jumped up and thrust his hand out to me. He was dressed in jeans and a rumpled white oxford open at the neck. I doubted his grandfather would approve. "You must be Ms. Blaine. How was your drive up?"

"It was fine," I replied, taking his hand.

"Would you like a cup of coffee? Or an espresso? I have a great little espresso machine."

"I would love a latte."

He whisked a pile of folders off a black lacquered chair with a school crest emblazoned across the back piece and pulled it up to his desk. "You sit right down and rest a minute. I'll be right back." He stepped into an alcove to the side of the room. A moment later I heard the whir of a burr grinder and the click of a doser. Mr. Longley spoke loudly over the hiss of the espresso machine, "I owe you an apology, Ms. Blaine. I was unaware of the situation with your property until your stepfather showed up shouting at me."

"So was I," I called back. He emerged from the alcove kitchen and handed me a hand-thrown mug with a leaf drawn in the foam of the latte. "Thank you, Mr. Longley."

"Please, it's Bill. My granddad was Mr. Longley. Even my

daddy was Billy."

"And I go by Lara. My name may appear as Larissa in the paperwork, but I had it legally changed."

"I saw that." He set his tiny espresso cup down and opened his laptop. "I know you probably don't remember me, but I remember you."

"You remember me?"

"My mom used to say you looked like a little angel sitting in the front pew beside your grandmother and my brother, Jimmy, said you were the smartest girl in the first grade." The little girl that lived in Alders all those years before was not completely gone. Happy memories of me had been living in the minds of the people here.

"Jimmy Longley? Does he have a big cowlick on the back of his head?"

"Totally bald now. He's a lawyer, too. Lives out west with his third wife."

I took a sip of my latte then placed it on the corner of the desk. I was afraid of what Bill would say to my next question and didn't want to risk dropping the lovely pottery. "What exactly did my stepfather tell you?"

The young lawyer tilted back in his chair and smiled broadly. "He had some interesting ideas. He claimed that he had right of survivorship to all the holdings and got quite *upset* when I pointed out that they were never your mother's to begin with. He tried to tell me that you had abandoned your mother—"

"Bullshit! I—"

Bill shrugged. "I didn't pay him any mind. I remember my mother saying how broken up your grandparents were after you moved away, and, well, some unkind things about your mother." Bill sat up and clicked his laptop to life. "Anyway, he said he was going to make you sign over the property. But I take it, since you're here and he's not, that didn't happen?"

"No. No, it didn't."

"My granddad was the executor of your grandparents' will and set up the agreement with the Methodist church."

"What agreement with the Methodist church?"

Bill shuffled through a stack of yellowing file folders on his desk. "Hold on, it's here somewhere. To be honest with you, when I took over the practice after my daddy's stroke two years back, I never looked into the history of that house. Daddy had a lot of irons in the fire that needed to be attended to right quick. I haven't even started to explore what's in those files over there." I followed his eyes to a wall of walnut file cabinets. "I'm afraid my daddy was not very organized."

I took another tentative sip of my latte as he continued to flip through the file folders. Bill was an excellent barista. "You might not have realized this, but I wasn't aware that my grandparents even had a will, never mind that I was the beneficiary, until I received those papers."

"My grandfather was supposed to inform you of your inheritance when you turned eighteen, but apparently we didn't have contact information for your mother."

"We moved a lot."

Bill drained his espresso cup. "I take it your mother was estranged from her parents?"

I nodded. "You could say that." I clicked the heels of my red shoes together for courage. "Does it say anything in the files about who my father was?"

Bill put a hand on top of the stack of files. "No, there isn't much about either of your parents in the files. I have a copy of your birth certificate and social security card but the father line is blank."

Typical, Mama. Just leave him out all together. Why think about his feelings? "How much do you know about my family?"

"Not a huge amount. I know that your grandparents and my grandparents were good friends and that you lived here for a while when you were little." Bill found the file he was looking for. He ran his hand through his sandy hair as if struggling to form the right words. "My grandfather was a good man but an unconventional lawyer."

"Unconventional? Is that what you meant when you referred to an agreement with a church?"

"Yeah, well, in order to cover the cost of maintaining the house and the property taxes, my grandfather allowed the Methodists to use the place to house unwed mothers."

"Your grandfather had a sense of humor."

Bill blushed and played with his empty cup. "Like I said, the church was using it to house unwed mothers, and for the past few years, they've been letting immigrant families stay there until they get on their feet. I can give them thirty days notice to vacate."

"No, don't do that," I said. "Not yet." I liked the idea of a family living in my grandparent's house. Grammy would have liked that. "I don't know what I want to do with the house. I won't be living in it, but I'm not sure if I want to sell it either."

"You don't need to make any decisions right away. I'll speak to the church council and get a full accounting of what they have done for upkeep and get an appraisal of the property value."

"Thank you, Bill. That would be helpful." I took out my laptop. "What I'm most interested in today is the other holdings. Exactly how much of a share do I own in those old mines?"

"That I know." Bill presented me with an exhaustive inventory of the holdings. "You have a small interest in the Howell mine and a large share of the old 43G2 mine."

"Why does that sound familiar?" I rustled through my memory banks. I knew I recognized that name.

"Do you know anything about minerals?"

I smiled sweetly at Bill. "Quite a bit actually," I replied.

"Then perhaps you've heard of olivine."

Olivine occurs naturally along with mica and feldspar. The other minerals have a steady market value but are relatively common minerals. Olivine, on the other hand, is rare. "Aren't people using that for carbon dioxide abatement?"

Bill's eyebrows shot up. "You do know your minerals."

"It's part of my work." I sat up straighter in my chair. "How much of that mine do I own?"

"51%," Bill said with a sly smile. "In your absence, my father reinvested your dividends." Although the Longleys were unconventional lawyers, they had been excellent executors. Those old mines made me a millionaire several times over.

***

On the way out of town, I drove past my grandparents' house, now my house. The house looked drab. It needed some paint around the windows and a good power washing. There was a blue Buick parked in front. A woman jumped out as I parked across the street and let Barkis out.

"Miss Larissa?" the woman said. "I'd recognize you anywhere. You look just like your grandmother in the pictures hanging in my mother-in-law's hallway."

"Should I know you?" I asked.

"I'm Jillian Longley. Bill's mom? He called me and said he

had a feeling you might come by the old place. We can't go inside, but we can poke around the yard. Do you remember me? My parents were the Oystermans?"

"I'm sorry."

"Never you mind. You were just a little bitty thing last I saw you."

"Did you know my grandparents well?"

"Sure, sure. My mom and Elise played bridge every week."

"Did you know my mother?"

Jillian's face colored. She looked away into the backyard. "Of course. It was a very small town back then."

"Did you know my father?"

"No, I can't say that I did. Your mother was away for several years and when she came back you were already walking. Oh, how your grandparents doted on you!" A renewed sense of loss tugged at my heart. Strangers had known I was loved, when I hadn't. "Oh, listen to me going on. Let me show you what's been done around here. You'll see the house has been made serviceable but the ladies of the church have maintained Elise's garden. Just the way she left it."

Jillian led me up the driveway to the backyard. It was exactly the way I remembered it. The rose bushes needed trimming, the lilies were bumping into each other, and lamb's ears covered every open space, but it was still Grammy's garden. For a moment, I felt like I was still six years old and nothing bad had happened yet.

29
Out to Pasture

My stomach dropped as soon as the plane's landing gear rumbled beneath my feet and thudded into position. Vanessa lifted the window shade to watch the plane emerge from clouds. The morning sun sparkled off the fishing boats and sailboats in Boston harbor. "Wow, we're coming in over the ocean."

"Several of the runways go out on long jetties." I checked the security of my seat belt for the tenth time in the last two hours. "One year, a plane slid right off in icy conditions. It was all over the news."

Vanessa put her hand over mine. "It's okay, honey. I'm here."

The plane banked slightly and landed with only a minor bump. An electronic symphony erupted around us as the businessmen fired up their smart phones. The 6:30 flight between Charlotte and Boston allowed them to fly up for a meeting and be home to watch their favorite sitcoms. We were some of the few people who had luggage with them. I stayed in my seat until the suits left, then eased my bag out from beneath the seat. I refused to put it in the overhead compartment; its contents were too valuable to me.

"So how long will it take us to drive up to Hawthorne?" Vanessa asked as we walked through the terminal toward the rental car desks.

"It's about two hours. I thought we could stop in Portsmouth and get some lunch and go on from there. I thought you might like poking around the outlets in Kittery, Maine tomorrow morning. We don't have to be back here until late afternoon."

"Yes, please!" Vanessa squealed. "Oh, can we rent a convertible? It's such a gorgeous day."

"Sure, I had forgotten how lovely it is in New England in July. I know, we'll get off in Seabrook and drive up Route 1 to Portsmouth. I bet we could find some fried clams somewhere. We don't have to get to Hawthorne at any particular time."

"Not really." Vanessa cleared her throat and gave me a guilty look. "We have an appointment at two."

I stopped in the middle of the terminal and demanded. "What did you do?"

Vanessa pushed me over to the side so we weren't mowed down by the stream of people heading for baggage claim. "I told you, I am not going to let you confront your stepfather alone. That's why I came with you, and that's why I called the police department in Hawthorne and told them we're coming."

"He knows I'm coming?" I turned to walk back down the terminal ramp. "If Dale knows I'm coming, I might as well get back on the plane now." Vanessa grabbed my arm. I shook her off. "I should have let Sebastian come with me."

"Yeah, right. And bringing a man wouldn't piss off your stepfather at all." Vanessa rolled her eyes and hooked my bag over her arm. "He won't know you're coming. The lovely woman I spoke to was very understanding. You keep telling me that your stepfather has that town in his back pocket but that was not the impression I got from the police dispatcher. She made it sound like Dale is a bit of a joke these days."

"Maybe," I replied. I stepped over to an empty gate area and sat down. My head was spinning. "Frankly, I'm not sure he was ever as powerful as he made himself out to be. That psychologist you bullied me into seeing says I may have inflated his power in my mind over the years."

Vanessa sat down beside me and put the bag down at my feet. "Are you sure you want to do this? I can call that lady at the police station and tell her we're not coming. We could spend the day in Boston instead. I'm sure there's lots of stuff to do here."

"No," I said. I grabbed my bag and stood up. "I need to see Dale's face when I tell him what I've done."

"That lawyer in Alders could do it for you."

"He could," I replied. "But according to that psychologist, I need to 'get closure.' I need to go back and see that old bedroom. See the farm. Tell Dale off to his face."

"All right then, let's go get a car. I want to try fried clams from a place right on the ocean."

***

Anxiety made my fried clams repeat in my mouth as we passed Jonatt's Dairy on the outskirts of Hawthorne. Mr. Jonatt's herd was bunched up along the stone wall waiting to be led back across the street to the barns for the midday milking. The overpowering smell of manure made me wish we had not splurged on the convertible after all.

"I don't know, Vanessa. Maybe this is a mistake."

"You need to do this. Do you want to go over what you're going to say again?" Vanessa's experience and training had been invaluable over the last few weeks. She and the psychologist at the Women's Crisis Center helped me focus my anger into words and actions. Once I said the words, "Dale raped me and my mother was complicit" a few hundred times, the actions began to lose their power over me.

"We've come this far," Vanessa said. "You had that lawyer draw up all those papers for you. Come on; let's see this thing through. Goodness, look how green it is here."

"It's all white in the winter. Cold and white."

The library and the Congregational church looked the same when I drove through the center of town. I pulled up in front of the municipal complex, which housed the police and fire departments as well as the tax collector. A tall deputy with a military crew cut greeted us in the parking lot. "Larissa! Welcome home!"

I got out of the car and shook his hand. "It's Lara Blaine now. Thank you Deputy—"

"Sanborn."

"Dickie Sanborn?" I stepped back and tried to imagine the imposing man standing in front of me as a gawky kid with a bad haircut. "You look so different."

"A decade and two tours in Afghanistan change a guy." Deputy Sanborn smiled. I now saw the boy who sat behind me in trigonometry. "Hawthorne and Whiteneck share my time."

"You're the half officer of Hawthorne's one and a half person police force?"

"Yup. Wow, you don't look that different than you did in

high school. Still as skinny as ever."

"We just did a triathlon," Vanessa interjected.

"I'm sorry," I said pulling Vanessa into the conversation. "Dickie Sanborn, this is my friend Vanessa Klaitner."

"You spoke to Evelyn on the phone," Dickie said. "She said you requested an escort out to Dale's place?" Deputy Sanborn and Vanessa spoke for a few minutes about the logistics of the afternoon while I looked at the center of town. It was shockingly the same as when I left. The Congregational church needed to be painted, the convenience store had changed names but still had a sign advertising homemade doughnuts, and the funeral home's window boxes were clogged with weeds.

"Lara," Vanessa said touching me on the shoulder. I jumped a foot. "Are you all right? You need to go inside and fill out some paperwork."

I followed Vanessa and Deputy Sanborn inside. As soon as I walked through the door, a plump woman with an awful wig scurried out of a back room. "Larissa Scott. As I live and breathe. We never thought we'd see you again. Becky Patterson is going to be sick that she's missing you!"

"Miss Patterson? Is she *still* at the library?"

"Yeah, but she and John, oh, you wouldn't know John—they got married after you, well, left. They're visiting Colton at UCLA."

"Her son is in college?"

"He's a history professor. Becky is so proud of him. But she talks about you as much as she does him. She was so glad to hear you were doing so well in North Carolina."

"You all know I live in North Carolina?"

"Well," Dickie said. "for years Old Dale's been telling everyone down at the Rusty Bucket that you're an ungrateful thief of a daughter." I opened my mouth to protest. "Oh, no one listens to him anymore. But when he mentioned to Nate Jewitt that you changed your name to Lara Blaine, Nate googled you. Congratulations on the new job."

"So much for hiding," Vanessa whispered in my ear. "You can be googled."

"What brings you back to Hawthorne after all this time?" Evelyn asked. "Did you come back to sort through your mother's things? There can't be much left after the fire."

"Fire?" I asked. "What fire?"

Dickie and Evelyn exchanged meaningful looks. "I told you, Dick," Evelyn said. "That Dale is full of shit." She turned back to me. "There was a fire at the farm the same weekend you *borrowed* Dale's truck. Your mother said she was doing some sewing and dropped a lit cigarette in a pile of old papers, but Dale claimed you tried to burn down the house."

"I never—"

"Nobody believed you did," Dickie said. "You would have burned the whole place down if you did it at all."

"I don't mean to speak ill of the dead, but your mother's story never did make sense. Why would Dale store old papers in an upstairs bedroom? Everyone knew that roof leaked like a sieve."

"Oh, I don't know about that. He kept all sorts of weird things up there."

I felt faint. *Upstairs bedroom?* Mama's note finally made sense. She said she fixed it so Dale wouldn't know I took his money. I thought she meant she had lied to him about where the money had gone or replaced it.

It hit me. I'd been looking over my shoulder for eleven years while no one had been looking for me. Mama had been covering my tracks all this time.

After some more chitchat, I signed an official request for a police escort and Deputy Sanborn followed us out to the farm in his cruiser. This part of town had changed. Strip malls lined the road between the center of town and Dale's farm.

"This doesn't look right," I said. I slowed down as we got to the beginning of Dale's property. There weren't any cows in the front fields. Judging from the amount of clover growing in the grass, there hadn't been any cows in those fields for several years. I'd planned to leave the rental car at the gate in the stone wall and walk up the long driveway, but the gate was open. Buttercups and Queen Anne's lace were growing though the rusted, broken pipes that made up the cattle stop in the ground. I turned in and slowly drove up the rutted, muddy driveway.

"Something's definitely wrong," I said. "When I lived here, Dale had fresh gravel spread on this driveway every year. And where are the cows? They should have been milked and in these front fields by now."

"You said the land was in foreclosure," Vanessa said. "Would you graze cattle on land you're losing to the bank?"

"Bill Longley said that according to the State of New Hampshire, Dale supposedly still has 500 head of dairy cows. That's obviously a made up number but I thought there'd still be a hundred or so out here." As we got closer to the house, we finally saw a few cows in the nursery field, although none had calves or obvious mastitis. They looked old and dry.

Dickie pulled around us and stopped in the circular driveway. He got out and signaled for Vanessa and me to stay in the car. He walked up a worn path in the weedy lawn and peeked in the window along the front porch. He returned and said, "He's passed out in the chair if you want to look around. I'll stay here and keep an eye on him."

The house looked different than in my memories—a simple farmhouse with a narrow porch, old twelve-paned windows, and blistered white paint. It was neither as prosperous or ghastly as I remembered. The patch of grass in front of the porch needed mowing and the lilac bush at the eastern corner was covered with blight. I got out and walked around to the back of the house. The addition was gone. Grass had slowly reclaimed the glass and rubble-filled foundation hole. Vanessa came up beside me and put her hand on my shoulder. "Is this where the fire was?"

"My bedroom was right here. It's just a hole in the ground now." I pointed to where tar paper and particle board covered the opening to where the addition had once stood. "Look, he never even fixed where the door was."

"This happened eleven years ago?" Vanessa asked. "Isn't that going to leak without siding?"

"Dale's not big on patching leaks. The roof always leaked in this section. I'm surprised it burned at all." *Mama must have used gasoline or something.*

I walked further on to the close barn and pulled on the heavy door. The rusted wheels resisted at first but rolled when I gave the door a shove. The leather thong attached to the bare bulb still hung from the ceiling. The doors at the far end stood open to the backfields. The barn was bright and completely empty. When I was a teenager there had been hundreds of cows in the barn. The cows were gone. The milking machines were gone. The bales of hay were gone. Even the rats were gone.

A thick layer of dust coated my hands and knees as I climbed up the old metal ladder to the hayloft. It didn't appear that anyone had been up there since I left. Beneath the southern window, my yellow leatherette beanbag chair was still there with an old tattered copy of *The Handmaid's Tale* still on the edge. A family of mice had moved in at some point and spread tiny foam pellets in a swath across the wide planked floor.

Vanessa poked her head through the hole in the floor. "You okay up there?"

"Yeah, it's just as I left it."

Vanessa stood on the ladder and looked around. "It's like an old western up here."

"More like a bad horror movie," I replied. "Come on, let's go over to the house. I want to find out what happened to the cows."

"Did you have a horse?"

"There were horses, but I never rode them. They lived in the barn in the far pasture. There was an old white one that used to get drunk eating the rotten apples that dropped from the trees in the orchard over there."

"No way," Vanessa said. We walked around the side of the house laughing only to find Dale pointing a shotgun at Dickie Sanborn's chest. Dale was wearing the same plaid flannel shirt he'd worn when he came to North Carolina over sweat pants with holes in the knees and old man slippers.

"Put the gun down, Dale," Dickie said.

"Get off my land, Sanborn," Dale shouted.

Dickie had his hand on his service revolver. "Put the gun down, Dale. I'm here on official police business."

"You here to serve me more tax liens or more papers from the bank?"

"Not today," Dickie said. He signaled for us to get back. "I'm here with Miss Blaine."

Dale seemed to notice me for the first time. He pointed

the gun at the ground but kept it in his hand. "You finally sign those papers?"

Dickie moved quickly to wrestle the shotgun from Dale's hand. It seemed remarkably easy to do. He nodded for me to move forward. I took my time climbing the three flagstone steps. Up close I saw Dale's eyes were bloodshot and his hands shook. I waved a large envelope in front of his face. "I do have papers for you." A smirk spread across Dale's sunken mouth making his gray stubble sparkle in the slanted afternoon sun.

Deputy Sanborn stepped to one side, staying close at hand.

"They're not the papers you think they are, though. That very nice lawyer down in Alders helped me with them." I took a step closer to Dale. He edged back toward the open door. "You really shouldn't have been such an asshole to him. He was very motivated to help me."

"I deserve that property in North Carolina!" Dale shouted.

"Don't yell at me, old man!" I stepped to the side and looked through the door into the kitchen. Plates filled the sink and covered the counter. "Anyway, your little visit to Bill Longley got us both thinking about property and rights of survivorship."

"She was my wife. I supported that bitch for fifteen years. I should get what's coming to me."

"Hell yeah, you deserve what's coming to you!" Vanessa yelled from beside the car. The sunset was the same color as her hair.

Dickie Sanborn looked back at her. "Get in the car. I can't keep an eye on Dale and you at the same time."

"Sorry Deputy," Vanessa said. "But this guy is a real ass." She got in the car.

"Anyway," I said as I took another step closer to Dale. His Brut cologne made my heart race. "Bill did a little search for any property that was in Mama's name that I might have claim to."

Dale spoke to Dickie when he said, "I was her husband! I should get anything that she had coming to her."

"Shut up, I'm talking!" Dale backed up into the porch post. "Dickie, you'll want to hear this. My lawyer finally got around to doing a search on this property, and low and behold, along with the second and third mortgages, you don't even own it anymore. The bank does."

"Damn banks. I'll show them." Dale wiped his face with his palm. He was sweating like a pig. "Once I get those properties in North Carolina, I can stop them from bleeding me dry."

Dickie Sanborn turned to me with a grin. I could see the gears working in his head. "Larissa, why are you here?"

"I wanted to see his face when I told him I've bought and sold his precious farm out from under him."

"To who?"

"A wind power operation."

"You can't do that!" Dale shouted. "I still own the house and the north forty acres."

"Yes, you do. For some bizarre reason you never mortgaged that land."

"It won't perk," Dickie said. "It isn't worth anything."

"Great, you can sit right here on this porch and watch the big blades go round and round over your personal swamp."

"Tell him the other stuff," Vanessa yelled from the car. "Tell him what you came to say." I turned to look at Vanessa. Her cheeks were flushed with anger and she was heaving breaths through flared nostrils. Her passion both fueled and quenched mine.

I spun back to Dale, ready to blast him with my prepared statement, and saw a feeble old man imprisoned on his hardscrabble farm. "You know what, I had a whole speech prepared, but I don't need to tell you to go to hell anymore. You're already there." I took a step back and looked out at the weed-ridden fields. "Look at this place. Look at you. You're an old, used up pathetic wreck. Nobody loves you. Your money is gone. Your power is gone. You're all alone."

"Ooh, listen to the big shot! Does it make you feel good to yell at an old man?"

I thought about it for a second. A sense of calm resolve washed over me. "Yup. It does. I do feel better." I turned around and patted Deputy Sanborn on the arm. "Thanks, Dickie. I appreciate you coming out here with us. We can go now. The lawyers can take care of the details of the sale. I'll settle up the back taxes with the town once we close."

I walked to the rental car and climbed in. I didn't look back. I told Vanessa to drive to Portsmouth where we'd find a hotel. I didn't want to spend another minute in Hawthorne.

30
New Digs

ebastian lived in a cookie-cutter condo complex, very much like the one I lived in, with rows of unused front porches and empty patches of grass behind each unit. The labyrinth of interconnected streets allowed us to run three miles without actually straying more than a half mile from his front door. One steamy evening in late July, Sebastian and I raced back to his door in hopes of outrunning the leaden clouds in the western sky.

We didn't make it.

We lurched into Sebastian's place and stood dripping in the tiled foyer. "I didn't know we were getting a hurricane today," Sebastian wheezed. He released Mitzi from her leash. She gave a quick shake then plopped down in the center of the living room.

Barkis yanked the leash out of my hand and spun around in circles trying to catch the flapping leash handle. I couldn't get a firm grip on his slippery dog flesh to unclasp his leash.

"We don't get many hurricanes in July and they usually come from the east anyway." I grabbed the leash to get Barkis to stop spinning. It was making me dizzy.

"Hyperbole, sweetie. Hyperbole." Sebastian hopped over to the couch on his running leg and threw himself down. "Water, must have water."

Barkis ran into the kitchen, back into the living room, and rolled over at my feet for a belly rub. I couldn't resist his slobbery smile. I slipped out of my sodden shoes and squatted down beside him to rub his belly.

Sebastian hauled himself up off the couch and hobbled into the kitchen. He ran far better than he walked on his running leg. "I can see whom you really love," he teased. "I'm dying of thirst over here while the dog gets a belly rub?" He returned a moment later with two tall glasses of iced tea.

I gratefully accepted my glass and joined Sebastian on the couch. Every available inch of Sebastian's walls was covered with books. I couldn't tell what color the walls were behind the cinder block and board shelving. "How long did it take you to build those book shelves?"

"Year and years." Sebastian slung his arm loosely over my shoulder. "The first set of cinder blocks traveled with me from my place in graduate school. I add a shelf or two every year or so."

"How do you keep them organized if you just keep tacking on shelves?"

He pulled me closer to him and I leaned my head against his shoulder as I continued to look at the books.

"How do you ever find anything? I'd have built the shelves all at once." A post-run torpor made my muscles feel heavy and loose. I let my eyelids droop. "I want a library in my house."

Sebastian settled into the couch and laid his head against the soft cushion. "You still thinking of moving closer to work?"

"I don't know, maybe."

"Why don't you buy one of the houses your buddy Tom is building? Those sounded cool. Then you could put bookshelves in every room. You could even get one of those antique card catalogs to keep track of everything," Sebastian murmured.

I imagined what it would be like to have every wall lined with books. I could keep books in the bathroom in a steam proof case. My growing pile of cookbooks could live in a glass front cabinet to keep food and grease from getting on their pages. The living room could have floor to ceiling bookcases with a brass railing along the top for a sliding ladder. I was imagining a glass-topped coffee table that could display large format illustrations when I realized Sebastian was snoring. I snuggled into his shoulder and drifted off to the sound of his heart beating. When I'd imagined us sleeping together at some point in the future, this wasn't exactly what I had in mind.

∗∗∗

Once the seed had been planted in my brain, I wanted to build my dream house as soon as possible. I woke up in the middle of the night with ideas. I wanted a skylight in the bathroom that let in fresh air, lots of white tile, and an oversized laundry room off the garage with a walk-in shower where I could easily bathe Barkis.

I made an appointment to talk to the illustrious Candace to get the process started, but when I arrived at Babcock Construction, Tom met me in the reception area. "Lara! I saw your name on the appointment book. Are you really serious about building?"

"Yes, it's time for me to move out of my place. You've told me so much about your new Rivers Edge project, I thought I'd check it out." I looked around the reception area. "I'm supposed to meet with Candace at 4:00?"

"I'll handle this one myself," Tom replied. Ever his mother's son, he was not asking but telling me what would happen. "After all, you're practically family now." He put a long arm around my shoulder and led me down a wide corridor. "If you don't mind, we can talk in Mom's office. Candy's on the phone in mine."

He opened a set of double doors at the end of the hall that opened into a vast office. The room was a showcase of Jane's accomplishments from the wall of awards to the collection of pictures of Tom through the years. The sleek blond desk and console were piled with files and tubes of blueprints. The room had a stale smell about it. When Tom and I sat down on the low cream leather sofa, I noticed two dead flies under the glass coffee table.

"These aren't very practical," he said when I showed him the list of things I wanted in my house.

"I'm not interested in practical. I'm not worried about resale value. I want to build a house for me."

"Do you really want a library with floor to ceiling book shelves? A rolling ladder?"

"You need a ladder to get to the top shelves," I replied. "Would it really be that expensive to have a fenced in backyard and a low maintenance lawn?"

"No, not really. A heated two car garage, very expensive." Tom pulled out several stock home plans and showed me how they could be modified for my needs. By the end of the hour, we had come up with a plan for a two-bedroom bungalow that fit both my needs and his vision for the neighborhood.

As I gathered up my copies of the preliminary sketches, Tom put his hand on my arm. "You know, Lara, I'm really glad you came into Mom's life. I'm sorry if I was a jerk to you. I resented that Mom was talking to you about her feelings instead of to me."

"She doesn't really say that much about her feelings to me."

"Well, she talks about you all the time at home. I'm a little jealous."

"That's funny. She talks about you to me all the time—at least when she's not needling me about my social life and giving me career advice."

Tom digested this for a moment and chuckled to himself as he gathered up his notes. "So she treats you like the daughter she never had? Does she give you crap about your clothes?"

"All the time."

"She's so full of shit. She wasn't always so sleek and sophisticated. I have pictures of her as a flower child to prove it." He opened the door for me. "Anyway, I'm glad you're her friend. I hope we can stay in touch, you know, after."

"Me too, Tom. We could both use a friend these days."

✳✳✳

Jane's house was less than a mile away from the Babcock Construction offices. I drove up and parked in front of the garage. A unfamiliar woman was struggling to lift a box from the back of the Ellery Home Healthcare van. I jumped out and asked, "What's going on? Where's Nancy?"

The nurse gave up her effort and turned to me. "Nancy needed a break so I came to check on your mother today. Is she expecting you?"

I didn't correct her mistake. I pulled the box marked "Medical Supplies" from the van and carried it toward the house. "Why aren't you inside watching her? Is she sleeping?"

"She's up, although still in her pajamas. She won't get dressed." The nurse opened the door for me. "You can put that on the dining table."

"Put something down first. I don't want to scratch the table."

The visiting nurse rolled her eyes and moved a placemat over to the end of the table. "I guess that's a good idea. She bites our heads off if we as much as touch anything in this house. She's one tough old bird."

I took the woman by the arm and led her back to the heavily carved front door. "Have you done just about everything you needed to do today? Good, we wouldn't want to keep you from your other sick and dying patients then." I shoved the nurse out the door and locked it. I watched her pull her cell phone out and gesture wildly as she spoke to someone on the other end of the call. I had probably made things even more difficult between Jane and the visiting nurse service, but it felt good to kick the woman out.

I tossed my soft leather tote on the foyer table and walked through the house. Jane was on the brick patio wrapped in a light shawl. "Lara! What a wonderful surprise," Jane said with a wide smile as I opened the French doors. "Come. Sit. Did that awful woman finally leave?"

"She's gone," I said with a guilty smile. "I may have been a bit rude to her just now."

"Good. She was even worse than Nancy. She kept pestering me to get dressed and go for a walk."

"She left a box in the dining room. What's in it?"

"Isn't it lovely out today? I don't think I have ever seen the roses as beautiful as this year." Pale yellow roses dotted the low brick walls around the patio.

"Very pretty. I'm surprised you have yellow roses. Everything else is red." I brushed some dead leaves off the teak chaise lounge next to Jane and sat down.

"They were a mistake. I asked for Mister Lincolns. These are Julia Childs. That landscaper lost my account. If they can't get my yard right, how could I trust them to do my client's new plantings?"

"Are you warm enough? I could go find you a blanket."

"Lara, it's eighty degrees out. I'm not cold. We'll go in shortly and you can make me some of that tea your friend sent over. It was sweet of her to think of me."

"Mrs. Lee is a one woman eastern medicine advocacy board," I said with a smile. "Her daughter-in-law assures me her concoctions won't hurt you, and they usually taste pretty good."

"I told Sanjay that I was drinking her tea. He said that if it made my chest feel looser or made it easier to sleep, he was all for it. He's a good man." A small smile tickled Jane's lips. "Did I tell you he dropped by the other day?"

I took off my blazer and turned my face to the sun. "Your doctor made a house call? Were you having trouble breathing?"

"No more than usual. His daughter was playing tennis at the park down at the bottom of the hill, so he dropped by to see how I was doing." Jane picked up my blazer and ran her fingers over the linen. "Poor guy. It's hard on him. So many of his patients don't make it. I think he came here to take another run at convincing me to do that new drug trial, but I told him—no more treatments."

"But Jane."

"No. No more. I've made my peace with it. I'm not afraid." My heart twisted in my chest. "Sanjay tells me he can make me comfortable."

I looked out at the view from the patio. Red day lilies had replaced the tulips Jane and Tom planted around the pond. "I met with Tom this afternoon about building a house in River's Edge."

"How were things at the office?"

I recalled the dead flies under the coffee table. "I think your office misses you."

"They'll be fine. Tom has it under control." Jane adjusted the shawl around her shoulders. "Did he tell you that he and that Candace are thinking of getting married?"

"Really? They haven't been dating very long."

"I think he's worried about being alone. I don't think he'll end up going through with it." Jane shifted her feet to the ground. "Did you bring a copy of the plans?"

"I've got some preliminary sketches in my bag. I love the way they've designed the subdivision. I've decided to take one of the large lots that back up to the woods. It should be very safe to walk or run on those paths, and I'm psyched about having solar cells on the roof to heat my hot water."

"Tom has worked very hard on that project." Jane no longer sounded jealous of his success. "The company's in good hands." Jane sighed deeply. She sounded tired.

"How about some of that tea?" I asked. "Can I heat up some soup for you?"

"You and Tom, you're always trying to get me to eat something." Jane pulled herself up from the chaise and laboriously walked into the house. I could see that even walking a few steps had become difficult for Jane. I took her elbow.

"Come on, let me show you those sketches."

31
Riding the Cloud

Salmon morning light cast eerie shadows across the floor of the deserted Radiation Therapy foyer. I was disappointed that Lorraine wasn't at her post yet doling out information and support like butter mints. I was back at the Cancer Center for the last portion of my treatment plan, the all day internal radiation treatment. I had met with Dr. Obatu a few days before and he felt I had healed enough to tolerate this one last treatment. He told me that after that day, I would not need to see him again. I would see my regular oncologist for all my post-treatment care. I asked him for a list of other doctors I could see instead of Dr. Lander. I wanted someone as kind as Dr. Obatu taking care of me.

The glass doors swooshed open behind me. A woman walked in and stopped under the slowly spinning mobiles as if afraid to walk any further into the building. She rolled and unrolled a yellow pamphlet in her hands. I pulled an identical brochure out of my coat pocket and tapped it against the leg of my jeans. The woman whispered, "Are you here for brachytherapy too?" I nodded. "They said to wait in the foyer. Is this the foyer? And why do we have to be here so early? The hospital isn't even open yet." The woman shoved the brochure in her bag next to a sippy cup and a box of crayons. "Aren't you nervous? You don't look nervous."

"I'm trying not to think about it."

"I wish I could do that. I haven't been able to think about anything else for weeks. Part of me wants to get this over with as quickly as possible but mostly it scares the bejesus out of me." Anxiety leeched out of her like wisps of steam. "I was so petrified this morning, my husband had to pull me out of the car and march me up to the door like I do with our three year old."

I recalled how helpful the other patients had been that day in the orange waiting room when I was so nervous. I could be helpful. I tried to smile reassuringly. "We aren't supposed to eat anything but there are bottles of water here. Would you like some water?" I stepped around the corner into the atrium and returned with two bottles. "I'm Lara, by the way."

The woman took a bottle of water and sighed, "Cindy. My husband will be glad to know there's someone else here. He didn't want to leave me here by myself but he had to run home to get the kids off to camp. He'll be back later." The woman took a sip of water and seemed to be calming down. "Is your husband parking the car?"

"No, it's just me. No husband, no kids." A twinge shot through my heart. *I should have asked Sebastian to come with me to this appointment.* He could have understood and shared my anxiety. I didn't need to be alone. Cindy and I waited quietly turning over the bottles in our hands and the thoughts in our minds until a woman in a lab coat emerged from the morning gloom to lead us through the hospital maze to the basement-level treatment rooms. The Internal Radiotherapy suite was a puddle of light at the end of the dim hallways. A young nurse greeted us warmly and introduced herself as Rachel. She left Cindy in the small waiting area and led me to my treatment room for the day. Someone had taken pains to make the room comfortable with pictures on the walls and padded hangers for me to hang my clothes on. Still, no amount of decorating could mask the oppressive thump of the lead door that signaled that this was yet another place where my body would be subjected to forces the rest of humanity needed to be shielded from.

Nurse Rachel handed me a soft cotton gown and a pair of thick athletic socks. Before she left, she asked, "Are you alone?"

There was that question again. "Yes," I replied. "At least today."

"I only ask because Rosaria over in Dr. Obatu's office wrote an order for a sedative that will knock you out and make it impossible for you to drive yourself home. Would you like to use that?"

The word "no" reflexively crouched on my tongue. I stopped, swallowed, and asked, "What would you do?"

Nurse Rachel's perky smile didn't extend to her eyes. "I'll keep it here in case we need it."

I changed into the gown and took a moment to explore the room before Rachel returned. The hospital bed had been modified for the treatment. Instead of cold metal cups to hold my heels up in the air and leave my knees flopping around while the radioactive probe was irradiating my cervix, soft sleeves had been attached to the bed to support my calves. I tried to count off all the ways the hospital staff was trying to make me feel comfortable to stave off the growing sense of panic slithering up my spine like a serpent.

A voice came over the intercom asking me if I was ready. My voice echoed off the walls as I called back in the affirmative. A curtain retracted and exposed a thick glass panel set in the upper portion of the wall. I could see a mass of braids and a pair of soft brown eyes above the edge. A young woman stepped on a stool or step and waved to me through the glass. I felt like a zoo exhibit. The intercom crackled again then I heard, "Hi, I'm Taye, your dosimetrist. I'll be administering your treatment from in here."

"Okay," I called.

Taye covered her ears with her hands. "I can hear everything you say just fine. You can talk in your normal voice."

"Sorry," I said in a whisper. Taye gave me a thumbs up and turned to manipulate the controls.

Within a minute, Nurse Rachel came in to help me into bed. Once in position, she pulled several heated blankets out of a low drawer in the wall and draped them over my body and legs like a warm hug. "If you get cold, I can change these out for you. We can hear you in the control room so just call out if you need anything." Nurse Rachel struck me as being very sweet but also very young. It seemed wrong for this young woman with her cute blond ponytail and remnants of teenage acne to be ministering to people going through day long radiation treatments. I worried that any radiation exposure could damage her chances to have children. All the terrible things that residual radiation could do to her young body pinged through my brain as Rachel quietly reviewed the day's procedure while inserting an IV in my arm and clipping a pulse monitor to my finger.

The serpent of anxiety slithered into my brain. "This is really happening," it hissed. "They are going to jam a radioactive probe up inside you." The serpent coiled its tail around my chest until I couldn't get any air into my lungs. An alarm went off beside my head and Taye's disembodied voice echoed through the room. "Rachel, is she okay? Her heart rate is way up."

I screwed my eyes shut and attempted to take a calming breath. *Concentrate on the nurse. Don't zone out. Concentrate.* I hung from a narrow ledge of consciousness. My fingers were slipping. The treatment room became a tunnel. The crone stood over me again, poised to strike. The light from the tunnel's distant opening glinted off her speculum fingers. Outside in the sunshine, Nurse Rosaria called my name. I struggled to pull myself toward her voice but my legs were chained to something under the table. I yanked at the heavy chain. Mama's yellowing foot with its ridiculous owl tattoo rose into sight. I pulled with all my might but the chain slipped through my fingers. It was slick with oozing anger and resentment. Rosaria's voice boomed in my head again. "Where is the lorazepam? I know we ordered it."

Suddenly, I was back in the treatment room with Taye, Nurse Rachel, and Rosaria standing around me. I started to sit up. "Watch the IV," Nurse Rachel said while pushing my shoulder down.

"When did you get here?" I asked Rosaria.

She leaned over the treatment table to look me in the face. "Taye called. I came right down." The recessed ceiling light surrounded her compassionate face like a halo. "So what's the problem?"

"Her heartbeat is coming down again," Nurse Rachel said from behind my head.

"I'm afraid," I forced out.

"Is that all?" A quiet smile graced Rosaria's face. "Let me give you something to help you relax." She signaled to Nurse Rachel to hand her the vial of sedative and injected it into my IV. She rubbed my arm as if hurrying the medicine into my blood stream. "I can stay a few minutes while Taye prepares for the treatment. Would that help?" I felt like my blood had been replaced with Cheerwine, bubbly and syrupy. Taye and Nurse Rachel swung a machine over my body. I was vaguely aware of Taye moving near my legs but was fixated on Rosaria gently stroking my hair with one hand and patting my arm with the other. It was probably the drugs, but I chose to believe it was Rosaria's touch that let me relax enough for Taye to position the probe without pulling away. Rosaria could not possibly treat all her patients with this level of attention. I felt special, valuable.

Once the probe was in and the equipment had been double and triple checked, Taye said, "Okay Miss Lara, we are about ready to begin the treatment. We need you to stay in this position for five hours. I have put straps across your abdomen and around your legs. They'll prevent you from moving, so just relax. Sleep if you can. Rachel and I have you covered. Ready?"

Thoughts floated through my foggy mind like dust motes. *What if I do move? What would happen?* "What if I have to pee?" I moaned.

"Lara dear, you are all right. Taye inserted a catheter to relieve your bladder," Rosaria said. "Didn't you feel her insert that?" I whimpered noncommittally. At that point, the serpent of anxiety gave up fighting against the pull of the tranquilizers and I drifted into a warm sleepy state. I heard Rosaria whisper as if from a distance, "If you need me, I am just down the hall." When I opened my eyes again, Taye, Nurse Rachel, and Rosaria were gone.

I was alone again.

✳✳✳

Two hours into the treatment, Taye's voice came through the wall speaker. She sounded flustered. "Miss Blaine, there is a woman here? She wants to sit with you, but you did not authorize any visitors on your intake form. Do you want visitors?"

I was enjoying the languor that the drugs brought on. "Who is it?"

"A Vanessa Klaitner? She says she's your friend. She's being kind of pushy with Lorraine out in the waiting room."

A bubble of laughter escaped from my mouth. I knew exactly how pushy Vanessa could be. I wished I could be a fly on the wall to see her going head to head with the gracious Lorraine. "Can she come in?"

"For a few minutes. Then she has to wait for you in the waiting room."

A moment later, Vanessa burst into the tiny room. "Wow, what a place you've got here! That cute little nurse—"

"Rachel."

"Yeah, her. She read me the riot act about how I can only come in for twenty minutes and I'm not supposed to touch you at all and I am supposed to sit way over there in the chair near the wall. They sure are protective of you around here."

"Why are you here?"

"To keep you company, silly. I couldn't bear the thought of you being all alone in here."

"But I'm radioactive," I slurred. "They're going to kick you out."

"That's okay. I'll wait outside until you're done," she

replied.

"You'll wait? It could take hours. Don't you have to be at work?"

"I have my laptop and cell phone. Hey, don't roll your eyes at me. I am not leaving you alone here."

Vanessa pulled the folding metal chair over to where I could see her. She had covered her wild hair with a scarf and was wearing a black tracksuit. She looked like a tabloid reporter trying to cover a mosque shooting.

"So how's Sebastian? Did you two have fun at the movies Sunday?"

I was not about to discuss my date with Sebastian with Vanessa. I didn't understand the way I felt when I was with him well enough to explain being both happy and terrified at the same time. "You are the nosiest person ever."

"Don't I know it," Vanessa chuckled.

My eyes felt hot and my throat felt dry. "Thank you, Vanessa."

Vanessa leaned against the wall and bubbled on about Barkis and how cute he was when she let herself into my condo and took him for his morning walk before she came to the hospital, but I wasn't really paying attention. I stared up at the ceiling and just let the happy noises wash over me.

Eventually Taye's voice came over the intercom telling Vanessa she would have to step out during the next section of the treatment that was about to begin. With dewy eyes, Vanessa said, "Okay honey, I'll be right outside. I'll see you later, and we'll get a pizza or something." Out of the corner of my eye, I watched Vanessa.

I was unclear of how much time was passing as I floated in and out of wakefulness. Occasionally, faint snippets of classical music came through the microphone when

Taye talked to the patient in the other treatment room. I recognized Chopin's *Nocturnes* at one point and floated away into a memory of sitting in the university music department's antiquated listening lab. The smell of late summer roses outside the tall windows of the oak-lined room mingled with the smell of dust covered LP's and old leather furniture replaced the smell of hospital disinfectant. Dr. Talbot, the music librarian, had been kind to me and allowed me to study at the wide wooden library tables far longer than the posted one hour limit. *I wonder what ever happened to Dr. Talbot? Could he still be working at the library?* I drifted off again to the sound of Taye and Nurse Rachel chatting softly in the control room. I felt safe knowing they were there watching over me.

∗∗∗

Some time later, Nurse Rachel propped open the door and pushed a wheelchair in. I turned my head to see Jane's face at eye level. She had a gray pallor under her baseball cap. *Am I dreaming?* "Jane? What are you doing here?" I mumbled. I was awake enough to be concerned for Jane. "Don't get too close."

"I know. They warned me. I can only stay a few minutes. You'd think with all the stuff they've done to me, what's a little more radiation?" She looked tired.

"But how—"

"That Vanessa woman called me a few hours ago." Jane rolled her eyes and sighed heavily. "She really doesn't take no for an answer, does she?"

"Sorry about that."

Nurse Rachel's voice came over the speaker saying, "Don't move, Lara!" Jane looked up and waved to Rachel in the control room.

"Big sister is watching." Jane held her hand in front of her mouth. "This place is like something out of Star Trek. I keep looking for Dr. Bones to come in and wave a little machine over you and make you all better. TV is so much simpler than real life."

"Yeah." I took a deep breath and relaxed. "Much simpler."

"So how long have you been here?" Jane whispered.

"Since 5:00."

"How much longer?"

"An hour or so maybe?"

"How has it been?"

"Not so bad, really. They've got me drugged up pretty well."

"Will there be any side effects from this treatment?"

"The doctor said I will probably feel really tired for a few days but that's about it. He made me promise to call if anything funky happens. He's really nice that way."

"Yeah, everyone has been very decent to me, too." Jane stepped closer. "Do you need anything?"

"No, I'm sure Vanessa will have planned for every possible eventuality."

"That girl is a trip." I appreciated the way Jane was acting like we were just two friends chatting over coffee instead of being in a lead lined room with my feet in the air.

"I should go. I'm going to try to see Sanjay about upping my pain medication while I'm here."

"Thanks for coming."

"Happy to do it. This will be the highlight of my day. Why don't we get together next week? I'll call you."

Jane leaned in so our faces were inches from each other. She looked up suspiciously at the observation window before whispering, "One more thing. I was reading more of that

Buddhism stuff and I got to thinking about all that has been going on with you lately. I am still not convinced that this cancer has any larger significance, but you seem to need it to mean something."

I turned my head to the side and whispered back, "It has to mean something. I can't believe that this has all just been random." The alarm went off again signaling that my heart rate was elevated again. Taye's voice echoed through the room saying that Jane would have to leave now.

"Okay, okay!" Jane shouted. I saw Taye flinch and touch her ear through the window. Jane coughed into a tissue. Her chest made a gurgling sound like a slow drain. "Sweetie, what if instead of seeing it as you being punished, you imagine something else? What if *you* decide what all this means?"

"What do you mean? Me decide?"

"I don't know. I don't have the answers. The more I read, the more questions I have myself. But I do keep coming back to one thing. I refuse to accept that you, or I, did anything to deserve any of this. I simply cannot accept that—I won't." She leaned forward and kissed me on the forehead before her visiting nurse came in and wheeled her away.

After Jane left, Taye and Rachel returned to begin the final section of the treatment. Before they left me alone again, Rachel draped fresh warm blankets over my body and injected another small vial of sedative in my IV. I let my mind relax into its soft embrace.

Could it be that simple? Can I decide what this last year has meant?

I floated on a cloud of sedation into my dream world. I returned to the tunnel from earlier. Instead of being afraid, I looped the chain attached to Mama's foot around the crone's neck and pulled. The crone crashed to the ground and shattered into a million tiny shards. I jumped off the table, stepped out of my chains, and into the sunshine.

The dream changed. I saw the probe deep inside me and wondered what it could mean. It morphed from a metal probe into a searchlight scouring my darkest folds and recesses. It searched back and forth until it reached a dusky fold in the healthy pink surface. A glossy green bug with Dale's face clambered out and scuttled away. The light let him go. It stopped over the hole. A flash of light blinded me. When I could see again, there was nothing but a rosy patch where the hole had been. The light shimmered in delight and moved on.

My eyes popped open. *That's it! The radiation is burning Dale, and Mama for that matter, out of my body. If I can see the cancer as a symbol of what they did to me, then I can see the radiation as burning all the traces of them out of me forever.* I lay on the table for the next hour feeling filled with light. Instead of being burned, I chose to see it as my wounds being cauterized, healed by the fire.

32
Full Circle

One year after my diagnosis, I was back at the Cancer Center. This time, I was there solely as Jane's friend.

Tom and I spoke almost every day about the house we were building together and to update me on Jane's health. After feeling quite well for months, Jane had been going downhill fast over the past several weeks. Most days she didn't even attempt to get out of bed. The visiting nurse Tom hired could only do so much. Everyone knew the time was coming when Jane would need around-the-clock care to manage the pain that had become more and more debilitating. Hospice would be the final stop on Jane's journey.

Tom could barely speak when he told me Jane was coming to see the Hospice coordinator to start putting things in place to allow them to step in. While he wanted his mother to be free from the pain, he couldn't manage coming with her to sign what amounted to her admission of defeat. If accompanying Jane that day eased Tom's burden, I was happy to rearrange my schedule to be there.

Now that I managed a team of six analysts, I left instructions with Greg Blankenshipp to text me if anyone needed me. I could no longer call Greg Garlic Breath since he and Peter were on a macrobiotic diet to help Peter recover after his cancer treatment. Things change. The two men who were my least favorite co-workers a year ago had turned out to be my most valuable team members. They worked well together and seemed to appreciate the freedom I gave them as members of my team.

The hospital reception lobby was bustling with activity that afternoon as I helped Jane through the door. "Do you need to sit down?" I asked. "Tom told me to put you in a wheelchair. Do you want me to get you one?"

"Maybe you could push me from here to the waiting room. When we get to the appointment though, I want to walk in there on my own steam." Jane looked at the long line of people waiting to check in. "If you don't mind checking me in, I think I might just sit over there on that bench for a while." Jane and I edged over to a low bench in front of the windows. Before I left her, I wrapped her favorite dove gray silk shawl over her shoulders to keep the air conditioning's chill from making her shiver more than she already was. I wished I could do more for her.

There were a dozen people ahead of me in the line. My mind wandered to my plans to run with Sebastian then go back to his place for tacos that evening. I felt guilty for feeling so happy when Jane was gravely ill, yet I knew Jane wanted me to be happy. Every time we spoke, Jane pumped me for details about our plans to visit London and Paris over Sebastian's Christmas vacation as well as the progress on the house.

After I finally collected Jane's itinerary, I located a wheelchair and disinfected it the way Tom had shown me. It was very important to avoid exposing Jane to germs. Her lungs were so weak at this point that the common cold could kill her. I got her settled in the chair and leisurely pushed her down the green path to the oncology waiting room.

I parked Jane in the corner of the room and sat on the moss-colored settee I was sitting on when we first met. "Do you want me to find one of those warm blankets for you?"

"No thanks, sweetie. I'm okay with my shawl." Jane laid her thin, cold hand on mine. "Have you made an appointment yet with your new oncologist?"

"Dr. Obatu gave me a few names. I want to interview them with my clothes on before I let them examine me. If I am going to have to see this person every few months for years on end, they better be nice."

"Good for you. Take charge." Jane leaned toward me. I could smell her gardenia perfume. "Can you believe it has been only a year since we met right over there? So much has happened."

"I know, I was thinking the same thing a few minutes ago."

"You were such a mess that day," Jane chuckled. Laughing brought on a coughing jag, but it passed quickly. I held Jane's shoulders while she coughed. I could feel each contour of her shoulder blade through her blouse. Eventually her breathing recovered and she patted my arm thankfully.

"I'm so glad we met," Jane smiled. "I don't know if I could have gotten through all this without you."

"I didn't do anything. You're the one who was always helping me. You called me and stood up for me and, well, gave a damn."

"Exactly, you gave me something else to think about when

things got too dicey inside my own head. When I got tired of brooding about my cancer, I could brood about yours, and, let's face it—yours turned out a whole lot better. It's been a tough year, but look at you now. You're healthy, you have a great new job, you're building your dream house, and you have a promising young man. What more could you want?"

I shook my head. "It's not quite a fairy tale ending."

"It never really is, sweetie." We watched a couple enter the room and sit down in the chairs across from us. They looked terrified.

"Oh my gosh, I almost forgot. I have something for you." Jane shifted in the wheelchair so she could pull a small envelope out of her pocket. She took my hand and shook into my palm the tiny Eiffel Tower that had been on her charm bracelet. "I want you to start your own charm bracelet with this. I want you to go to so many places that your bracelet ends up even more crowded than mine."

"I'll make an effort." I pulled my grandmother's chain from beneath my blouse and slid the charm on next to Grammy's silver cross as I blinked back the tears that burned behind my eyes. Jane had forbidden me to cry for her. I slipped the chain back over my head. "You know, I told Sebastian that we have to climb the Eiffel Tower when we're in Paris."

Jane bit her lip as she squeezed my hand. Her grip was still strong. "Make sure you leave plenty of time to eat croissants and drink lots of wine, too. Live the whole experience, not just the hard parts."

Author's Note

Cancer is a very personal disease—every individual requires his or her own treatment plan. Throughout this book, I have merely skimmed the surface of what it is like to experience cervical cancer treatment. I made a conscious decision to not discuss the staging and specific details of Lara's cancer. Although I did extensive research and spoke with many cancer patients, this book is at heart a work of fiction. My primary goal is to guide the reader on a journey through the characters' lives; therefore, I have intentionally left out some of the more graphic parts of cancer treatment to allow the reader to focus on the personal transformations of the individual characters.

If you would like additional information on cancer and its treatment, I recommend the following resources: The American Cancer Society, National Cancer Institute, the Foundation for Women's Cancer, and the CDC.

About the Author

Elizabeth Hein is a mother, author, and cancer survivor. She grew up in Massachusetts and now lives in Durham, North Carolina. She writes about the people who go unnoticed in life—the woman standing in line at the bank, the mousy gal in the last cubicle, the PTA mom. She wants you to care about these women and think twice before ignoring the people you meet each day. When not writing, she is trying to raise two young women and a husband.

How to Climb the Eiffel Tower

ELIZABETH HEIN

a reader's guide

Light Messages

Discussion Questions for *How to Climb the Eiffel Tower*

1. When we first meet Lara, her only friends are the characters in her books. Are there any fictional characters that you consider friends?

2. Lara and Jane ease each other through their cancer experiences, yet they met entirely by chance. How do you think their experiences would have been different if Jane and Lara had not run into each other several times?

3. Lara suffers from severe social anxiety. Although she is the best analyst in her department and has been there for seven years, no one in the office knows her. She further distances herself from her co-workers by not learning their names. Instead, she gives them nicknames like Garlic Breath, Short Red Head, Bald Guy, and Pathetic Dog Owner. Why do you think she objectifies her co-workers? (Hint: Elizabeth Hein addresses this question on her writer's blog at scribblinginthestorageroom.wordpress.com.)

4. When you first met Garlic Breath and Pathetic Dog Owner, did you think they would be working for Lara by the end of the novel? Why do you think Lara wanted them on her team?

5. Lara's mother knew about Lara's inheritance all along. Why do you think she stayed with Dale? Do you think Dale knew that Lara was a wealthy girl when he was abusing her? Would it have changed anything?

6. Several young men show interest in Lara, but she is not interested in any of them. Why do you think she found Sebastian attractive?

7. The opportunity to be part of a team changes the way Lara sees herself in relation to other people. How has being part of a team changed the way you look at yourself?

8. Many times, cancer survivors will say that their experiences have given them wisdom and insight. What experiences in your life have left you wiser? Was that knowledge worth the suffering you endured to acquire it?

9. This book is titled *How to Climb the Eiffel Tower* and yet the actual Eiffel Tower doesn't appear in the book. What roll do you think the Eiffel Tower plays in the novel? What does it represent? (Hint: Elizabeth Hein addresses this question on her writer's blog at scribblinginthestorageroom.wordpress.com.)

10. While in a waiting room, Lara and Jane form the beginning of what turns out to be a beautiful friendship. Have you ever made any waiting room friendships? Elizabeth Hein is collecting waiting room stories. You can share yours at: elizabethhein. com.

For more discussion questions, an interview with the author, and a "Clubbing Guide" made especially for book clubs, visit Elizabeth Hein's official author page at lightmessages.com/elizabethhein.

If you liked this book...

Check out these other women's fiction titles from Light Messages Publishing:

A Sinner in Paradise by Deborah Hining
Winner of the *IndieFab Book of the Year Bronze Medal* in Romance and the *Benjamin Franklin Award Silver Medal*. Readers will quickly fall for Geneva in this exquisitely written, uproarious affair with love in all its forms, set in the stunning landscape of the West Virginia mountains.

Can't Buy Me Love by Summer Kinard
A Top 5 women's fiction novel on Amazon. This is a tale of romance, friendship, and healing the hurts of the past. Fans of *The Sugar Queen* (Sarah Addison Allen), *The Lost Recipe for Happiness* (Barbara O'Neal), or *Julia's Chocolates* (Cathy Lamb) are sure to wrap themselves around *Can't Buy Me Love*.

A Theory of Expanded Love by Caitlin Hicks
A dazzling debut novel. This coming-of-age story features Annie, a feisty yet gullible adolescent, trapped in her enormous, devout Catholic family in 1963. Questioning all she has believed, and torn between her own gut instinct and years of Catholic guilt, Annie takes courageous risks to wrest salvation from a tragic sequence of events set in motion by her parents' betrayal. **Coming June 2015.**

CPSIA information can be obtained
at www.ICGtesting.com
Printed in the USA
FFOW02n2121081014
7890FF